Sherlock Holmes
in Paris

IN THE SAME SERIES

Séamas Duffy

Sherlock Holmes
in Paris

BLACK COAT PRESS

Visit our website at www.blackcoatpress.com

ISBN 978-1-61227-148-4. Printing. February 2013. Published by Black Coat Press, an imprint of Hollywood Comics.com, LLC, P.O. Box 17270, Encino, CA 91416. All rights reserved. Except for review purposes, no part of this book may be reproduced or transmitted in any form or by any means, electronic or mechanical, including photocopying, recording or by any information storage and retrieval system, without permission in writing from the publisher. The stories and characters depicted in this anthology are entirely fictional. Printed in the United States of America.

For Ellen

TABLE OF CONTENTS

Foreword

The idea that I might write this book occurred to me when I enrolled as a candidate member of the Sherlock Holmes Society of Scotland. I drew up an inventory of essential features which I thought the ideal Sherlock Holmes stories ought to comprise, and finally settled upon the following list: references to previously undocumented cases (which reader, after all, has not been tantalized by the spectre of the "giant rat of Sumatra" or intrigued by "Wilson, the notorious canary trainer," or has not pondered precisely what Holmes's involvement was in the case of the Two Coptic Patriarchs?); a litany of astounding on-the-spot deductions in which Holmes demonstrates the equivalent of "inferring a Niagara from a drop of water;" secret codes (upon which Holmes has, naturally enough, written a monograph); Holmes and Watson trotting off cheerfully in a growler to the scene of the action—whether it be robbery, murder, or a case of mere mistaken identity; the Baker Street Irregulars on covert twenty-four hour surveillance and the District Messenger dispatched urgently to look for a needle in a haystack; manifestations of the superior intellectual power of the omniscient, yet shadowy, Mycroft Holmes; the privacy or safety of some august, usually aristocratic, occasionally royal, personage threatened; Holmes and Watson sharing a pipe round a roaring fire in a fog-girt Baker Street sitting room; an appetizing and jolly repast, always described in Dickensian detail,[1] usually partaken just prior to the two heroes launching their final offensive upon some unsuspecting guilty party, and often accompanied by the impartation of spectacularly pointless information on some bizarrely obscure topic (the Chaldean roots of the Cornish language, early English charters, Buddhism of Ceylon, etc.); gratuitous philosophical speculation by Holmes on the meaning of life—judiciously sprinkled with quotations from Horace, Hafiz, Goethe, Pope, and Shakespeare (and, more rarely, from Scripture); and finally, of course, mystery, horror, and suspense. I trust this book contains all of the above, and more.

There are other features of a classic Sherlock Holmes story which makes the canon stand out from the rest of detective fiction. For instance, Doctor Watson does not always, or even often, feel the need to "play fair" with the reader, and we are not invariably presented with *all* the clues which Holmes himself holds, thereby preventing us from reaching the same brilliant conclusions as to the identity and motive of the suspect, the method of commission of the crime, and so on, that he does: "...it was by *concealing* such links in the chain that Watson was enabled to produce his meretricious finales..." says Holmes in *The Blanched Solider*; somewhat hypocritically, since Holmes himself occasionally

---

[1] One modern reviewer estimated that in *Pickwick Papers* alone, there are references to five breakfasts (full English, of course), ten luncheons, and 32 dinners (there seems to be a tendency for these descriptions to increase in quantity in direct proportion to the lateness of the hour!), as well as, apparently 249 (not 250, mind you!), references to excisable liquor—which equates to an average of one on every second page.

achieves the same effect by clandestinely dispatching a probing telegram to which only he will see the reply, or by descending, pseudonymous and incognito, into London's criminal underworld and returning with secret incontrovertible evidence which will be presented with a flourish as he both traps the unwary suspect in his finely woven net and astonishes the reader with his brilliance.

I have made one trifling departure from Holmesian convention. One frequent complaint about Doctor Watson's longer stories—particularly *The Hound of the Baskervilles*—is that the plot is unraveled, and the culprits unmasked, too soon. In this book, I have tried to ensure that the full denouement is held back until the last possible moment.

Séamas Duffy

The Adventure of the Nebrodi Sapphire

Chapter I
The Cipher from Porlock

In the spring of 1894, I returned to my old quarters at 221B Baker Street. I well remember the unalloyed joy I felt at being back once again in that sitting room with my friend, Sherlock Holmes, beneath the enormous shelves of reference books, amidst the detritus of our bohemian existence, amongst the old familiar land-marks: the violin case, the pipe rack, the coal scuttle and the stained table where he occasionally diverted his powerful intellect with abstruse and, to Mrs. Hudson's annoyance, invariably malodorous chemical experiments.

The year had been a singularly busy one for Holmes for, although the published accounts of his adventures amount to a mere four cases, in point of fact the calls upon him were many, constant and varied. Throughout the early summer of that year, a series of events occurred in Paris which kept him constantly occupied for two months on end. Although it ended with Holmes saving the life of the French President [2] (becoming one of the very few Englishmen ever to wear the *cordon rouge* of

---

[2] Following Holmes's departure from Paris in June, Monsieur Sadi Carnot was assassinated, allegedly by Italian anarchists.

the *Légion d'Honneur* on account of his bravery), he came very close to complete physical and mental breakdown as a result of the exertions expended upon this, and upon his many other cases. His state of health on return from France at that time recalled to me a similar condition in which I found him at the conclusion of Baron Maupertuis affair some eight years previously. I am bound to record, with regret, and no small degree of irritation, that he remained completely deaf to my best and soundest advice offered to him at various junctures throughout most of that year, as both physician and friend, that he should take some form of rest, lest the overworking of his mind and body result in permanent detriment to his unique, magnificent, and celebrated powers. It was well into late autumn before I managed to prevail upon him to ease back upon his excruciating schedule, and I finally succeeded in persuading him to come with me for a fortnight's ramble in the fastness of the South Downs until the events at Yoxley Old Place[3] intruded upon us.

My friend's physical deterioration had been compounded by a grave professional disappointment: in September 1894, Colonel Sebastian Moran, lieutenant of the infamous Professor Moriarty—who was presumed to be dead at that juncture—was acquitted on the charge of murdering the Honorable Ronald Adair, a series of events which I recorded contemporaneously in *The Adventure of the Empty House*. The acquittal obtained by Colonel Moran's defense counsel was founded entirely upon a legal-procedural technicality, and not due to the lack of material evidence—for it was Holmes himself

---

[3] Recorded as *The Adventure of the Golden Pince-Nez.*

who brought to justice the person whom he had once described as "the second most dangerous man in London;" and although Moran had confounded the mediocre abilities of the official forces of law and order from the start, it was the Metropolitan Police, of course, who ultimately claimed the credit for the capture of Moran at the time, just as they had done for the resolution of many criminal cases of the period, something to which Holmes had become inured and upon which, at times, he waxed sardonic. In fairness it must be said that, at least through the persons of Inspector Lestrade and Inspector Gregson, who had both made several visits (perhaps pilgrimages is a better word) to 221B Baker Street to record their thanks, the gratitude of the official force towards Holmes was neither grudged nor feigned, albeit it was conveyed in the privacy of the sitting room rather than publicized in the columns of the Press.

Following Moran's acquittal and subsequent release from prison, it was a treat to the ears to hear Holmes damning and blasting with a very fine assortment of oaths the incompetent Crown officials responsible. He fairly shocked Inspector Lestrade, who had come to give him the unpalatable news of Moran's acquittal, with the robustness of his language. The fault lay entirely with the mandarins of the prosecution service, and it was neither from want of diligence, nor lack of competence by the Metropolitan Police in the preparation of their case, that enabled Colonel Moran to slip through the net and return to his criminal milieu. But worse was to come: during the autumn and winter of 1894, the steady rise in London crime was remarked upon intermittently by the leader columns of the Press. Of particular note was the occurrence of a spate of robberies committed by apparently well organized gangs of young men who, according to the Illustrated Police News of October 1894 were said to have "paid officials and who make a weekly contribution to defray the cost of the fines inflicted for assault and outrage; they are fined by the secretary if they were found without a belt or a stick." By the spring of 1895, the scale and subtlety of these operations, and the fact that they all remained unsolved, began not only to cause Holmes grave concern but also, as his tentacles stretched out into every nook and cranny of the city's teeming underworld to sense the merest whisper of organized crime, to give rise to a bizarre and unsettling suspicion. Following his investigation of the affair of the Cleveland Street Picture Gallery, in which low farce alternated with tragedy, and which culminated in the defenestration, and ultimate public disgrace, of a Privy Councilor, it became obvious that only one explanation, albeit a startling one, could possibly meet the facts—Professor Moriarty had returned!

Yet, how could Moriarty possibly have avoided death during that struggle between himself and Holmes was a deep mystery to both of us? Holmes had a clear recollection of his enemy plummeting to his death into that chasm of the Reichenbach Falls, and it seemed impossible that anyone could have survived such a fall. Nevertheless a tip-off from one of Holmes's criminal contacts in the East End finally cleared up the mystery: it transpired that, on the day of that fateful meeting, Moriarty had sent an accomplice who bore a more than passable resemblance to him on the errand to meet Holmes on that narrow deserted mountain pass. Holmes admitted to me privately, and much to his chagrin, that, in the fading light of the late afternoon, in the deep gorge, he may have misrecognized his old adversary under that darkening sky. In fact, Holmes's only proper recollection was of what he thought at the time to be the Professor's grey eyes under a hat which covered most of his face. It must be remembered that prior to their rendezvous at the Reichenbach Falls, Holmes had only met Moriarty in person once, and that was under circumstances where he had surprised Holmes in his sitting room, and so had had the advantage of him. Subsequent events seem to have confirmed suspicions that, as Holmes himself had done after their meeting, Moriarty had allowed the rumors of his apparent demise to circulate, until he determined the most propitious time for his eventual resurrection.

Looking back upon my notes of the period, I see that I have happily recorded that, by the spring of the following year, Holmes had recovered fully and had once again attained that peak of brilliance for which he had had become renowned. From then until the turn of the century, he fairly threw himself into his work for there was never any of shortage of clients, and throughout the nineties, an abundance of cases followed in rapid succession, not all of which I have had the opportunity, or, in some cases, the inclination, to publish the accounts of in detail.

My records show that Holmes investigated the cause of the curious bouts of madness which afflicted the well-known philanthropist Count Dom Agostinho Mendoça of Braganza, and effected a most singular cure. There was the sad, but rather comical, case of the White-chapel Contortionist which had vexed the Police for months, but perhaps most notable was the series of events surrounding the Bognor Prestidigitation Circle, beginning with an incident which had been brought to Holmes's attention by a Harley Street colleague of mine, Doctor Moore Agar.

In fact, it is another of these, as yet unchronicled, cases from 1895 which I now address in these pages. I had returned from my holiday on the Continent on the first day of the grouse season, and I clearly recall that it was rather more than two full calendar months later before I clapped eyes on Holmes. Save on those occasions when he had left London completely, I can scarcely recall his having been absent from Baker Street for such a long period in pursuit of his quarry. On this occasion, it seemed that he had once again descended, pseudonymous and incognito, into some stratum of the criminal fraternity and had been holed up in one of his many refuges in the East End.

It was a fine warm day in mid October and the streets were already hot and dusty from an unseasonably long dry spell. Although I had given up my own private practice the previous year, I had been looking after my old colleague Jackson's patients in his absence, and was returning to Baker Street at the end of a busy morning round, with the prospect of a pot of Mrs. Hudson's best Javanese, followed by a leisurely perusal of the morning newspapers. In fact, as it happened, when I arrived in the sitting room, I was rather surprised to find Holmes there. He had evidently dispensed with his disguise and, having removed his seaman's clothes, had donned his normal apparel, and was now bustling around with the air of a man about to depart; a portmanteau in the corner by the door mutely proclaimed that his departure was both imminent and meant to be a lengthy one. He had that alert and eager look and his eyes a certain hard glitter which I had come to recognize: for all the impassivity of countenance which he cultivated, it was not difficult for me to read the signs. I was reminded of the problems with his constitution the previous year and felt a vague sense of unease at his slightly overwrought appearance. As Holmes grew older I was less inclined to be so indulgent with the games he played with his physical health. Although I had succeeded in prevailing upon him to desist from the dreadful cocaine habit, nevertheless there still lingered on his part a morbid tendency to deprive himself of food for long periods of time in order, as he once told me airily, that his brain should not be starved of the blood supply diverted to use by his digestive system. I am afraid that his understanding of the intricacies of the human anatomy was unsystematic to the point of absurdity.

"My dear Holmes," I began, "I really must warn you that if you overwork yourself again as you did…"

"Ah! The same old Watson, solicitous for my health as ever," he broke in, "and reproachful in equal quantity!" he added with a twinkle waving me to the armchair by the fire which, although set, remained unlit.

Indeed so warm was the morning that, although my constitution can rather better stand a rising than a falling thermometer, I had begun to regret donning the heavy overcoat inside which I was beginning to swelter uncomfortably. The yellow brick houses opposite seemed, even at that early hour, to be baking in the Indian summer which was the delight of all London, save those, like myself, whose duties compelled them to be abroad in formal attire. "Nevertheless, I am delighted to see that I am not the only person who has been busy. I assume Doctor Jackson has gone to Switzerland again?" he chuckled.

"How on Earth did you know? Why, you have been gone for several weeks and I have just…"

"Come, come, Watson, I know your methods as well as you ought to know mine. You have no regular practice. What would take you out on such a morning dressed so formally? It was obvious that you were covering your friend's practice in his absence. Look at the glossy sheen upon your boots, untainted by the dust and grit of our infernally hot and chokingly dusty London streets: further inference—that Doctor Watson is too busy to make his calls on foot, therefore he takes a cab. How many times used I to gauge the quantum of your calls by the state of your shoes?"

I perceived a small pile of papers on the coffee table, and I knew instantly that any homily I might deliver to him regarding overtaxing himself would be futile. I nodded towards the pile, "You do have another case in hand, then?" I inquired rather ruefully.

"Yes, I seem to have returned from my bolt hole in Ratcliff at exactly the right time. As you may or may not know, I had been exceedingly busy of late with the affair of the *Quatuor Coronati* which detained me rather longer than I expected."

"The Quatuor Coronati!" I repeated, "The Four Crowned Ones? Is that not the name of a Freemason's Lodge?"

"Yes, it is exactly that. It has been a most curious case, Watson; never before in any of my hundred odd weighty cases have I seen the interests of so many revered organizations of civil society inextricably entangled to such a degree. It is no exaggeration to say that were certain facts to be made public with unpropitious timing, it would shake the English Freemasonry establishment to its very foundations; unfortunately I suspect that, considering the many high ranking and august persons implicated in the matter, it will not suffer to be recounted to the general public for quite some time; indeed it will, rightly or wrongly, be questioned by some as to whether the facts should ever be exposed to public scrutiny."

"And your other case?" I asked.

"*Cases*," he corrected me. "I have in fact several others maturing at the moment, the effects of which upon my person were immediately apprehended by yourself upon your entry, and which aroused your professional concern. Amongst these, one concerns the Athanasian Scroll which has gone missing, presumably stolen, from Saint Mark's and his Holiness Pope Kyrillos has requested my urgent assistance in an attempt to retrieve it. However, if my theory is correct, no harm is likely to arise to the document, and a few thousand piastres will not only guarantee its return, but will also keep the matter hushed up. Perhaps the most pressing case is one which may possibly entail a visit to France."

"What could possibly take you there?" I asked.

"Perhaps the most intriguing moment of my career, Watson! You have heard the rumors of the return to England of Professor Moriarty—the signs are everywhere. If there were any doubts, they have almost been dispelled by the papers you observe on the table which arrived this morning by the second post after you had gone out on your round."

"Well, Holmes, it is no more than you deserve," I replied, "for only a year or so ago I recall, when investigating young McFarlane's predicament,[4] that you were lamenting the dreary monotony caused by the Professor's supposed demise."

"Yes, Watson I admit it," Holmes smiled ruefully and continued. "The correspondence which you perceive on the table emanates from our old friend Porlock,

---

[4] In *The Adventure of the Norwood Builder*.

whose enigmatic, yet prophetic, epistle you may recall, provoked a charge of witchcraft against me from your countryman MacDonald some years ago. Porlock seems to have been retained by our returned adversary, but his altruistic instincts remain the same."

"What does it involve?"

"At present, it involves a slaughtered lamb, three kings and the ancient city of Jerusalem."

"Upon my word, Holmes… but what…?"

"Come along with me and you shall find out."

I glanced at the portmanteau by the door, "Come with you? *To Jerusalem?*"

"No, to Clerkenwell," he replied impatiently, "I shall explain in the cab. As you have none of Jackson's patients to see this afternoon…"

"*Dash it*, Holmes! How could you *possibly* know that I have no patients to see this afternoon?"

"Oh, that's simple enough Watson, had you intended going back out after lunch, you would have simply left your wicker basket on the table by the door where I could see it, whereas it is presumably packed away in the hallway cupboard."

"Well, it would be a pleasure to accompany you Holmes, for, as you suggest, I am anticipating quite a bit of a lull."

"Excellent, Watson! Is this lull likely to extend as far as a week perhaps?"

"Very likely, I think, since my colleague returns to London tomorrow, after which I revert to my life as a leisured gentleman."

"Then that's settled! A week in Paris—first class tickets, all expenses paid, and the prospect of a substantial reward at the end. We shall leave Victoria station this evening on the ten o'clock boat train to Calais, and thence to Paris. I had already taken the liberty of sending young Cartwright [5] down to reserve us a first class carriage, for I knew you would not fail me."

"There must be something urgent or extraordinary about the case for you to leave so suddenly."

"Quite urgent yes, but not, on the whole, unusual. Porlock merely warns of an impending jewel robbery in Paris, and we may arrive in time to avert it, rather than avenge it. Still, you may judge for yourself," said Holmes, handing me two envelopes inside which the cipher and the cipher key had arrived. They were identical, printed in rough characters, no doubt with the object of disguising the sender's original handwriting, and read as follows:

Sherlock P. Holmes,
221B Baker Street,
Marylebone,
London W1

"What does the middle initial 'P' stand for? I was not aware that you had a middle name, Holmes."

"You are correct, Watson, I have no middle name, and therefore no middle initial. The P is purely a protocol between myself and Porlock, which we agreed to adopt after the events at Birlstone some time ago, which you recorded in a somewhat sensational and romanticized vein, if I may say so. I warned Porlock then of the dangers to his person should any message to me be intercepted, and it also occurred to me that certain parties might wish to usurp his pseudonym out of a desire to

---

[5] Cartwright works for the District Messenger Service and makes only one other named appearance in the canon, in *The Hound of the Baskervilles*, although Holmes makes use of an anonymous District Messenger service on other occasions.

mislead me, so this, then, is Porlock's unique mark of authenticity; should any communication arrive at this address purporting to be from that quarter, which does not contain my fictional middle initial in the address, then I shall know it immediately to be a forgery. It is a simple but effective device, since the P may be seen by anyone, and yet be neither noticed, nor remarked upon, whereas only yourself and brother Mycroft would know for certain that I have no middle initial."

"Rather clever, Holmes."

"Oh, perfectly simple, Watson. I have also taken the trouble to refine my method of his remuneration, as well as increasing the quantum thereof; the ten pound note in a plain envelope to Camberwell Post Office was becoming rather too risky and, frankly, smacked of amateurism," Holmes continued. "Still, despite the rather crude attempt to disguise his handwriting, certain features of his, certain idiosyncrasies remain and the Camberwell postmark is unmistakable. There are one or two, admittedly exceedingly minor, indications of a departure from Porlock's normal methods, for he has employed a cipher which I hazard would scarcely trouble even the most dull-witted schoolboy."

"Perhaps the explanation is that he may have been forced to act in haste to avoid discovery of his treachery?" I replied.

"By Moriarty? [6] Indeed, Watson, very probable, and one would hardly blame him."

---

[6] Incongruously, in *The Adventure of the Final Problem*, Watson states on 24 April 1891 that he had "never heard of Moriarty." We can accept that Watson may have decided to draw a discreet veil over previous cases which he was not ready, at that point, to publish. However one of the great unsolved ca-

Holmes went to the table again and, picking out two slips of paper from the pile, handed them to me. The first was an inscription in cipher similar to that which we had received from Porlock eight years ago, warning us of the impending danger to Jack Douglas. It ran:

534 C2 43 27

"I assumed as usual that the solution to Porlock's conundrum is to be found in the *Almanac*," said Holmes, "on turning to page 534, column 2 thereof, the forty-third and twenty-seventh words are respectively 'Pig' and 'Pen.' Now, here is the actual cipher, the important part. Please tell me what you make of it..."

The paper contained several lines of strange-looking symbols printed in black ink on a plain un-marked sheet of writing paper. The pen had spluttered a few times during the printing.

The message ran as follows:

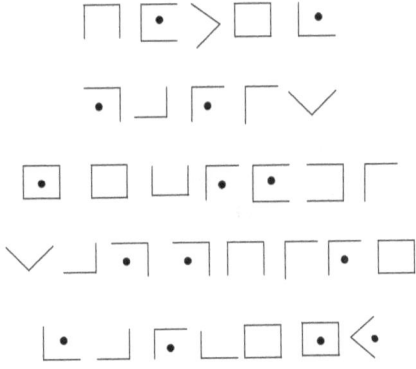

---

nonical puzzles is how Watson can describe Moriarty as "the famous scientific criminal" in *The Valley of Fear*, generally regarded as having taken place in January 1888... three years earlier!

I studied the cipher for some minutes whilst Holmes sat with an amused expression but, apart from detecting a vague resemblance to some of the letters of the Cyrillic alphabet, I was quite unable to make any sense of it. Holmes continued to smile across the table at my discomfiture. As for the words "Pig" and "Pen," I had absolutely no clue as to their possible meaning.

"My dear Holmes, I know you well enough to appreciate that you are not being facetious when you say this code can be broken by a schoolboy, and a dull-witted one at that. Yet, I confess I am forced to place myself intellectually rather below that level; it is completely impenetrable to me."

"As I have had occasion to remark before, Watson, I really ought to get you to write that down and sign it in the presence of witnesses, for in several moments from now, you will declare the solution to be perfectly obvious."

"Well, I am at your mercy as usual, so please do explain," I answered with some asperity.

"Porlock has sent two separate messages. The first message contained the key in essence: the words 'pig' and 'pen.' Initially, neither 'pig' nor 'pen' seemed to me to be leading me in anywhere like the right direction. In fact, I instantly recalled how in the Birlstone case, when we had made an initial attempt to decipher Porlock's communication, our inquiries led us somewhat disappointingly, and erroneously as it turned out, to the term 'Pig's Bristles.' Thus, I had begun to think that I had once again misread the key to the cipher in some similar way, but on opening the second envelope, and seeing the message which you have just read, I realized immediately that it represented a variant of what are called the *Pig-*

Pen symbols derived from the Aik Bekar cipher, which has been used by various secret societies over the centuries, or at least societies who wished to keep their communications secret. It is many centuries old, and is thought to have been invented by the Knights Templar, though it fell out of favor until around the 17th century, when it was resurrected. It appears also to have been used by the Confederate forces in the American Civil War, and was very probably the mode of communication employed by those members of the evil society which persecuted the unfortunate John Openshaw[7] in '87.

"As you are aware", Holmes continued, "I am presently engaged in the authorship of a short treatise [8] upon analyses of ciphers and codes, having studied scores of specimens from various parts of the world, and from various historical epochs. As I stated, Porlock's cipher is of such banality that I would have been able to crack it with little effort for, although considered useful in its day, the steady progress of mass literacy amongst all classes has rendered it more fit for the amusement of schoolboys than for serious cryptology. Essentially, each cipher represents a cell on a grid which corresponds to a letter of the alphabet. The dot in the cell, as in the first cipher in Porlock's message, merely represents second series of

---

[7] John Openshaw, the nephew of a former Ku Klux Klan member, was harassed and finally assassinated by that organization in the autumn of the previous year, in the story of *The Adventure of the Five Orange Pips*. The KKK was known to have used the Pig Pen cipher.

[8] One of the many topics upon which Holmes has produced a monograph or treatise. By the time that Holmes had come to investigate *The Dancing Men*, three years after the events recorded here, his treatise on cryptology had grown to encompass "one hundred and sixty separate ciphers."

letters, repeated in order to avoid unnecessarily lengthening or complicating the cipher. The *pig pen* is merely a fanciful description of the grid, which superficially resembles the pens in which those beasts are herded."

Holmes handed me a slip of paper, "Here is the key to the message," he remarked.

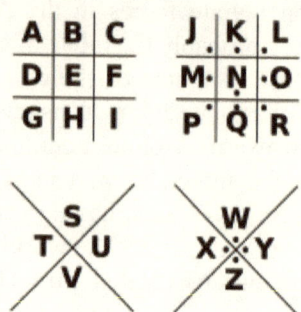

"You see, Watson, although there are a number of potential variations in the configuration of the code, it is really a very simple cipher."

"Yes, you are correct Holmes; it does seem remarkably, almost childishly, simple. So what then does this message from Porlock actually convey?" I asked.

Holmes handed me yet another slip of paper, which contained a transcription of Porlock's cipher into Holmes' own writing. It read:

Hotel Paris—Nebrodi Sapphire — Larceny

"Posted at 07:15 a.m., 21 October—today, postmarked SE 5. Unless some other arcane meaning can be attached to this, Watson, I assume that Porlock's message is intended to warn us the Nebrodi Sapphire belonging—if my reference book is correct—to the Countess of Milazzo, presumably resident in Paris at this moment, is in danger of being removed by some nefarious person. The unmistakable inference, of course, is that Moriarty is behind this. Now, Watson, it is almost twelve o'clock, we must be off to Clerkenwell."

Chapter II
A Trip to Clerkenwell

It was one of the traits of my friend to make me feel, despite my superior or, at least, more systematic education, very obtuse at certain of his more obscure allusions. As we rattled down in the cab through the noisy crowded thoroughfares of Marylebone and Bloomsbury, I resolved to try to puzzle out the meaning of something he had said to me earlier.

"Holmes, you have yet to enlighten me as to which three kings you referred to, and how the city of Jerusalem comes into this. And what was that other reference...? The butchered pig?"

"Ah, Watson, you must excuse my twitting you— The Three Kings and The City of Jerusalem, as well as The Slaughtered Lamb, are taverns in the Clerkenwell area which constitute the natural habitat of one Gioacchino Ricoletti. You recall him surely?"

"Yes, that was one of your cases from the eighties. I am unlikely to forget... He was the chap with the club foot, married to that dreadful Scotchwoman, wasn't he?"

"Yes, a slatternly, incurable, and unpresentable drunkard; it was she who drove him to crime, and brought about his downfall. It was difficult not to have sympathy with him. He ran a small but flourishing jeweler's business in those days, and had set up house several times in Eyre Street—each time, it ended with her pawning the furniture or the silver. Finally, she pawned one of his client's pearl sets and, on that occasion, desperately needing the money to redeem the chaplet, he turned to crime. He was involved in the theft of the Mondragon Emerald, and when he came out of prison, a few years ago, he separated from her and resolved never to return. With some assistance from well-meaning acquaintances, he was able to set himself up in a small commission business, and now frequents the taverns of Clerkenwell in the afternoon to conduct his trade.

"Of course, with his former contacts, there is little he does not know about the commerce of stolen gems. In point of fact, he was wrongfully accused in the Mondragon case, and I forwarded some papers to his solicitor which, I believe, assisted in proving that his culpability was limited to reselling the proceeds of the crime, rather than actually stealing the booty. Thus, he happens to owe me a small favor."

We disembarked from the cab in Britton Street, outside the narrow frontage of a tavern which bore the inscription: *"City Of Jerusalem Tavern Anno 1720."* Once inside, we ordered two glasses of porter and, when the white-aproned curate returned with the change, Holmes asked him in an offhand manner if Ricoletti was about. The curate nodded towards a room at the back and, as it happened, Ricoletti was found inside at a table playing a hand of cards. At a sign from Holmes, he threw in his cards, left the school, and we three retreated to a quiet corner of the low-beamed, smoky tavern.

"Now then, Mr. Holmes," said Ricoletti coming straight to the point, "while I am delighted to see you, and have never forgotten your great kindness to me, I know you have not come all the way down here from Baker Street to sample the porter."

"Indeed, I have not, though it is rather fine," replied Holmes. "I wanted to know what you could tell me about the Nebrodi Sapphire."

"The Nebrodi Sapphire?" Ricoletti thought for a moment. "Well, it is rather unusual of its type, being a very pale blue, almost colorless in fact. It is perhaps not the most handsome of jewels, but it is very highly prized, and certainly worth a small fortune, possibly as much as sixty thousand pounds. Let me guess, it has been stolen and you have come here to see if it has appeared on the market?"

"No, not quite. I must bind you to silence here, for that is what I am hoping to prevent."

"To prevent?" Ricoletti looked surprised. "In that case, you would have to go to Sicily to prevent it!"

"How much do you know about it?"

"The Nebrodi Sapphire or *La Stella Zaffiro di Nebrodi*, to give it its proper name, was mined in the Kashmir. It has changed hands over the years due to the usual skullduggery, but it has belonged to the Milazzo family now for several generations. They are landowners and own large estates near the Nebrodi Mountains in north-eastern Sicily: olive groves, vineyards, orchards, and so on. If I remember correctly, the entire collection of jewels, of which the Nebrodi Sapphire was but one, passed to the Contessa Di Milazzo on the death of her husband several years ago. I would have thought that there would be little chance of its being stolen in Sicily, as the family had cordial relations with the local Mafiosi. In fact, I would say that it would be tantamount to committing suicide for anyone to steal it."

"But if it happened to be, say, in Paris at the moment?"

"Ah, that would be different. The tentacles of the Mafia do not usually stretch that far. Even so, only a really big fish would be prepared to touch a jewel as well known as the Nebrodi Sapphire. It would be too difficult for the smaller fry to get rid of it, especially in one piece."

"Of course. But if they cut it into smaller stones and sold it that way?"

"It is possible, I suppose. I wouldn't have thought so though… You see, it would realize only a fraction of its proper value if it were cut. But only someone with the right connections could possibly hope to sell it in one piece, and you would assume that this person had an interested buyer beforehand."

"Someone of Professor Moriarty's standing?"

Ricoletti looked surprised and a spasm of alarm shot across his face.

"Ah-ha, I see a mere mention of that man's name still inspires fear!" said Holmes.

"Then you have heard?" asked Ricoletti.

"That Moriarty has made a return? I did not doubt that the rumors were true."

Ricoletti nodded his head. "You must have heard of that business in Cleveland Street."

"Yes, I recognized the signature."

"And you think Moriarty is after the Nebrodi Sapphire which is now in Paris?"

"I believe that to be the case. Again, I must bind you to absolute secrecy."

"Of course. Well, you don't need me to tell you, Mr. Holmes, that if that man has set his sights on it, he will allow nothing, and no one, to baulk him. Besides, he now has a reputation to rebuild. I know you have no fear of danger, Mr. Holmes, but I do counsel you to be careful."

"Thank you for your advice, Gioacchino."

"It is a pleasure to be able to repay you. There is just one small thing Mr. Holmes, you won't, er, mention…"

"Your name will not appear."

Ricoletti shook hands with us and went back to the deck of cribbage he had been playing when we had arrived.

"We shall also call upon Sergeant Hill," said Holmes as we left the tavern. "He is a plain clothes colleague of Lestrade's from the Holborn station whose beat is around the Italian Quarter. He is a veritable encyclopedia of the Italian criminal underworld, both in England and on the Continent. Thanks to his having been brought up by his Italian grandmother, he is practically a native speaker, and there is hardly an ice-cream seller, organ grinder, or scissors sharpener in Saffron Hill that he does not know personally."

"Yes, I seem to remember that his name was in the newspapers a year or two ago."

"That is correct, Watson, you have an excellent memory. It was in '92. Although it was a minor misdemeanor—a shop window smashing I believe—the incident was well publicized at the time due to the bizarre combination of the tragic and the ridiculous. On being alerted to the crime, Hill and his younger colleague, Constable Daniels, had dashed immediately from the Holborn station to the shop at the corner of King's Mews but, sadly, Daniels choked to death after swallowing his false teeth."

It was a pleasant walk westwards along Clerkenwell Road, and we strolled, in no particular hurry, through the noisy crowded streets and byways of Saffron Hill with its Italian cafés and fascinating, quaint little shops. Holmes was ever at his most discursive on such excursions, and such a neighborhood as this one had the effect of stimulating his imagination: he kept me continually diverted by his clever and illuminating deductions drawn from sharp apprehension of the most minute and subtle detail of the individuals in the thronging pavements and cobbled lanes. On this occasion, in the space on a quarter of a mile of road, he was able, by recognizing a faint smell of paraffin, a smudge of ink on a shirt cuff, or a characteristic posture fashioned by occupational habit, to point out that this fellow was a lamplighter, that one was a printer's laborer, or yet another was a clockmaker.

Passing a low, smoke-blackened building with iron railings enclosing a small paved courtyard, he then fell to discoursing about the origin of English Almshouses and their dissolution under the Tudor monarchs.

It now being close to our usual luncheon hour, we turned into John Street and stopped briefly at Theobald's Coffee House for sustenance, before going on to the Police station in Lamb's Conduit Street. Sergeant Hill welcomed us warmly and he confirmed Ricoletti's story in all its essentials, but he also adverted to the possibility of a connection with one of the Italian cartels of organized crime.

"You mean the Mafia or the Camorra?" Holmes asked.

"No. The Camorra is largely of Neapolitan origin, and the Count's family is believed to have owed its wealth to connections with the Mafia. There is another organization known as the *Veste Nere.*"

"*Veste Nere?* The Black Coats?"

"Yes, you have heard of them?"

"No, not at all, for as far as I am aware, they do not appear in Heckethorne's famous book of reference. They sound quite fantastical, like something out of a novel!"

"I can assure you they are very real, Mr. Holmes," said Sergeant Hill, "and they will have agents in Paris, of that you can be sure. It is not as big an organization as the Mafia, and seem to have come into existence much more recently—around the 17th century, possibly as a result of a schism within the dreaded Camorra, of whose activities you are obviously be well aware. The *Veste Nere* were active mostly in Sardinia and Sicily, but the movement spread to Corsica during the Napoleonic Wars, where they gained a stronghold in Bastia and in Sartene through a number of wealthy families, the Coronas and the Monteleones principally, who still wield influence there. They were known as the *Habits Noirs* in France and as the *Gentlemen of the Night* in England..."

"Ah, I *have* heard of them! They were involved in organized crime in the '40s and '50s. There was an internecine feud which began in London, I think, and ended in a shoot-out in Australia during the gold rush there. The murders were never solved."

"And never will be due to the code of silence which is enforced rigidly. As an organization, they seem to have waxed and waned over the years, occasionally vanishing from public view, often due to bloody vendettas, then re-appearing dramatically in other places. At one point, they were running a religious order called, rather ironically, the Brotherhood of Mercy, for mercy is not one of their better known qualities. This served, of course, merely as a cover for their criminal activities. During the Peninsular War, they were led by the aristocratic Monteleone family who formed the *Companions of Silence*, and they joined forces with the Bourbons against Napoleon."

"But they still survive?"

"They faded away after the restoration of the monarchy, but to the best of my knowledge, they still have connections with the Corona family, whose *paterfamilias*, *Il Padre d'Ogni*, remains the chief. Sometimes, the organization operates with military precision; at other times, it degenerates into sheer banditry. But one thing never changes—the iron discipline of the *Conclave Supremo*, the High Council, and the code of honor. You have heard the expression *Omerta*? No one has ever impeached them publicly, and it is unlikely that anyone ever will. You will recall the case of the train robbery on the Riviera Train De-luxe a year or two ago?"

"Yes, very well."

"That was the work of the *Habits Noirs*."

"Indeed?"

"Yes, a certain Giovanni Negroni, half Corsican, half Italian, was the brains behind that," said Sergeant Hill. "Although the Sûreté could find no evidence, there is no doubt that it was the Corsican *Habits Noirs* who carried out that robbery. It was quite a remarkable crime, almost a text book example of how to rob a train populated entirely by rich folk, without harming a hair of anyone's head—and very much an inside job. The *Habits Noirs* had infiltrated every nook and cranny of the railway company's operations at the time. Many of the Corsican immigrants in Paris belong to the organization, and they had agents in every important railway post on the overnight train from the Gare de Lyon: they had the engine driver and firemen on the engine; the sleeping car and Pullman car stewards and the guards inside the train; the signalman who stopped the train on the pretext of a fire and the station master at the remote countryside station. As you know, they stripped every piece of valuable jewelry and currency from every cabin on the train, and disappeared into the night at a small country station out-side Toulon. They got away with several million francs—the amount was never verified—no doubt, they had a boat waiting off the coast at La Garrione to take them across to Propriano."

"I know the Sûreté never managed to lay hands on the culprits."

"Not one person admitted to seeing or hearing any-thing, that is the sort of fear that they inspire. You can begin to appreciate how well organized and disciplined they are. After the robbery, Negroni came to England where he appears to have posed as an Italian nobleman under the name of Count Negretto Sylvius."[9]

"Ah, yes," said Holmes. "Watson and I crossed his path not so long ago."

"Well, a job such as stealing the Nebrodi Sapphire from the Countess would be child's play to the *Habits Noirs*. They play for large stakes and plan their cam-paigns well in advance. You say the Nebrodi Sapphire is now in Paris with the Contessa Di Milazzo; should the *Habits Noirs* decide to go after it there, half the hotel staff will be in their employ. I must say honestly that I believe that the men and—beware!—in some cases, the *women,* of the *Habits Noirs* would be more than a match for the Parisian Police."

"Of course, there is no certainty that the *Habits Noirs* are behind it," replied Holmes, "it is merely one of the possibilities. We shall have to try to establish the lie of the land once we get to Paris, but it is useful to know. Of course, my own suspicions naturally fall on Mori-arty's organization, since it is from that quarter that the warning emanates; it now occurs to me, however, that it

---

[9] From *The Adventure of the Mazarin Stone*.

is not beyond the bounds of credibility that having moved the focus of his operations to Paris, Moriarty may have decided to, shall we say, co-opt the local specialists in crime…"

"It is not impossible," said Sergeant Hill. "I hardly need warn you of the personal danger that you would risk from not one, but two societies which enforce their decrees by murder and brook no interference from without and no disloyalty from within."

Holmes smiled and said, "You are the second person within the last hour to warn me of that. Well, Watson, this certainly has all the potential to be an interesting, if somewhat hazardous, adventure—it certainly bears out my judgment in giving preference to this case, as opposed to chasing around trying to retrieve some dusty old scroll."

Our cab called promptly at nine and, soon afterwards, we found ourselves settled comfortably in a first-class carriage bowling along through the darkness on the London Chatham and Dover railway. I sat drawing upon my cigar in the corner by the window as we steamed through Rochester, and Holmes reached for his flask and poured two large glasses of whisky. He then began to fill his cherry wood pipe [10] with tobacco and, once the wisps of smoke had begun to curl up from the bowl, he looked across at me and he began to sketch what he had discovered since our visit to Clerkenwell and Holborn in the afternoon.

---

[10] Holmes possessed a whole range of pipes, which he chose according to whether his mood was discursive, disputatious, imaginative, and so on. The cherry wood appears to signify a mood of quite reflection.

"To be perfectly honest, Watson," he began, "I had originally considered whether the message purporting to come from Porlock might have been a hoax..."

"But why a hoax, Holmes?"

"To get me out of London, of course! To set up a decoy—it is an old stratagem, and a simple one, amongst the criminal fraternity. Start a commotion at Clapham or Lambeth, and whilst attention is diverted there, marshal your forces to rob a bank in the City, or make a smash and grab raid on a jeweler's in the Whitechapel High Street. The footpads and highwaymen used to do in the days of the Bow Street Runners. With Sherlock Holmes known to be on the continent, on the trail of the culprits of some imaginary jewel robbery, who knows what depredations Moriarty's organization may get themselves up to whilst the coast is clear? However, two facts persuaded me that message was a genuine one: one was the protocol which Porlock employed, which is, admittedly, by no means foolproof; and the other was because I reasoned that, since Moriarty has his standing in the criminal fraternity to consider, he may well wish to make a name for himself very soon by carrying out something on this scale. Until now, his return has been marked largely by petty robberies and the like. But think what a prize the *Stella Zaffiro* would be—the largest and most expensive Sapphire in Europe!

"I spent an instructive afternoon in investigation of the facts, which I have now established beyond doubt. It happens that this very rich Italian noblewoman, the Contessa Di Milazzo from Sicily, is presently residing in the luxurious Hotel des Mamelouks in Paris. It seems that her husband was much older than she was—some twenty odd years—and many people at the time believed that she married the Count purely for his money. There is nothing unusual in that, one would suppose. Her present company, that is to say, her entire traveling entourage, as distinct from her domestic establishment in Sicily, consists of the Contessa herself, her secretary, an Englishman called Michael Carter, her personal maid, Giulianna Peretti, and a general factotum, Giuseppe Gazzano—the latter is also Sicilian. The maid is a Corsican, and as soon as I heard that, my ears pricked up. You recall the conversation with Hill, of course, about the women of the *Habits Noirs*?

"The Contessa is a very eligible widow of forty-two, and spends much of her time, and large amounts of her late husband's legacy, drifting through the fashionable watering places of Europe: Paris, the Riviera, Milan, London, with occasional forays to New York. She has pretensions toward the arts—indeed, in the society columns of the respectable Parisian newspapers, she carries a reputation as something of a benefactor of various *avant-garde* artistic societies. By all accounts, she is a very beautiful woman, and reports are that she looks almost twenty years younger than her actual age.

"That she is very rich is beyond doubt, but she is also very vulnerable; decidedly of the sort which appeals to sycophantic admirers, and who unhappily attracts voracious swindlers and criminal types as a magnet attracts iron filings. Her current passion is for sculpture, and if the society columns in the more salacious newspapers are to be believed, for sculptors—but that is another story. She has come to Paris, apparently, to attend, or at least, to be seen at, the *Exposition des Sculptures Modernes* at the Galerie Jonquin, a very exclusive private gallery. Rumor has it that she modeled, *d'après modèle vivant,* for one of the pieces on show, created by a young sculptor from an obscure coterie of Bohemian artists—wearing nothing but the *Stella Zaffiro!* A sort of aristocratic *grisette*, though her own social origins are markedly lower than her late husband's. Having ample means to indulge her most ridiculous whims, she is, by all accounts, the very personification of vanity and capriciousness, preferring to keep her precious collection of jewels, of which the Nebrodi Sapphire is, as Ricoletti said, but one—albeit the most precious—with her at all times, rather than entrust them to any bank. This must be the terror of the Hotel Managers wherever she chooses to reside. The society columns rumored that it was her intention to wear this Sapphire to the *Exposition* on Friday night."

"There have been no attempts on this valuable collection so far?" I asked.

"Not to my knowledge. Probably for the reason which Hill explained—the fact that any attempt to steal the jewel in Sicily would result in certain retribution would be enough to deter most ordinary criminals."

"But Moriarty is no ordinary criminal, and as Hill pointed out, the writ of the Mafia does not run in Paris."

"Indeed."

"What if we should arrive there and the Sapphire has already been stolen?"

"Good Lord, Watson, you do not think I had left that to chance! Before you arrived this morning, I had already detailed Cartwright to send a couple of telegrams from the Wigmore Street Post Office on his way to the railway station. I have informed my friend Monsieur François Le Villard, who is now head of the Préfecture de Police in Paris, and also the Contessa Di Milazzo herself, as to the contents of Porlock's message."

"But then, surely, having informed both the owner and the Parisian police, you need have done no more?"

"Indeed, I could have left the matter there, and may have considered my duty done. But the involvement of a certain Professor has kindled my professional curiosity. Having escaped my clutches once before, I am, as you might imagine, quite keen to even the score. I would want to be in at the kill, so to speak, if there is to be such a thing as a kill. After all, I owe Moriarty's establishment a bad turn or two. Quite apart from the matter of my professional pride, the Contessa, on receiving my message, seems to have become quite agitated. She requested my personal advice on how to proceed, and made a most princely offer to engage our services instantly."

"*Our* services?"

"Indeed, Watson. I informed her ladyship that I would be lost without my faithful chronicler," Holmes smiled. "The Contessa has engaged us to protect the Sapphire until she leaves Paris at the end of the week. My initial suggestion was that she should deposit the entire collection in a bank vault straight away, until we arrive and are in a position to decide the best course of action. I gave her the names of a few reliable Paris banks who are accustomed to holding such valuable cargoes in their vaults and who may be trusted. In the fashion of such persons, she was most insistent upon my dropping all my other cases and, quite dramatically, implored me to come to Paris right away. If we can ensure that she leaves Paris with the Sapphire intact, we shall benefit to the order of some thirty thousand francs—providing, as you suggest, that it has not already disappeared by the time we arrive."

"It is unlike you to be influenced by mere lucre, Holmes."

"As to the money, Watson, I may as well tell you that I have begun preparations for my retirement. I foresee a remote cottage somewhere on the south coast, or perhaps Devon or Cornwall, and it must be financed somehow. In perhaps... five years time, I shall be in a position to do so, but not, of course, until I have put Moriarty away where he can do no further harm. That is the real reason for my visit."

"Excellent news, Holmes! I heartily congratulate you. Incidentally, what did Monsieur Le Villard have to say on the matter?"

"He has taken the threat very seriously, although his reply was, naturally, more decorously worded than that of the Contessa's. He gave me his personal thanks for the warning and invited me to discuss the matter with him personally at the Préfecture first thing tomorrow morning. Now, I have told you all that I know, and really there the matter stands: further speculation would be futile until we arrive."

Chapter III
A Surprise in Paris

Once the train had pulled in to the Gare du Nord, we hastened, with the assistance of a porter, to the left luggage office to deposit our suitcases. Once we had collected our tickets, we then proceeded to have breakfast or, as Holmes put it with some asperity, what passes for breakfast in Parisian establishments, in the station buffet. Once revivified after our long night's journey, we hailed a cab and were soon crawling slowly through the busy morning traffic along the Boulevard de Sébastopol towards the Préfecture de Police in the Île de la Cité.

We were taken, on our arrival, to meet the celebrated Parisian detective, Monsieur François Le Villard, Préfet de Police, and his deputy, Monsieur Jérôme Dubuque. Monsieur le Préfet was a slim dapper middle-aged man, fair-haired, with a most intense manner; Monsieur Dubuque, whom neither Holmes I had heard of previously, was a much younger fellow, dark-haired, sallow and portly in the extreme: clearly, a man who was very fond of *Cordon Bleu* cuisine—a subject upon which, it later turned out, he held the reputation of being something of an expert.

My comprehension of the French language has never been of the first order, but I was nevertheless able to follow the opening of the conversation which Holmes, who was, of course, perfectly fluent, conducted with Monsieur Le Villard.

"Too late? *Too late!*" Holmes almost screamed, momentarily losing his normal impassivity.

The Préfet looked from one to the other of us intently, "Just so, Monsieur Holmes. As I say, you have arrived several hours too late, I am afraid."

"Then, despite all my warnings, the Nebrodi Sapphire has been stolen?" asked Holmes in dismay.

"No, it is worse than that."

"Worse?"

"Yes. The Sapphire remains intact, at least as far as can be determined, but Monsieur Michael Carter, the Contessa's secretary, appears to have been murdered during the night."

"Precisely what construction may I put on *appears to have been*?" replied Holmes.

"Well, the facts are these, Monsieur Holmes. On receipt of your message, I visited the Contessa personally and I impressed upon her your stature as a detective in England, and also the reputation which you have made here in France. I understood from her that she had not only had a note from you, but that she had already engaged your services. Although she had received your reply, containing quite definite instructions as to the arrangements which she ought to have followed as to the security of the Sapphire, frankly, she equivocated for such a long time about which course of action to take that the banks were closed by the time she had come to a decision, so there was no opportunity to put the jewel into safe-keeping. The decision was made that Monsieur Carter, her trusted secretary, would take the jewel case containing the Sapphire into his room during the night and place it in his own safe deposit box. He was a light sleeper for one thing and, if any attempt was made to enter the premises for the purposes of robbery, he would be sure to awaken. For another, he carried a revolver, and apparently knew how to use it.

"This morning, about seven o'clock, the Contessa's household awoke to find Monsieur Carter stone dead in his room. He was in bed, fully dressed in his night-clothes, and yet the strange thing is..." Here, Le Villard paused for effect, "...that there was not a mark upon him."

"Who discovered him?" asked Holmes.

"It happened this way," replied Le Villard. "Carter was an early riser on weekdays, who had normally breakfasted and was to be found at work in the office an hour or so before the rest of the household. At seven, he would go out for a walk along the Seine and bring back an English newspaper. Just before seven this morning, the maid, Giulianna, awoke and went along to Carter's room to ensure that everything was in order. She found the door locked, as might have been expected, but Carter would not reply to her knocking. Not only was his door locked, she could see the key inside the lock; therefore, she assumed that Carter was still inside. But why would he not answer? She became concerned and went straight away to talk to the manservant, Gazzano, to help her as-certain the cause of Carter's silence. There was some de-lay as a member of the hotel staff had to be summoned to dislodge the key on the inside. Then, on entering the room by using the master key, they found Carter in bed as I described.

"At first, they thought he was in a stupor, having possibly been drugged, but when it was found that he could not be awakened by the shouts and cries and the shaking of Gazzano, there was some alarm. Gazzano no-ticed how cold he was; then, he felt for his pulse and, on closer inspection, discovered that the man was dead. As the jewel case lay on the table beside the safe deposit box, they immediately assumed the Sapphire had been stolen, but on opening the jewel case, the maid found that it was still there."

"One moment—has it been verified as the genuine Nebrodi Sapphire?" asked Holmes.

"It has. One of the first things we did was to call in Monsieur Bernheim of the well-known firm Bernheim & Blum. He verified it immediately, as did Monsieur Cahen-Mervith, who was called in for a second opinion. Both men are at the heads of their profession, and are authorities on the subject, and indeed they each charged the Contessa over one thousand francs merely for a two minute valuation. The circumstances were reported to us immediately. It was just over two hours ago…" Le Villard broke off to consult his watch, then resumed speaking, "…when I received an urgent message from Inspector Faverges, the station officer in the fourth arrondissement. Remembering your note from the previous day, I decided to attend personally and I was at the Hotel des Mamelouks within minutes of being informed of the crime.

"I immediately made my own examination, of course, and I noticed that there were no signs of violence upon Carter's body—nothing, not even the slightest pin prick. On the contrary, it looked to me—and I have seen the corpses of many murdered men and women—as though he had experienced a natural death. The Medical Examiner, who arrived soon after, was undecided on this point and naturally wished to make a more detailed inspection before he would express an opinion. So the body was taken away for a *post mortem* examination to the Morgue. As I intimated in my telegram, I am grateful for your assistance in this case, and it would be foolish of me not to take advantage of your experience and wisdom, particularly as you have had some premonition of the crime. Would you care to examine the body at the Morgue?"

"It would be rather impertinent of me to do so, Monsieur Le Villard, after you have made such an exhausting examination. In any case, as the body has now been removed, I might as well wait until the results of the *post mortem*. I would ask one question however, whether there was any indication of poison?"

"I checked for that and found no evidence whatsoever. Even a poison dart leaves a pin prick and there was no mark. As you will know, however, by no means are all poisons traceable by smell, though I strongly suspect that was indeed the cause of death. Accordingly, my colleague, Monsieur Dubuque, immediately questioned the hotel staff as to the dining arrangements of the Contessa's party last night; by whom the food was prepared, and by whom it was served. He speaks the same language as the *chefs cuisiniers,* for he once graced their ranks before becoming a detective."

"You had great presence of mind," said Holmes to Dubuque. "What was the result?"

"The party, with the exception of the Contessa herself," Dubuque replied, "were in the habit of eating together in a reserved section of the Hotel Dining Room. The Contessa usually has Italian food specially prepared and sent up to her room. She eats like a sparrow, by all accounts, picks at her food, and constantly complains that the chefs here are not as good as in Italy, and that the hotel food has no taste. Last night, the members of the party all ate together at about seven o'clock in the evening, in the Hotel Dining Room. They each chose freely, as is usual, from the standard dishes on the menu—three courses."

"This menu is the same one as is provided to the rest of the Hotel residents?"

"Yes, always."

"Who chose the dishes for the menu?"

"On this occasion, the *sous-chef* chose them first thing yesterday morning once the day's consignment of fresh food arrived from the markets—usually it would be the *chef cuisinier,* who did this, but this was his day off, and it is common practice for the senior *sous-chef* to do this in his absence. He chose all of the dishes on the menu and cooked the ones containing meat; another *sous-chef* cooked the fish; yet another cooked the desserts—again, this is common in a large hotel. Of course, there are other persons present in the kitchen, the *plongeurs* for instance, but they do not normally handle the food other than peeling potatoes and onions and carrying out other menial tasks. The party was served by Antoine, a waiter who has been employed in the hotel for five years, assisted by Léontine, a new girl for this season who served all the wine, the desserts, and the after-dinner coffee and liqueurs. Monsieur Carter, on this occasion, chose, as was usual, the plainer dishes: clear consommé, *sole Véronique*, and *meringue glacée*."

"None of which was highly flavored and therefore unlikely to have masked the taste of any poison?" said Holmes.

"That was precisely my line of inquiry," said Dubuque.

"Did Carter have anything sent up to his room before or after dinner?"

"No food at all," replied Dubuque, "only a pot of tea, Earl Grey, which he took, of course, without any milk. This was also prepared in the still room by Léontine, and carried up to the room by Joseph, the page, at about three o'clock in the afternoon. According to Joseph, who came back some time later to retrieve the tea tray, the teacup remained unused; so, it is unlikely that any poison could have slipped into the tea. Unfortunately, the teapot was taken back to the still room to be washed then used again; so, we cannot perform an analysis of the contents."

"Nevertheless, it seems unlikely than anything containing poison, or at least any traceable poison, came from the kitchen."

"Inconceivable, I should say," assented Dubuque.

"Was anything else sent up to his room?" asked Holmes.

"No, not as far as we can ascertain," replied Dubuque.

Le Villard continued, "Not only was the door of Carter's bedroom locked on the inside, the windows had been locked on the inside too, and, as there was no connecting door to any of the other rooms, it would seem impossible on the face of it that there could have been any foul play from an outside party. However, I was of course immediately suspicious, not the least because of the telegram I received from you yesterday, but also because Carter is a relatively young man of thirty-seven, who seemed fit and healthy with no known medical conditions."

"And there is no sign that even an attempt was made to steal the Sapphire?" asked Holmes.

"None whatsoever, although the strangest part is that the jewel case seems to have been removed from the safe deposit box, which is built against the wall on a table."

"Removed from the safe! Why, that's odd."

"Yes, we thought so too. Still the jewel remains."

"And the two jewelers who confirmed the authenticity of the Sapphire are beyond suspicion?"

"Absolutely. Now, if you are agreeable, Monsieur Holmes, we shall go along to the Hotel des Mamelouks and you may examine the premises and question, as well as interview some of the people connected with this mysterious occurrence."

"Do I understand," inquired Holmes "that yourself have taken the case on?"

"Yes, Monsieur Dubuque and I are dealing with the case personally. We have had a spate of valuable jewel robberies recently, and I am afraid that the officials from the *Ministère* have been hounding us privately—and the press publicly. I felt that, if I could at least thwart this robbery, I would at least prevent the situation from worsening. That is why I was most delighted that you agreed to come to Paris. We may have averted the robbery, but now we have murder to solve," said Le Villard dismally as we prepared to leave the building.

A journey of a few minutes brought the four of us from the gloomy Préfecture across the Pont Saint-Louis to the Hotel des Mamelouks, a fine establishment located in the Rue St-Louis-en-l'Île—one of those very select places where a night's board without breakfast costs the equivalent of an artisan's weekly wage. The Contessa Di Milazzo and her party occupied a magnificent suite right at the very top of the hotel.

We were ushered there straight away by the Manager, and the Contessa welcomed us most demonstratively to her sitting-room, which was richly furnished with an almost oriental opulence. She made a great exhibition of thanking us for coming to her assistance. She had, as soon as Holmes had consented to come to Paris, immediately reserved, at her own expense, a smaller suite for my friend and I on the fourth floor, which saved us the trouble of finding our own accommodation. She was indeed a very attractive woman: olive skin, raven black hair, drawn back to reveal dark luscious eyes, and sensuous carmine lips. The curves of her bare neck, shoulders and bosom, were set off to perfection by a magnificent gown of turquoise silk. One could see without difficulty how she would make an excellent, if distracting, subject for a sculptor.

"Signore Holmes, I am glad to have not one, but two Englishmen to help me. My secretary, Signore Carter, he too was English. I should have acted straight away as you suggested, and I feel that I am responsible for his death." She spoke very good English, albeit with a strong Italian accent.

"In what way, Contessa?"

"Because he died defending the jewels which he was guarding on my behalf. I know it was very foolish of me not to place them in the bank, but I cannot bear to be parted with them. Signore Carter was very brave and…"

"With the greatest respect, Contessa," interrupted Holmes, "there is no evidence yet that there has been any murder, and far less evidence that any attempt was made to steal the Sapphire last night."

"Evidence!" she cried in surprise. "What more evidence could anyone need? Signore Carter lies dead and *La Stella Zaffiro* was taken out of the safe by someone who came in here last night to try to steal it. I know that Signore Carter was murdered by someone who was after my jewels. A woman's intuition—is not that good enough?"

Holmes smiled indulgently. "As a male of the species, I am disadvantaged, Contessa, in not sharing this intuition, so I would prefer to begin with a few facts. May I ask you some questions?"

The Contessa nodded.

"My apologies if you have already been asked this, but how long have each of your employees been with you?"

"Giuseppe Gazzano and his family have been with us for generations, Signore Holmes. His father, mother and sister, still work on the estate in Milazzo. Signore Carter was with me for almost two years—from London, he came to work with me after my previous secretary left. Giulianna Peretti has been my traveling maid for about six months—I found her here in Paris, just after I arrived earlier this year."

"Leaving aside Giuseppe Gazzano, what has been your experience of the other two employees?"

"I have found no fault with them. They are both very efficient in their own ways. Signore Carter was typical of the Englishman—he *was* very reserved, always polite, and most efficient. Giulianna is a wonderful companion to me: clever, amusing... in such a short time, she has become like Giuseppe, one of the family. And she is fluent in Italian in addition to the other languages which she speaks. Those qualities are very useful when one travels as much as I do. "

"I will ask you frankly, Contessa, to put aside any preconceptions you may have. Assuming there had been an attempt to steal the Sapphire last night, would you suspect any of your servants?"

"That is a terrible thing to ask, Signore Holmes! How can you expect me to accuse my own servants and employees? Big cities like Paris are full of criminals and robbers, why should I suspect my own people?"

"Contessa, these are not strictly your own people. Carter, as you say, was English…"

"An English gentleman!"

"The maid, Peretti, is Corsican."

"Yes, a very decent girl, I cannot believe that she would do anything dishonest or disloyal."

"But she is the most recent arrival?"

There was some hesitancy on the Contessa's part. "Yes, but what difference should that make?"

Holmes continued, "Have you ever had any reason, even the merest suspicion whatsoever, to doubt the honesty of either Mister Carter or Mademoiselle Peretti?"

"No, none at all."

"I will require to question both Peretti and Gazzano at some point."

"By all means. Do you wish me to summon them?"

"Not until I have examined the premises. I suppose the practical point upon which we now have to decide is whether or not it is prudent for you to wear the Sapphire to the *Exposition* on Friday evening."

"My mind is made up, Signore Holmes," said the Contessa, flushing. "I did not bring this beautiful thing all the way from Sicily to hide it away in a bank. *Of course* I shall wear it, and you will accompany me to ensure my safety, will you not?"

"Indeed, Contessa, I shall."

"But surely," interrupted Le Villard, "after what has happened, it would be madness to take such a chance?"

"Not at all, we have a full three days in which to clear the matter up," replied Holmes. "And after all, that is what I have come here to do."

"I knew you would not fail me, Signore Holmes."

"May I ask you one final question, Contessa?" said Holmes. "Have you ever had any reason to suspect that either Mr. Carter or Miss Peretti might have been planted in your household by someone or some organization?

"Impossible. Signore Carter came to me through a respectable international agency. Giulianna Peretti, I selected myself from a number of applicants in Paris. When I saw the name 'Peretti,' I thought she must be of Italian descent, but once we had had a short interview, I felt she was perfect for me in every way. It mattered not that she was Corsican, even though I have heard of their dastardly reputation."

"Can you remember the name of the agency from which you recruited Mr. Carter?"

"I cannot recall it, Signore Holmes, but I will ask Giulianna to find it for me, and I will let you know."

"Monsieur Holmes has a theory that a certain master criminal with international connections may have been involved in a conspiracy to steal the Sapphire," explained Le Villard.

"A theory which is, at least, partly borne out by recent developments," Holmes added. "Incidentally, Contessa, may I be permitted to see this little gemstone on account of which one person may already have lost his life?"

The Contessa rose and went to a locked cabinet and withdrew a black rectangular box, which she handed to Holmes.

"It is beautiful, would you not say so, Signore Holmes?"

"Hm, a rare coloration, certainly," said Holmes, holding it up to the light, "and a remarkable translucence; no doubt, due to the peculiar chemical composition of trace elements such as titanium in combination with corundum and, of course, the notable absence of chromium…"

"I am very grateful that you have consented to come. You will not regret it, I assure you."

"I will do my best, Contessa," replied Holmes. "My advice remains to lose no time in handing it over to one of the banks whose names I have given you, where it can be placed in an impregnable vault until Friday evening. However, I must warn you that, if my information is correct, the man who is out to get the Sapphire will stop at nothing until he succeeds and, perhaps, even when you leave Paris, your troubles will not be over."

"It is to be collected and taken to the bank within the hour. But surely, this man is no match for the great Sherlock Holmes?" she asked.

Holmes smiled indulgently. "In my experience, this man seems to have been more than a match for the combined police forces of two continents, but I can guarantee you that I will do all that is in my power, Contessa. It has been a lifetime's ambition to bring that man to justice: it remains so. In the meantime, I should prefer if you did not discuss any aspect of the affair with your staff."

As we took our leave of the Contessa, it was clear that Le Villard remained skeptical about the role of Moriarty in this affair, and the connection with Porlock.

"Despite your disbelief, Monsieur Le Villard," said Holmes, "I can assure you that this Porlock character does exist, and that he is part of Professor Moriarty's shady empire. I have never known Porlock to have committed any actual crime; indeed, he appears to have the status of a kind of manservant and general dogsbody to the Professor. He knows a little about the Professor's depredations, of that we can be certain, though I suspect scarcely sufficient to secure a conviction in a court of law. In some way, that is his only guarantee of safety.

You can be sure, however, that should he either discover anything which the Professor would regard as compromising, or engage in activity which the Professor might consider disloyal—including coded messages to a certain private consulting detective—there would be no more of friend Porlock."

"Meaning that he would be done away with?" asked Le Villard.

"Just so. Eliminated swiftly and without leaving the slightest trace, which is why I have never made any attempt to communicate with the man personally. Whether motivated by material gain, or by the occasional stirrings of conscience, it is impossible to say; however, Porlock's communications tend to be anticipatory to the crime, rather than *post-facto*, and it is correct to say that, on a number of occasions, he has succeeded in preventing some tragedy befalling an innocent party."

"He seems to have left it very late in this case," said Dubuque rather ruefully.

"Late perhaps, but he was nevertheless quite accurate in his premonition that something was afoot. In the present circumstances," Holmes continued, "the likelihood is that he sent his message as soon as he humanly could do so. To the best of my knowledge, the fellow who goes by the name 'Fred Porlock' has no stomach for violence. Although I have never met the man, I have a vague idea of his background, an intelligence gained, I may say, from one of my contacts in the criminal underworld of the East End. He is a Russian Jew, born Klesmesh Porloch, who anglicized his surname to 'Porlock' after fleeing Czar Alexander's pogroms with thousands of others at the same time. The 'Fred' part was a cognomen he picked up—thanks to the unpronounceability of his forename to our cockney, that is to say our London, tongue—whilst working in the textile trade, until more lucrative opportunities presented themselves in the criminal underworld of London's East End. His Camberwell address is a mere flag of convenience, so to speak, a district of London south of the river where he may, presumably, come and go safely without being recognized. As to Porlock's lord and master, let me assure you, that forgery, fraud, robbery, arson and murder are all but a job of journeywork to the man. Now, gentlemen," he continued, "let me bring the matter within your own purview: you will recall last spring the assassination attempt on *Monsieur le Président* by Georges Huret?"

"Indeed, Monsieur Holmes, how could we forget how you singlehandedly saved Monsieur Sadi Carnot's life and managed to capture his intended murderer who had eluded us for months?"

"I suspected, even at that point, although I was unable to prove it, that Huret belonged to that shady organization which was being run by Moriarty's lieutenant, Colonel Sebastian Moran. Huret, as you will recall, refused to talk at the trial and, at the time, most people, including, if I remember correctly, the head of the Sûreté, believed the second successful attempt on Monsieur Carnot's life to be the work of Anarchists. It was not; it is now clear to me that was the work of Moriarty. His motive? He is one of the most ruthless, but also the most vindictive, master criminals I have ever come up against. I am sure that Moriarty held your President personally responsible for the disastrous failure of the Panama Canal Scheme in which he was almost ruined—a mysterious investor was known to have lost over a million francs in the collapse, more than thirty thousand pounds, a small fortune. That investor was undoubtedly Moriarty.

"At the bribery trial which followed the collapse, as you no doubt recall, Minister Berthaut received five years' imprisonment, and the financial adviser to the scheme, Baron Reinach, was supposed to have committed suicide. It was no suicide, I can assure you, but a very cleverly planned murder made to look like suicide—one which bore every hallmark of Moriarty's work. Some of the other defendants implicated in the fraud managed to escape from prison before they gave evidence—it was no co-incidence that they fled to England. Believing themselves to be fleeing from justice, they were no doubt lured there by Moriarty's organization, and were never seen again. By that, I mean their bodies were never found.

"Each generation seems to throw up some variety of arch-villain: Jonathan Wild, Adam Worth, Charlie Peace, James Saward, but the prototype has been perfected with Moriarty—he's an enemy of mankind. Now, let us proceed to examine the actual scene of the crime."

Chapter IV
At the Hotel des Mamelouks

Le Villard led us out of the Contessa's sitting-room and began to describe the layout of the rest of the suite occupied by the party. The Contessa's suite comprised her own bedroom and a sitting-room, linked by a door to her maid's bedroom; there was a bedroom for Gazzano, the general manservant, and another for the secretary, Carter, both of which were completely self-contained. There was a communal sitting-room, which was used by all of the employees from time to time, and a smaller room temporarily converted to an office which was used mainly by Carter, and occasionally by the maid Giulianna.

Le Villard showed us into Carter's bedchamber, a large, airy room into which bright morning sunshine now streamed through the full length windows. On entering, we saw the ruffled bedclothes where the man had lain until being discovered in the morning, and the miniature safe deposit box on a table against the wall. Holmes bustled around the room as a bloodhound trails a scent. He tiptoed back and forth a number of times, stopped, and made a note or two in his notebook, then finally crouched and gazed at the carpet for some time with a mixture of concentration and puzzlement on his features. He looked under the bed, and in every cupboard and drawer, and then began scribbling away again. He examined minutely the surface of the bedside dresser, turned to Le Villard and said sharply, "A water glass and some other larger heavier object appear to have been placed here quite recently."

"Ah, yes indeed. We have also taken away for chemical analysis the water glass and carafe which stood on the bedside table," replied the Préfet.

"The indentation of the glass was unmistakable," said Holmes. "Now, let me just be certain that, in order to steal the Sapphire, a thief would have had to get into the hotel unobserved, then get through Carter's locked bedroom door, or come in through the window, which was also apparently locked. Then the thief would have to subdue Carter..."

"Or had already subdued Carter by some other means," interjected Le Villard.

"Fine, he would have to subdue Carter if he had not already done so, then abstract the jewel case from the locked deposit box, pocket the gem or the case, which implies the possession of the necessary keys."

"Carter had the keys to both the box and the case in the drawer beside his bed. Either the intruder could have taken them from him and replaced them, or he could have had duplicates made beforehand."

"He would then have to retrace his steps again unobserved?"

"Yes, it is as you say, although getting into the hotel unobserved is perhaps not so difficult... As you saw, the foyer is always busy..."

"But to come in during the night?"

"He could have come in during the previous day—it would be the easiest thing to conceal oneself in a linen cupboard or such like for several hours," said Dubuque. "These hotels are labyrinthine; one can work in a place like this for several years and never see all of it."

Le Villard continued, "Now, when the Contessa's maid arrived this morning, the room was locked and the key was in the lock inside—proof, I think you will agree,

Monsieur Holmes, that if there were any intruders, they did not escape this way. This is confirmed by the fact that the hotel staff had to knock the key out of the lock from the outside before the room door could be opened with a master key. The windows, as it has been stated, were also locked on the inside."

"That is proof then surely, Monsieur Le Villard, that there were no intruders at all, since if they did not escape through the doors or the windows, then no escape was at all possible."

"Not necessarily, because the windows may have been locked by someone in the general confusion when the room was entered and the dead man found."

"In which case, you suspect a confederate amongst the people who entered the room?"

"I do not rule out the possibility, and I have a reason for doing so which will become apparent presently. You see, this confederate would have known what to expect to find inside the room and would not have been in the same state of confusion as the rest of the party. He or *she*..." Le Villard added with emphasis "...could have surreptitiously slipped across to the window and turned the key in the lock whilst attention was being diverted to the corpse in the bed."

"An escape through the window?" mused Holmes. "Well, let us take a look then, shall we?"

Holmes walked over to the windows and threw them open. They led onto a shallow balcony, from which there was a sheer drop into the busy Rue St-Louis-en-l'Île below. He took out his magnifying glass, examined the balcony and inspected the doors minutely, then went over the ironwork of the railings with great care; finally, he gazed upwards towards the roof of the hotel. After a few minutes, he returned to the room, shaking his head emphatically.

"As you can see, Monsieur Le Villard, from the balcony, it is a sixty foot drop to a busy street, and there is scarcely a foothold on the surface of the wall. I'm afraid I cannot discern the slightest trace of disturbance anywhere, either on the balcony or on the adjacent brickwork. It would be inestimably difficult for anyone to have entered or left that way, and a virtual impossibility to have done so without leaving any trace behind."

"I believe it is not impossible for… for someone who was used to it, but I will return to that presently," Le Villard continued. "Monsieur Carter was found in the bed, fully attired in nightclothes. As I said, the jewel case which the dead man was guarding was not in the safe deposit box, where it would have been placed until proper arrangements could be made for its safe keeping, but had been removed and was placed adjacent to it."

"But the safe deposit box remained closed and locked?"

"Yes."

"Indeed! Then the implication is that someone removed the jewel case, but they did not steal the jewel?" asked Holmes.

"Yes. It struck me as being extremely strange— definitely suggestive that the culprit, or culprits, were disturbed by something or someone. Perhaps he or they lost their nerve and fled immediately?"

Holmes shook his head decisively, "No, I doubt it. Having got the jewel case out of the deposit box, it would take only a second or two to pocket it and disappear."

Le Villard said, "We have since checked up on some of the family connections of the maid Peretti—she has two cousins who live in the Paris suburbs, on the Rue des Lyanes, near Bagnolet, to be precise. Two gentlemen to whom a sheer wall and a sixty foot drop would be a child's game, Monsieur Holmes, for they were once circus acrobats, although they are too old for the high wire nowadays. They would have the skill and the nerve to carry out such an operation; furthermore, they both have a record for burglary in Corsica."

"You suspect they were the intruders, and you suspect Mademoiselle Peretti of being the confederate who, as you put it, subdued Carter."

"It is certainly possible that she may have poisoned him."

"Ah, you have formed your theory already then?"

"To a certain extent—a theory which is supported by the known facts."

Holmes pondered for a moment. "What does the Contessa think about this?"

"She believes the maid to be completely innocent!"

"And you do not?"

"By no means."

"Then, how do you consider that she managed to poison Carter?"

"There are a number of possibilities: she could have slipped something into his food or drink beforehand. She could have insinuated herself into his room on some pretext—after all, she is by no means an unattractive girl as you will no doubt see."

"In fact, I make it a point not to notice such things, Monsieur Le Villard. It biases the judgment," replied Holmes, much to the Préfet's and to Dubuque's incredulity.

"Let us suppose that she had a secret rendezvous with Carter in his room late last night," Le Villard continued, "who knows what may have happened. Either she could have slipped him the poison, or she made it possible somehow for her cousins to gain entry in order to execute their own plan and they disposed of Carter."

"But surely there are a number of objections to that theory, apart from the impossibility of having come in through the balcony. If the Peretti brothers had managed to steal the Sapphire sometime during the night and then disappeared, they must have known that the hue and cry would have gone up at once. Assuming they made for Corsica then, before they would even reach Lyon, their names and descriptions would be in every railway station and ferry port in the country; the trail would be very hot."

"Criminals are often arrogant, sometimes stupid, and even occasionally quite mad. And they may have intended to steal the jewel and sit on it until the heat died down."

"Yet, according to your own investigation, there is no sign of the forced administration of poison. And even if there were, why was the jewel still in the case? If there was time to commit murder by poison, then why not the robbery? We can hardly believe that the intruders, if indeed there were any intruders, took the case out of the deposit box in order simply to admire it."

"No. There is another, more remote, possibility: that Carter may have been in league with the Corsicans and then either had a change of heart, or tried to cross them."

Holmes shook his head severely, "We can hardly believe that there were two parties out to steal the Sapphire and that they were both in the very same room as it, and yet somehow managed to leave without taking it. But are these two Corsicans big enough to handle such a job as a jewel worth two million francs?"

"That is a minor question. They may have been acting for others, who would be able to dispose of such a piece it with no trouble. Chief amongst these is one Raoul d'Andrésy, who arrived in Paris recently; there is also Bertrand de Beauharnais, Be-Bo as he is known in the underworld, although he has not been seen in Paris for some time. More to the point, there are bigger and more powerful Corsican criminal connections in Paris with whom the Perettis may be connected and for whom they may be working."

"The *Habits Noirs*?"

Le Villard laughed. "There is no getting past you, Monsieur Holmes. So you know of the *Habits Noirs*?"

"Yes, I was warned by a colleague in the London Police, a Sergeant Hill."

"He must be very well informed, if he knows of the *Habits Noirs*."

"Indeed, he has done a great deal of work amongst the immigrants in the Italian quarter of London—the *Veste Nere*, he called them, but it is in essence a branch of the same organization. He also warned me that some of the Hotel staff might be in the employ of the *Habits Noirs*, so I have taken nothing for granted. He also warned me of the personal danger I would be running if I were to cross swords with them."

"He did not exaggerate, Monsieur Holmes. Last year, there were two fatal stabbings and a garroting. And these two Corsicans—Petru and Ghjuvan Peretti—were suspected of membership of the *Habits Noirs* at the time of their conviction for burglary; of course, nothing was ever proven against them."

"They may have left that organization and be acting so to speak in a freelance capacity, for example, Professor Moriarty."

"No one ever leaves the *Habits Noirs*, Monsieur Holmes, except in a coffin."

"Who are these two other gentlemen to whom you referred?"

"Raoul d'Andrésy has come to our attention in recent years; he is a rising young confidence artist and jewel thief. We have kept a watch on him since we received your message. Our information is that Be-Bo has not left Marseilles since 1892."

"I have not heard of either."

"There is no doubt that you will if you keep your eyes on the crime reports from France. De Beauharnais is perhaps in the twilight of his career—a man of sixty—but he was a desperate character in his day and he still has connections to the jewel trade. D'Andrésy is a most intriguing individual, certainly not the common type of criminal. He is a lone wolf with an almost aristocratic background, albeit an impoverished one—a sort of gentleman thief. He is learned in law and medicine, and once spent a year touring in a drama company. He has even studied with stage magicians and worked with would you believe... circus acrobats! He began by cracking safes. We trailed him last year to Nice, to Menton, and then to Normandy, and we know that he arrived in Paris only last week. You can see why we were suspicious when we considered a possible connection between d'Andrésy and the Perettis, who had been acrobats."

"Yes, it must be admitted that it seems a very singular coincidence, though coincidences do happen. Nevertheless, whichever way you look at it, whoever was responsible for Carter's death, whoever may have had a design on that Sapphire—and none of the suspects you named are exactly novices—how comes it to remain in the case?"

Le Villard shrugged. "That is the greatest enigma of the whole affair. We placed a watch on all the Contessa's staff as soon as I had received your message. Gazzano remained in the hotel all day, but the maid left almost immediately after lunch and went off to meet her cousins in La Villette."

"I thought you said they lived in Bagnolet?"

"Yes, the Perettis live near the Porte de Bagnolet, but their workshop is in La Villette; they have a statuary and reliquary business which seems to do well enough amongst the Italian immigrants there, though of course, given their antecedents, it has occurred to us that it may simply be a front. However, the shop was closed in the afternoon, for the Perettis seem still to follow the southern habit of siesta. Then, the maid came back to the hotel for some time, waited for a while, then hurried off again to La Villette when the shop re-opened."

"What did she say as to the purpose of her visit?" asked Holmes.

"She explains the pretext as having gone there on impulse simply to visit her cousins, but there is no doubt that she went there to arrange the robbery, in haste, because of the warning which was received," replied Le Villard.

Holmes's brows furrowed even further. "But the Porte de Bagnolet is almost en route to La Villette, is it not? You mean that she passed their residence twice and went back to the workshop later, when it would possibly have been easier to visit them in Bagnolet? Well, it may or may not be important."

Le Villard laughed again, "Your knowledge of Paris amazes me, Monsieur Holmes!"

"It is not impeccable, but I spent several weeks disguised as a jarvey trailing around the less salubrious parts of the city in a fiacre in pursuit of our friend Huret and his accomplices."

Le Villard continued, "Monsieur Carter left the hotel at two o'clock. Although our man lost him briefly at the junction on the Rue Maître-Albert, he picked Carter up again a few minutes later on his way back at the hotel. It turned out that all he had done was to go out to buy a newspaper."

"Did you find anything else of interest in Carter's room?"

"There were a few odds and ends in the pockets of a suit of clothes hanging in the wardrobe, but nothing incriminating—they are all in here," said Le Villard, handing Holmes an envelope.

"Yes, nothing very much here," commented Holmes. "A stub of a theatre ticket, a map of Paris, and postcards from a friend. Incidentally, did Carter make any mention of having friends in Paris?"

"Not that we know of. But why should you ask?"

Holmes shrugged, "I may be mistaken; perhaps I am reading too much into such an apparent trifle."

"I believe so, for I can see nothing of any importance there."

"This collection of articles, they were all found in Carter's clothes, the clothes which he would be wearing today if he were still alive?"

"No, only the postcards; the rest were in the drawer alongside the keys to the safe and the jewel case."

"I should like to take a closer look at these, if that is possible."

"Yes, by all means. Once we have examined them in detail, I shall send them on to you."

"Now, how exactly were the things in this room arranged?"

"According to Gazzano and Peretti, everything was where you would expect to find it and where you see it now—apart from the body, of course, and the locked jewel case. Naturally, we have only the maid's and Gazzano's word for that. If they were part of the conspiracy..." Le Villard made a significant gesture with his hand.

"How many people had keys to the deposit box?"

"Only Carter and the Hotel Manager."

"And the jewel case?"

"Normally only the Contessa, though her maid has a duplicate of all her keys—for her employer is dedicated to the habit of losing them. She gave her own key to Carter that night."

"Now you said that Carter owned a gun; a pistol I presume?"

"Yes, here it is," said Dubuque.

Holmes examined the weapon for a moment or two. "Very interesting. What explanation did Carter give for possessing a professional's weapon?"

"That he was acting not only as secretary to the Contessa, but also as her bodyguard; and the Sapphire was, after all, worth over two million francs," replied Dubuque.

"It feels empty. Have you unloaded it?" Holmes asked.

"No."

"You mean, it was not loaded?" asked Holmes with surprise.

"No, it was not," replied Le Villard, interrupting. "The first thing I intended to do was to carry out a test in

71

order to establish whether or not it had been fired recently."

"Not only had it not been fired, it had not even been loaded," said Dubuque.

"Hm. Not loaded. Most singular indeed, do you not consider it so, Monsieur Le Villard?"

"It is impossible to say. Perhaps Monsieur Carter did not take the warning very seriously? Perhaps he felt that, with the door locked, he was unassailable?"

Le Villard and Dubuque seemed puzzled at Holmes's question. They had obviously not grasped the point that, not only was Holmes not accustomed to taking even the smallest detail for granted, but that he was apt to test even the most infinitesimal link in his chain of reasoning when attempting to unravel the thread from some visible effect to the initial hidden cause.

"I had thought this case to be fairly straightforward," continued Holmes, "but now it begins to appear rather more complicated than I had imagined at first..."

Le Villard and Dubuque registered further confusion at this statement.

"Now, Monsieur Le Villard, would you be so good as to furnish me with a description of the dead man?" continued Holmes

"Of course. He was over six foot tall, very slightly built, which made him appear much taller, with fair, medium length hair, brown eyes; otherwise, very pleasant features. He bore a livid scar below the line of his collar on the left side of his neck, so that it would not be normally be noticed. He was deeply tanned from having spent the summer in Sicily. I can arrange for you to have a photograph after the *post mortem* if that is of any use to you."

"Yes, that would be of inestimable value. Well, I think we have done enough here, for the moment at least. Now, if you are agreeable, Monsieur Le Villard, I will proceed to question the Contessa's staff."

Chapter V
An Adumbration

Le Villard rang for the page and sent him to ask the manservant Giuseppe Gazzano to join us in the small room which Carter had been using as an office. Gazzano was in his late forties, dark, slow and heavy, with that obsequious demeanor that comes from a lifetime of servitude. Holmes explained that we were assisting the Paris Police in investigating the suspicious circumstances of Carter's death, and that Gazzano's employer had retained Holmes's services. He then asked the man, who spoke only very poor French, to recall what happened when he had entered the room when the alarm had first been raised.

"Well, Signore Holmes, I went in alone first because I did not want Signorina Peretti to see… to see anything; you understand, at that time, we thought that Signore Carter had been murdered, and that the Sapphire had been stolen. I thought it might be a very bloody sight. I was surprised to find him in bed. I then called to Signorina Peretti to come in."

"Can you tell me exactly what Signorina Peretti did as soon as you both entered the room?"

"Yes, she followed me to the bed where Carter lay, and then she went straight to the safe deposit box because the jewel case had already been taken out by someone and it was lying on the table."

"Did she seem surprised to find Carter dead?"

Gazzano seemed confused, "We did not know he was dead at that point."

"What did she do next?"

"She opened the jewel case and we found, to our surprise, that the Sapphire was still there."

"Did she go across at any time to the windows?

"No."

"You are absolutely certain that at no point she went near the windows?"

"I am sure, but I was quite shocked at what had happened, so I may not have noticed."

"Then what did she do?"

"Nothing. Once I found that Signore Carter was dead, I told her and she turned very pale and fainted."

"At what point did the Contessa arrive?"

"Just as I was trying to find Carter's pulse."

"Where was Signorina Peretti at that point?"

"Closing the jewel case."

"And the Contessa took the Sapphire back into her possession then?"

"Yes Signorina Peretti handed it over and then she was so overcome by the shock that she fainted."

"One final question: did you know if Signore Carter had any friends in Paris, or whether he had mentioned anyone coming to visit him?"

"No, but he was a very private person; he was not the type who would discuss such things with people like me or the Signorina; he saw us as common servants; but I heard of no friends of his in Paris."

"That will be all, thank you."

Le Villard then brought the maid into the room. She looked a very spirited young woman; her figure was slight, petite in fact, her movements graceful and, though one would have hesitated to describe her as beautiful, her countenance was striking, and her shrewd eyes shone with character and determination. Her mood was one of deferential sullenness, and her answers to Holmes's questions conveyed only the minimum of information.

He began by asking her to recount what had happened when the Contessa received the warning message that the Sapphire was in danger of being stolen; he particularly wanted to know why she had gone out. She replied that she had wanted to go for a walk and that, when she was passing the tram stop, she had decided to go to see her cousins, who were only a short ride away.

"What made you decide to go to visit your cousins in La Villette?" Holmes asked.

"I have already told the Police that I have Monday afternoons and Tuesday evenings free. I may go where I please. As I have only two relatives in Paris, it is hardly unusual that I go to visit them on my day off."

"When did you last see them?"

"About six weeks ago."

"Then it seems a strange coincidence that you went to see them on the very day that this message was received."

She merely shrugged.

"And even stranger that you went to visit them, not in at home but in their workshop."

"What difference does it make whether I see them at the shop or at home?" she asked.

I was certain that I saw just a flash of alarm as she answered.

"The difference is that you went out to La Villette, which is further away and necessitates changing to a second tram at Menilmontant, instead of going to the Porte de Bagnolet, which is closer."

She seemed confused, "I had forgotten that they still take the siesta."

"Yes, but when you found the workshop closed, you did not call in on them at home in Bagnolet. After all, it was no further to go than making your way back to the city, and would have avoided you having to make the trip again."

She shrugged again, "I cannot see that it is of any importance."

"I believe you fainted when you discovered that Signore Carter was dead?" Holmes continued.

"Yes, it was a terrible shock."

"What was the terrible shock, Signorina?"

She looked hesitant as if afraid to betray herself, "When we found Signore Carter dead. That was the great shock."

"Do you know of any reason why anyone would wish to kill him?"

"No."

"Did you ever know Signore Carter to receive much in the way of personal mail—letters or postcards for instance?"

"I know nothing about his private life."

"And you had never been in his room prior to this morning?"

She flushed angrily, "What do you mean? He was not my lover if that is what you suggest!"

"In point of fact that was not my meaning. But…"

"I did not kill Signore Carter, and I have already told the Police everything!" she interrupted hotly. "You are wasting your time, I cannot tell you anymore."

"On the contrary, Signorina, I believe that you could tell me very much more, if you chose to."

She relapsed into a glowering silence and Holmes signaled to Le Villard that the interview was over. Once the girl had left the room, the Préfet asked:

"What do you think, Monsieur Holmes?"

"That I am once again indebted to our friend Porlock for providing me with such strenuous mental exercise," replied Holmes with an enigmatic smile.

"Quite an interesting case, is it not?"

"Indeed. A locked room mystery—one of my favorites."

"Do you think the girl is guilty?" asked Dubuque.

"She knows more than she says, of that I am absolutely certain."

"Undoubtedly," agreed Dubuque.

"Yes, no doubt that she is holding something back, but of her guilt in either doing away with Carter, or of being involved in an attempt to steal the jewel, frankly, I am not so sure. Circumstantial evidence," continued Holmes, "is a strange thing, as I have remarked before on many occasions. After all, the Sapphire has not been stolen, and it is yet to be proven that Carter was murdered."

"All the same, it seems an odd coincidence, does it not, that she went immediately to see her cousins on the very day that a warning had been received that the jewel would be stolen," said Le Villard.

Holmes nodded in agreement. "I assume you have questioned the two Peretti brothers?" he asked.

"Yes, Monsieur Dubuque sent a couple of gendarmes to their shop and brought them in," replied Le Villard. "They had very little to say; they completely denied any involvement in the incident. They denied having been anywhere near the hotel last night and said that they had an alibi: after closing the workshop at eight o'clock, they went to a Corsican café on the Rue Rouvet for sandwiches and a glass or two of beer; then, they played cards with some friends for a few *sous* until closing time, and went straight home. They say their concierge can vouch that they did not leave the building until they returned to work this morning. At present, one of our men is checking these facts. Is there anything more you wish to know?"

"No, I think that will be all for now, gentlemen. It has been a most instructive episode which has provided me with three obvious clues, and I have been able to draw a number of other inferences from the data I have collected; however, I need to assess their significance. I would be greatly obliged if you would alert me should anything else come to light, however unimportant, trifling, or irrelevant it might seem."

"Certainly."

"In the meantime, I shall go off and contemplate what I have learned this morning. As you know, Monsieur Le Villard, 'art for art's sake' has always been my motto, though you will recall that, once I have given you my preliminary account of the case, I would prefer to work along my own lines and shall say very little until I have the case practically wrapped up. At which point, however, I shall retire, as I have done in the past, into the background."

"Yes, Monsieur Holmes, I recollect that you have your own *unorthodox* means of pursuing a line of inquiry—methods that are not always open to us in the Sûreté," said Le Villard with a wry smile to Dubuque.

"Of course," replied the latter smiling, "and I have also heard that you are something of a *gourmet*, Monsieur Holmes. So, I really must insist upon you and Doctor Watson dining with us this evening."

"Certainly," said Holmes.

"I should be delighted," I added.

"At *La Maison Normande*, Rue Lepic, just off the Rue Caulaincourt," replied Dubuque. "Shall we say, eight-thirty?"

Holmes and I took our leave of the Frenchmen and returned to the Gare du Nord to collect our luggage.

Holmes was completely silent throughout lunch, which we had taken rather later than usual, but once our table was cleared, and we had repaired to the quiet calm of the smoking-room, he began to discourse over the coffee. Although he had refused to be drawn in front of our French colleagues, he settled himself down upon the sofa and embarked upon an adumbration of the affair.

"Well, Holmes, I can see that you are still puzzling over the events of this morning," I said by way of an opening.

"I now have the photograph of Carter, which I had requested, and also the name of the international agency through whom he was recruited, and have set some inquiries afoot that may or may not clear up those particular aspects. But it is the strangest of cases: we have an abundance of information, yet a dearth of absolutely solid clues; a profusion of suspects, and yet a complete absence of any motive—indeed, perhaps an absence of any crime, though I am sure Le Villard's suspicions as to the actual cause of death will be borne out. Still, that doesn't take us very far. Now, to begin with, this is one of those occasions where one must pare down everything to the barest essential, and make no assumptions—Occam's razor is a most useful intellectual weapon in detection. Facts, Watson, hard facts.

"So, let us for a moment leave the official Police to look after their own investigation and separate what we know to be absolutely indisputable facts from all the conjectures and theories. We are warned that a robbery is about to take place; a young and apparently healthy man, given the charge of guarding the jewel, is found dead; the jewel has not been stolen. That is the sum of our definite knowledge. Now, let us consider the probabilities. Did Carter die defending the jewel? If so, then, we are on the trail of a murderer, and a murderer for whom it was more important to kill Carter than to steal a jewel worth a small fortune. If his death is unrelated to the attempt on the jewel, a suicide for instance, then that would be a monstrous coincidence. From the outset, I am going to rule out that coincidence. Let us assume, then, that there is some relation between Carter's death and the attempted theft of the Sapphire, and that his death was indeed intended. Either he tried to avert the theft of the jewel and perished in the attempt, or we must consider Le Villard's theory that he may have been one of a number of parties who had an interest in the jewel, and that he met his death at the hands of his rivals..."

"In either case, then, Carter was murdered by the Perettis who were acting for the *Habits Noirs*?"

"According to Le Villard's theory, yes, but I can see nothing but difficulties with it. The idea that the two former acrobats came across the roof and went in through the window is by no means an absurd one—I can think of a number of cases where this has been done. There was the Meier case in New York in '84, and the Kensington robberies in '92. All cases involved trained acrobats scaling sheer walls and using a high wire to make an entry—as Le Villard suggested, it would be a piece of cake, even for a couple of retired acrobats, to perform such a feat. But the evidence conflates it. It is impossible to carry out such an operation without leaving a trace, and I *saw* no trace—therefore, there *was* no trace.

"I mentioned three clues to Le Villard. These are events that do not follow, or conform to, any expected pattern or sequence. For instance, let us take the assumption that Carter died defending the jewel. A fairly probable one, but not without its own difficulties, because, if this were so, then who removed the jewel case from the deposit box, and why?"

"Perhaps the jewel case was never in the safe in the first place?"

"Excellent, Watson! You are improving with age. But again, why? If someone was able to get into Carter's room and murder him, why not then take the Sapphire? We do not know the answer to that yet, but it is something to label and docket. Why did the man who was supposed to be guarding the Sapphire with his life not even bother to load his gun? He was certainly singularly unprepared for any attempt on the jewel, yet he must have known that he was putting his own life in danger. For his negligence in omitting to load the gun, he may have paid with his life. Yet again, if he, too, was involved in some conspiracy which went wrong, then how do we explain that fact that the Sapphire remained in the jewel case when he was in the same room alone with it all night. All he had to do was walk out of the Hotel."

"But surely he knew he was being watched by the Police?"

"Indeed, it is highly likely that he would have known this, but there would have been a number of ways around that. For one, if he had been involved in stealing the jewel, he would have been unlikely to have undertaken the job without the assistance of some accomplice. Knowing he would be followed by the Police, he would have arranged some rendezvous with this person to whom the Sapphire could have been surreptitiously passed. Or he could have simply disappeared—after all, it is not difficult to shake off even an experienced policeman once one knows one is being followed—I have done it myself many times.

"Then, there is the maid, into whose surly brooding silence one can read only guilt. Clue number three: she chose, of all days, the very day that the warning is received to visit her cousins, but she made a much longer journey to their shop in La Villette rather than the shorter one to their house in Bagnolet. Who, or what, did she want to find at La Villette which made it imperative for her to go there?"

"But if she is not actually guilty, whom is she shielding and why?"

"There, Watson, I believe you have put your finger on what is perhaps the key to the whole mystery. And yet, if she is innocent, why does she persist in denying that her visit to La Villette was connected to the warning about the Sapphire. Of course, it *must* be connected, otherwise we have a preposterous coincidence. Yet, my instincts tell me that, whatever the Corsicans were up to, assuming they were up to anything, it did not start off as murder. Something went wrong somewhere. Yes, I am definitely coming round to the view that, somewhere in the middle of all this contradictory evidence, there has been some unsuspected occurrence."

"Most puzzlingly, Holmes, where does Moriarty fit into this, if at all?"

"Where indeed! Moriarty is no bungler and he does not employ amateurs. We are presently at an impasse, Watson, and require more data. I shall have to go off and smoke a few pipes if I am to unravel this convoluted chain of events which began with Porlock's message and ended with Carter's corpse. In the meantime…"

"In the meantime, Holmes" I interrupted, "as it is such a pleasant afternoon, I suggest that, since you are unable to immerse yourself in your usual means of diversion, we take a stroll along the Seine, then go and view the street artists in Montmartre. Do not forget we have agreed to meet Messieurs Le Villard and Dubuque for dinner there tonight."

"Watson, I think you have hit the nail on the head! A slight cooling breeze has got up and there is, after all, little I can do until I receive an answer to my inquiries."

So it was that Holmes and I wandered for several hours through the city streets. We passed along the banks of the Seine and up through the district of Les Halles with its market stalls selling every imaginable commodity. Though the enormous structure with its cast iron and glass was grandiose in its conception, and magnificent in its execution, the architecture was nothing compared to the bustle of commerce in all its noisy, picturesque squalor. We bore with delight the assault upon our senses: the bright colors of the vegetables and *charcuterie*; the salty tang of the seafood stalls; pie-sellers extolling their pastries, the braying of asses, the shrill cries of the costermongers and the fishwives haggling with customers over a couple of *sous*. It seemed to me more entertaining than anything devised for theater. We stopped for a *café crème*, at the Bistro Rimiaudière on the corner of the Rue Lamartine; then, we began the steady climb up the Rue des Martyrs towards the heights of the of Montmartre, meandering through the narrow and crowded cobbled lanes and squares.

We stopped often to look over works by street artists. Although I maintain that Holmes's ideas on art were as crude and idiosyncratic as his notions of anatomy, he commented on each piece as though he had come to Paris to make a special study of it. Soon, it was time to make our way up to the Rue Lepic to meet the two Frenchmen whom, it turned out, had procured a table by the window at *La Maison Normande*. We turned in the door of the rustic-looking restaurant.

"Well, Watson, here we are at last. I am keen to sample the *andouillettes* which are apparently a particular specialty of the kitchen."

"And I, the bouillabaisse," I replied as the intoxicating aroma of fish, garlic and aniseed wafted through the air.

It turned out to be a most memorable repast. Dubuque, who ate like a horse, was a childhood friend of the proprietor, Monsieur Le Couillard, who appeared alongside each course to inquire as to whether we were enjoying the food. Throughout the meal, Holmes discoursed on a number of topics: the invention of a new mechanical engine by Herr Diesel in Germany, the amazing developments in moving photography by the brothers Lumière, and, finally, on one of the subjects in which he had recently become interested—medieval music, and so, for a while, he rattled away about motets and madrigals.

Le Villard and Dubuque were exceptional hosts, and the table talk inevitably drifted to comparisons between the French and English methods of crime detection, and to recent advances and discoveries in medicolegal science. Le Villard elaborated on both the cleverness, but also the defects, in the theories and practices of Monsieur Bertillon, the famous scientist whom I knew Holmes held in great regard.

"We British should have followed the example of your Monsieur Vidocq. He had the Sûreté set up in 1812, wasn't it?" Holmes asked.

"Yes," replied Le Villard.

"It took us more than fifteen years to catch up. We—that's to say, Scotland Yard—are still a decade behind," my friend continued.

"You know, Holmes, you are beginning to sound like a character out of a book—Podsnap, I think was his name—only upside down, as it were," I said.

Dubuque, who turned out to be a most sociable dinner partner in every way, regaled us with unabridged tales of the spectacular criminal careers of Eugène Vidocq, prior to his redemption, and of the incomparable Rocambole. Later, I wished I had recorded the conversation in detail, for it would have distilled into a most useful thesis on criminal detection. After our dessert plates had been cleared away, we lingered over a glass of the best Calvados in the house and, from the window of the restaurant, we watched dozily as the tide of humanity ebbed and flowed over the narrow hilly street in this most picturesque corner of the city. During the meal, not a word had been spoken of the case in hand, but now, Le Villard brought us back to earth by referring to the subject of the Nebrodi Sapphire.

"We now have the results of our forensic tests, Monsieur Holmes: firstly, it has been confirmed, as expected, that Monsieur Carter died by means of poison, whether administered forcibly by a third party, or taken by himself, we have not yet established—I incline strongly to the former. The *post mortem* has also confirmed that there were no other marks on the corpse. It has also been ascertained that there were no traces of any poison in the water carafe or in the glass which were found at Carter's bedside."

Holmes's eyes brightened. "What was the poison?" he asked.

"It was a compound which is found in certain industrial preparations."

"Then, it is not entirely an uncommon one?"

"No, that is true, but its legitimate possession would be fairly limited."

"Nevertheless, it would be fairly readily obtainable and, unlike, say, arsenic and strychnine, one would not expect it to be so strictly regulated."

"One would not have to sign a register, no."

"What is its precise use?"

"At the present, it is limited to certain types of manufacturing. It is not yet ready for the wider market, although it is being continually researched for it has commercial possibilities since it can be molded, colored, dissolved, and made to resemble other materials and substances. When the gendarmes brought the Perettis in for questioning, Monsieur Dubuque had the presence of mind to take a sample from their hands, clothes, and other personal effects…"

"And it matched the poisonous substance!" interjected Holmes.

"Yes," replied Dubuque, rather astonished.

"And what inference do you draw from that?" asked Holmes.

"That it is fairly solid proof, if any were needed, of the Perettis' guilt. I have been certain of it from the outset."

"You have arrested them then?"

"No, not just yet," replied Le Villard. "I thought it would be more instructive to keep a continual watch on them. Firstly, if they are acting on behalf of the *Habits Noirs*, they may lead us to their *complices*, or to the one who gives them their orders."

"I think that it would be ten to one against the Perettis receiving their instruction in person—more likely, they would be sent messages," said Holmes.

"All the same, we wish to be certain that we have enough evidence to convince the Magistrate. After all, they did not actually get the Sapphire, and they may yet make another attempt. In which case, we could take them red-handed."

"And we know exactly where we can lay our hands on them, should we need to, and the maid too," added Dubuque.

"Yes, I think that the best course of action at present is to do nothing precipitate," Holmes answered diplomatically. Yet, I had more than a mild suspicion that he was far from convinced.

After dinner, we found a cab outside and, though it was well after eleven o'clock when we returned to the Hotel des Mamelouks, Holmes had the Hotel Manager send up coffee and Curaçao to our room.

Chapter VI
The Mysterious Visitor

When we arrived in our suite on the fourth floor, we were astonished to find a young man already seated in our antechamber, clearly awaiting our presence. I assumed that one of the Hotel staff had admitted him, and I was therefore somewhat surprised that his arrival had not been mentioned to us when we collected our keys and had given our order to the Hotel Manager. As we entered, the man immediately stood up and favored us with a most elegant bow. He was finely featured, pale skinned and fair, but his mode of attire was undeniably Gallic. His age, I would have put at no more than about twenty-two, though his manner was anything but nervous or shy; for all his extreme youth, he held the bearing of a refined gentleman.

"Pray, allow me to introduce myself, I am Raoul d'Andrésy, although I suspect you may already have heard of me. I trust I have the honor of addressing Monsieur Holmes. Perhaps I should say *Chevalier* Holmes?"

"Indeed, I was favored with that singular honor some time ago."

"And this must be Doctor Watson, the Dumas of Baker Street." He bowed again and smiled. "I trust you will forgive my taking the liberty of letting myself in…"

"Providing you can furnish me with an explanation for your unannounced visit," replied Holmes.

"I am sure your friend and colleague, Monsieur Le Villard, will have alerted you to my presence in Paris."

Holmes did not reply. D'Andrésy continued, "Partly, I was curious to meet the gentleman who has the title of the most successful detective in England, possibly even Europe; and also, I have come to offer you some advice based on my assumption that you are here to investigate this affair of the Nebrodi Sapphire."

"I am sure you will understand, Monsieur d'Andrésy, that in addition to my investigative capacities, first and foremost I extend to all my clients my absolute discretion," replied Holmes suavely.

The young man smiled, "No doubt you are correct with respect to the Contessa, and to her ladyship's business; but there is no point in pretending that you are not here to assist Monsieur Le Villard in tracking down the murderer of Monsieur Carter, and that is what I have come to speak to you about."

"I am afraid I am not at liberty to discuss the…"

"Monsieur Holmes," d'Andrésy interrupted, "I would not dream of soliciting confidences; on the contrary, you need not say anything. I have come here simply to save your valuable time and effort, discreetly of course; the Préfet de Police will have been no more aware of my presence here than the Hotel staff."

"You seem very sure that they did not follow you here."

"Follow me?" the young man laughed indulgently, "but of course, they followed me here, Monsieur Holmes! However, like yourself, I have perfected a method of circumventing any official surveillance. I only permit Policemen to follow me when I wish to mislead them." He laughed again like a mischievous child revealing his latest trick. "A lesson it seems the Sûreté have yet to learn. No, I am afraid the man who was detailed to track me around Paris is probably still waiting across the river in the Gare de Lyon where I left him. He shall wait for a further hour or two before I go to retrieve him on my return. He can then follow me back and sit in my hotel foyer, under the impression that he is still invisible to me. They really ought to send someone who is up to the job, don't you think?"

"I am hardly inclined to debate the limitations of the Parisian Police."

"Of course, I understand. Still, were it not for the fact that I am receiving tonight a visit from my friend Comte de Mirepoix to discuss some important private business, I might be tempted to reward this preposterous public servant with a twenty kilometer trudge around the suburbs of Paris. Not out of any malice, you understand, merely to emphasize the stupidity of it all."

"To come to the point, Monsieur d'Andrésy—the point of your visit, that is—you hinted that you had come here to render some assistance to me?"

"I did not put it quite as strongly as that, but yes, I suppose you could say that I believe I might assist you in helping to eliminate one of the suspects from your inquiries—myself!"

Holmes laughed.

"No, this is not a jest. I can assure you that, if I had been after the Nebrodi Sapphire, I would at least have had the decency to warn the Contessa first. I give you my word as a gentleman that I would certainly not have bungled it, nor would I have harmed a hair of anyone's head. Murder is a crime to which I do not stoop, for there is rarely any justification for violence. And so, I suggest to you that you may as well have your friend Monsieur Le Villard call off his sleuthhound to avoid a waste of his own resources."

"What makes you think that you are under suspicion, Monsieur d'Andrésy? A guilty conscience perhaps?"

"Do not bluff me, Monsieur Holmes, it will not work. It is my business to know what goes on in the world of the Sûreté—my natural predator. How did I know that Monsieur Le Villard and his corpulent *bras droit* have mentioned my name in connection with this crime? Why, by the same means as I knew that yourself and Doctor Watson were residing on the fourth floor of this Hotel—but I trust that you will not expect me to be so unchivalrous as to reveal my sources," the young man smiled charmingly. "Now, I give you my word that I have nothing to do with the Nebrodi Sapphire. Is that not good enough for you?"

"And you are not working for Moriarty?"

D'Andrésy sneered. "You obviously do not know me, Monsieur Holmes. I have aristocratic antecedents, I work for no one, I submit to no one's orders. To use a rustic phrase, I plough my own furrow. I called in order to pay my respects to you and to, shall we say, assist in shortening your list of suspects. But I do caution you that we may find ourselves on different sides of the law on the next occasion on which we have the honor to meet. Well, I trust you all enjoyed Monsieur Le Couillard's superb cuisine Rue Lepic—the *Tripes à la mode de Caen* there are quite the best in Paris. Please convey my compliments to Monsieur Dubuque on his excellent taste. And now, good evening to you gentlemen both."

And with a sweeping bow, he turned on his heels and was off into the night.

The next morning, Holmes had risen and departed well before I had breakfasted. It transpired that he had gone to seek an answer to the telegram he had dispatched a day earlier, although he was as close as ever about the details. He returned about ten o'clock waving an envelope and beaming with satisfaction.

"I decided to collect this personally," he said by way of explanation. "Too many people seem to be familiar with Sherlock Holmes's movements these days, and I should not want the contents to be known. It is my reply from Lestrade," he continued, "which confirms what I had already begun to suspect: that Carter was working for Moriarty, and had managed to infiltrate the Contessa's household; he was the one sent to steal the Sapphire, and therefore friend Porlock has been proven correct as usual. In fact, Watson, according to Lestrade, we have already made this man's acquaintance."

"How so, Holmes?"

"You surely recall Charley Hayes, from the Blessington case?"

"Blessington? Ah, the Worthingdon bank robbers? That was nearly ten years ago... I do not recall the name Hayes."

"He was the page in the house of Blessington, or Sutton to give him his correct name, who fled after the murder. He was eventually tracked down, but the Crown case against him collapsed when the rest of the gang disappeared. I had never met him face to face, thus I was unable to recognize him from the photograph, but I knew of his reputation. He has borne a plethora of aliases since then, and is a most gifted actor. He could portray a count or a costermonger with equal facility, and his criminal record for grand frauds is rather impressive. I must say, for the son of a Blackwall docker, he seemed to have carried off the part of the English gentleman very well, even down to his choice of Earl Grey tea. I afterwards discovered that, in order to get himself taken on by Sutton as a page, he was obliged to take some five years off his age, so that he looked like a lad of thirteen. After the trial, he was recruited by Moriarty who appreciated his precocious talents. Ironically, he survived an assassination attempt by Badeczosky and Perkoff —hence the scar to which Le Villard alluded—after which he rose both in the Professor's estimation and in the ranks. Moriarty will be greatly displeased to have lost him; indeed, he may even now be out to avenge him, for Lestrade's letter concludes with a rather chilling warning—see here, this last line struck me with alarm."

I read the final words of Lestrade's note: *Parker has left his post*. "Who is Parker?" I asked.

"Montague Parker was the sentinel appointed by Sebastian Moran to dog my footsteps on my return from my skirmish at the Reichenbach Falls—a garrotter by trade and an extraordinarily efficient one at that. Dear me, this is much deeper than I had thought."

"It seems that things are beginning to happen at last, Holmes, for when you were out, this note from Le Villard was delivered; he requests our presence as soon as possible."

"Excellent," said Holmes, rubbing his hand in glee, "then let us hasten straight to the Préfecture. Don't bother to call a cab; it will be quicker to walk."

Dubuque handed Holmes the envelope which he had spoken of the day before.

"These have been examined by our specialists, but there does not seem to be anything incriminating in them, and nothing which gives us any kind of lead. You can return them once you have completed your own examination."

"Thank you. You have some news for us, I presume?"

"Yes, there have been some quite dramatic developments in the case," said Le Villard, "and I thought you would wish to be apprised of the facts immediately."

"Well, it is always good to have some news to barter," Holmes chuckled.

"You also have something to tell?"

"It relates to your plainclothes policeman who was spent most of the evening at the Gare de Lyon last night–"

"How could you possibly know about that? You were with us at *La Maison Normande* at the time!"

Holmes laughed, "I got it straight from the man who marooned him there."

"Marooned him?"

"Yes, Raoul d'Andrésy."

"*D'Andrésy?!* Well, by the name of—quite incredible! And how did you manage to find d'Andrésy?"

"Find him? Oh, that was no effort at all! You see, he was already occupying our quarters when we arrived last evening. Without having troubled to inform the Hotel staff that he would be waiting for us, as you may understand."

"What insufferable impudence!"

"A most courteous young man nevertheless, despite his, shall we say, reluctance to acknowledge the usual social conventions. He went out of his way to visit me in order to offer some advice in the conduct of the case."

"We shall have him arrested for this! All you have to do is file a complaint, breaking and entering…"

Holmes waved away the idea, laughing.

"Not for the world, Monsieur Le Villard. I found that whimsical little incident most amusing. Of course, he denied all involvement in the affair."

"He would, of course," said Le Villard with some asperity.

"His words had a certain ring of sincerity, although I well understand that sincerity is the confidence trickster's stock in trade. I'm afraid that he led your man a merry dance largely due to his resentment of the fact that he may have come under suspicion of having committed the crime, or more accurately having *failed* to commit the crime. You see, he was at great pains to point out that, had he set his sights on the Nebrodi Sapphire, it would certainly not still be in the Contessa's possession by now. He was quite incensed at the thought that his name might be associated with such incompetence. I must say that, for all his bombast, I am inclined to believe him. He abjured all violence, and also took the trouble to assure me that he had no connection with a certain Professor Moriarty. Incidentally, he asked me to pass on his congratulations to Monsieur Dubuque in his choice of restaurant!"

Dubuque shook his head in disbelief, and then began to smile. "I think we can accept his protestation of innocence on this occasion," he said glancing at Le Villard.

The Préfet nodded, then, with obvious satisfaction, said, "Now then, Monsieur Holmes, we have information which has established the guilt of the Perettis quite beyond doubt."

"I see. And you now have them safely under lock and key, they have admitted their part in the affair, and so Sherlock Holmes and Doctor Watson may now return to London?" replied Holmes with just the faintest touch of mockery.

"No, not exactly," replied Le Villard. "To tell the truth, they seem to have got clean away, just as we were about to arrest them."

"Why did you suddenly decide to arrest them?"

"Despite your belief in Mademoiselle Peretti's innocence, we decided, as I told you, to keep up our discreet watch on her. At five o'clock last night, she left the Hotel and went to visit her two brothers in La Villette—what a very close family they seem to have suddenly become! Our man, Meurant, followed in the guise of a dealer, and, on the pretext of looking over the contents of the shop, managed to get close enough to them to hear what was being said. He reported that it sounded like a council of war, and the conversation seemed not only to establish the guilt of the Perettis, but indicated that the directing mind behind the affair was not the two men but the girl herself! Of course, some of the most dangerous characters in the *Habits Noirs* are women."

"I was warned of that," replied Holmes. "One moment though—presumably, they conducted this conversation in their own dialect; how was your man able to follow it?"

"Meurant is fluent in Corsú," replied Dubuque with a smile.

"Once again, I must congratulate you gentlemen on your thoroughness. What precisely was said?" asked Holmes.

"Mademoiselle Peretti began by remonstrating passionately with her brothers; she sounded very angry and stamped around furiously. She said words to the effect that 'We will all now be had up for murder because of your stupidity.'

"Then, one of them men retorted, 'It was your idea, Giulianna, not ours, don't forget that.'

"The other man added, 'Yes, we told you to leave it well alone, but you wouldn't listen. See what your haughty pride has brought you.'

"The girl replied, 'Yes, it was my idea to secure the Sapphire, but not to kill Carter!'

" 'But we couldn't have known how he would act,' one of the brothers replied.

" 'And it is too late now,' said the other.

" 'They have no proof against us as yet; only a suspicion,' the first one continued, 'and they can't convict us on suspicion. The Contessa still has her Sapphire, doesn't she? Isn't that all these rich people care about? After all, what is the death of one foreigner to her?'

" 'How stupid you are!' the girl cried, 'how little you understand! She has brought here a private detective from England, the best in Europe, to investigate the death of this foreigner! I have sat before this man, under his gaze. He has such a penetrating eye that seems to look right into your soul, and see what is going on in your mind. It is as though he has supernatural powers. He read the guilt in my eyes, I know he did, and he told the policemen so too. Now we face the guillotine, because of your stupidity!' Then, she burst into tears.

" 'You know the old saying—at the end of many disasters, there's always an Italian,' said the second man, and they sat quiet for a while.

" 'If we keep silent, they will prove nothing,' the other one finally said. 'They haven't any proof, or they would have arrested us already.'

"There was some desultory talk, then the girl dried her eyes, left the shop and returned to the hotel."

"A fairly clear admission of guilt, Monsieur Holmes, do you not think?" asked Dubuque.

"On the face of it, yes. But…"

"*On the face of it?*" Le Villard laughed incredulously.

"Surely, there can be no room for doubt?" interjected Dubuque.

"Come, come, now, Monsieur Holmes," said Le Villard, "we all get our theories wrong from time to time; there is no harm in admitting that."

"It was perfectly clear to me that the maid was not telling all she knew, and if she is guilty of anything, it is of withholding information which may or may not lead to the arrest of the murderer of Carter," said Holmes. "However, I can think of several interpretations of that conversation, not all of which would indicate the guilt of the Perettis in the murder or the robbery. But how did they manage to escape?"

Le Villard continued, "It was this way. Meurant debated whether to try to arrest the two brothers there and then, but he was not armed and he could not guarantee to take both men in. He also considered the danger of alerting them prematurely to his suspicion, so he left and went straight to the local *commissariat* to seek assistance. Unfortunately for us, the Perettis must have become suspicious themselves, or perhaps they had seen through his disguise, for when he returned with his men, just as dusk was beginning to fall, the birds had already flown."

"The maid too?"

"No. She returned to the hotel. We had intended to arrest her too, but we have agreed to place her under house arrest due to the Contessa's objections…"

"She still believes her to be innocent?"

"Strangely enough, she is adamant that the girl is innocent, despite the facts—her feminine intuition apparently," said Le Villard with a smile.

"Perhaps it is more that she foresees some difficulty in finding a replacement for her at such short notice," added Dubuque with a trace of asperity.

"How does the girl explain this apparently incriminating conversation?" asked Holmes.

"She doesn't—she refuses to speak," replied Le Villard.

"But if the maid is, in fact, the leader of this little gang," Holmes went on, "then what is the sense of only her brothers fleeing and leaving her behind?"

Le Villard shrugged, "I cannot say, but it seems from what they said that they are the ones who actually committed the murder. I think we have all the evidence we need."

Holmes shook his head, "It is merely circumstantial."

"Well, let me reconstruct the crime to you, Monsieur Holmes: on Monday, the maid scurried off to La Villette to tell her brothers that a warning had been received and they had to act now, or the Sapphire would disappear into the bank vault, and their opportunity might be gone for good. They hatched out their plan—the Peretti brothers would come in through the Hotel window and take Carter by surprise. No doubt, when they got there, Carter refused to hand over the keys, and they forced him at gunpoint to swallow the poison. You will recall the Joseph Leturier case in Montpellier in '85, and the case of Marco Gandolfi in Imperia the same year, *n'est-ce-pas*? These Corsicans are slyest and subtlest assassins in Europe—no bloodied knives or hatchets this time. However, I assume that they must have been disturbed after killing Carter, lost their nerve, and fled the way that they came without taking the jewel. The maid surreptitiously locked the window on the inside on her arrival in the room—there was great confusion, and Gazzano may have missed her doing it. The facts all fit, and together with the conversation which Meurant overheard, I think that is enough to convict the Perettis."

"I do not believe so. A clever attorney would derail your case quite easily. For as start, how did the Perettis obtain the poison?"

"It is in common industrial use."

"Precisely—it is relatively simple to obtain, and anyone with the right connection could have obtained it easily. As to the forcible administration of poison at gunpoint—did you find a pistol or a knife in the Peretti's premises?"

"No, but they could easily have thrown it into the river or the Canal Saint-Martin, which runs right though La Villette, or in the basin itself."

"So after forcing this poison on Carter, they then waited until he was dead, put him neatly back into bed and tucked him up? Most considerate! Then they mysteriously forgot to take the Sapphire. No, I rather think the solution is much more convoluted than we have imagined so far."

"Well, it was complicated enough, although the disappearance of the Perettis supplies us with a further and unexpected complication..."

"But does it?" interjected Holmes. "No, what a fool I have been, for I should perhaps have anticipated this... Ah, yes, it becomes clearer now!"

Chapter VII
Holmes Sets a Trap

We all three looked at Holmes in astonishment.

"*Clearer*?" asked Le Villard.

"Yes. You see, I received information this morning from Scotland Yard to the effect that this Michael Carter was none other than Charley Hayes—a confidence trickster, amongst other things, who seems to have infiltrated the Contessa's household. He was one of Professor Moriarty's top men. And the indications are that Moriarty has now sent one of his killers to Paris, a fellow I know called Montague Parker."

"Then there must have been two rival organizations out to steal the Sapphire," said Le Villard."

"I remain to be convinced that the *Habits Noirs* had anything to do with it"

"But who else could have murdered Carter?"

"Let us leave that aside for the moment, Monsieur Le Villard," Holmes said. "Has the disappearance of the Perettis been reported to the Press?"

"No, not yet."

"Then, perhaps there is still time."

"Time for what? You are speaking in riddles, Monsieur Holmes."

"I am going to ask you to do something which I think may bring us closer to the solution of this mystery. I want to test a theory which I have begun to formulate, and I would ask you to place your trust in me on this occasion. I wish you to inform the Press by your normal channels that two men have gone missing, presumably abducted."

"*Abducted?*"

"Abducted from the neighborhood of La Villette; and that you believe these two men, who were Corsicans and were employed at the Perettis' workshop, have been mistaken for the Peretti brothers"

"But…"

"Mistaken for the Peretti brothers. Your strong suspicion is that they have been involved in some kind of vendetta within the Corsican community involving some secret society, they have offended someone's honor—you know the sort of thing."

"So, you incline to the theory that they have not escaped, but that they have been abducted. It seems rather a wild guess, if I may say so."

Holmes smiled, "Tut-tut, Monsieur Le Villard, I thought you knew that, although I may occasionally bluff, I rarely gamble and I *never* guess. No, I incline to the theory that Parker has been sent here to finish the job, by which I mean to get the Sapphire, and to exact revenge for the murder of Hayes. It is unlikely that he will be acting alone, and I had already considered that, on the balance of probabilities, Hayes was working with an accomplice who remains in Paris. The departure of Parker from London has convinced me that this assumption was correct. I believe the Perettis have been abducted by Parker and this accomplice, who want to find out what really happened on Monday night.

"What may happen to them now, we can only surmise, but the Professor is not known for his clemency towards those who transgress him. Their life probably depends upon them observing their time honored code of *Omerta*. If we can deceive Moriarty's men into thinking that they picked up the wrong men, there is a chance, albeit a slim one, that they may be released unharmed. I would counsel you to keep a constant watch on their workshop and their apartment. Should they turn up, arrest them immediately, but do so discreetly."

Le Villard threw up his hands in confusion, "But Monsieur Holmes, you had told us that you believed in their innocence, and now you tell me to arrest them!"

"I have good reason for that. If I have erred in my estimation, then no harm shall come of it, but it may already be too late. However, should my little stratagem be successful, I hope that you will soon find the Perettis back in circulation. Then, we can put the second part of my plan into operation."

"The *second* part?!"

"Yes, let us leave that in the meantime. As soon as you have any news, please let me know."

"Well, it is difficult for us to refuse a favor of the man who saved the life of our President, but I must say it all sounds unlikely. However, I shall certainly be happy to see these men again, and if we can lay our hands on them, they shall not get away a second time."

"All the same, I can assure you that the arrest of the Perettis will not help you solve the mystery of Hayes' murder."

"Then, who do you think committed the crime?"

Holmes paused briefly before returning an answer. I had long been inured to that facet of his artistic nature which tended to accentuating the dramatic. But, even allowing for his penchant for sensational and mysterious utterances, I must confess that I was just as astonished as our French colleagues at his parting shot on this occasion.

"I remain to be convinced that any actual crime was committed on Monday night. On the whole, I am coming round to the conviction that, if anything, a serious crime was averted. Now, it may take a day or so for my stratagem to bear fruit. Until then, good day."

And with that he walked off, leaving a bemused Le Villard and Dubuque staring after him.

"Well, Watson, here we have some information, the significance of which seems to have been lost on Le Villard and Dubuque, and which we are now in the fortunate position of being able to pursue. I am convinced that there must be something amongst this lot which will help to clear up some of the mystery."

He smoothed out the papers which he pulled out of the envelope given to him by Le Villard. He enumerated the articles again to me.

"Now, here is a man known to be friendless who rarely receives personal mail; yet, on this particular day, within hours of my sending the Contessa a warning, he receives not one but two postcards from a friend recently arrived in Paris."

He went through each item in turn, examining it closely, and finally took up two postcards and read them out:

"The first one was posted at 11 o'clock on Monday in the Rue de Clignancourt in the eighteenth arrondissement; it reads: *Just arrived today. Meet for lunch tomorrow at Gaultier's once I have seen the sights. James.*"

Then he took the second one.

"Posted just over two hours later in the same place; it says: *View from the top of Eiffel Tower quite marvelous, but heady. James.* What do you make of those, Watson?"

"I can make neither head nor tail of them."

"Nor I, Watson," he confessed to my surprise. "One thing is certain, however; the writer can hardly have traveled from the eighteenth arrondissement to the top of the Eiffel Tower and back in two hours, so the content is obviously spurious. There must be some hidden message, some type of code. Surely it is far too much of a coincidence not to be related, for I have already enumerated seventeen separate coincidences in this case. I shall have to work a bit harder on this, Watson—it is a one man job, I am afraid, and a cerebral one at that."

Knowing Holmes's need for solitary seclusion, I said, "I shall make myself scarce then, there is an inviting looking Turkish bath on the Rue des Rosiers. It is but a ten minute walk."

"And I have a full pound of Ships' blend to see me though the afternoon."

I returned to the Hotel within an hour and a half. The air was blue with pipe smoke and the table was littered with a score of papers, scribbled on and crossed out in various colors of ink. Holmes sat with on the sofa with an air of frustration.

He shook his head as I entered, "It is no good, Watson, I have got precisely nowhere. Now, as you know, I am fairly well up in my cryptology, but I cannot fathom these out. In the last two hours, I have applied every type of analysis with which I am familiar: acronymics, numerous substitution ciphers, homophonic analysis, and the polyalphabetic methods of Della Porta and De Vigenère. The results of this fruitless labor, you see scattered around you. I am afraid to say that I can get neither of these messages to make the slightest sense, yet it must have made sense to both the person who wrote it and the person who received it, or my entire chain of reasoning is erroneous from beginning to end."

I glanced at the postcards again.

"I am afraid if it is beyond your powers, Holmes, then it is certainly well beyond mine," I replied. "Shall I order us some coffee or, perhaps, tea for a change?"

"Yes, a capital idea. Tea for a change."

After I had rung for the boy, Holmes sat for some time in silence, the picture of utmost disappointment. He turned the postcards over and over with irritation, examined again them with his magnifying glass and finally held them up to the light. Then, he relit his pipe and began muttering to himself. He had hardly drawn a few mouthfuls of smoke when he suddenly sat up as if stung. He rushed to the table and pulled out the postcards.

"Watson," he cried, "Watson, you have done it again! It was the *tea*, of course. Dash it, I ought to have known all along."

"The tea?" I asked, mystified.

"Yes, Hayes ordered tea on the day that he died."

"So Hayes was poisoned by the tea?"

"No, no, Watson," he cried impatiently, "not poisoned, it was the…"

At that moment, we were interrupted by the bell ringing: the boy had arrived with a large pot of tea.

"You are in the presence of an educated idiot Watson," he continued, "I have paid the price for being rather too intellectual in my approach in this instance. The message was not written code at all, but was concealed within the postcard itself!"

"*Within* the postcard? But how?"

"You recall when I asked if Hayes had ordered anything from the kitchen, it turned out that he had ordered a pot of tea to be sent to his room. Now, the page said the tea had not been drunk—because it was never meant to be drunk!"

"I confess I did not pay much attention at the time."

"Nor did I, Watson, because we were looking for a potential source of poison."

I gazed in amazement at Holmes, "Then what was the purpose of the tea?"

"I will show you presently. I deserve to be horse-whipped for being so dull witted, for it may have cost two innocent men their lives. Now, do you know what I intend to do with this teapot?"

"I cannot possibly imagine."

"Then observe!"

He laid the first postcard flat on the table and placed the large teapot on top of it. Then, he stood back for a few moments, checked his watch and finally lifted the pot. The following words appeared very faintly between the lines of the written message: *Holmes has left London. Act Tonight.*

"Invisible ink, Watson, a schoolboy trick!"

"Good Lord, Holmes, someone was watching us and sent this warning to Hayes!"

"That is how I read it. Yes, now for this one!" He did the same with the second postcard and the following message appeared: *GDN W C-D 113.*

"Hm, not so simple this time, Watson. We are almost back to where we started. Let us reason this out. Hayes received the first message as a warning that we were on his trail, with an instruction to act instantly. The original plan must be discarded and a second plan adopted—possibly one that had been agreed as a fallback in the event of adversity. What does he do next? Prepare to strike immediately. Then what further information does he need from this James?"

"He has to effect an escape with the booty?"

"Brilliant again, Watson! The second postcard therefore a concerns the getaway plan, as Lestrade would call it. *GDN W C-D 113*... where does that lead us?"

"I must confess, Holmes, I am completely in the dark.

"And I, too. Still, we have the answer even if we don't have the original question. And we must be able to narrow the range of possibilities."

"I am certain I have seen those initials *GDN* very recently, yet I cannot recall precisely where."

"Watson, you are scintillating this afternoon!"

"Is it a code?"

"Sort of."

"Whose?" I asked.

"The *Compagnie des Chemins de Fer du Nord*, to be precise," answered Holmes.

"*GDN*! *Gare du Nord*! But what is the significance of the other letters and the numbers?"

"You recall when we arrived at the Gare du Nord and deposited our luggage before we went to meet Le Villard?"

"Yes."

"There were lockers on both the east and west sides of the concourse. This *W* refers to the west side obviously. The columns were alphabetically ordered—that is the *C-D* for Column D; the lockers were numbered and so *113* is the number of the locker. Since Hayes was unable to keep this appointment, it is possible that whatever was placed in locker 113 at the Gare du Nord remains there. We shall soon know for it is a mere twenty minute walk from here. And more importantly, this postcard may lead us to the identity of the person who sent these messages, this mysterious James."

"Not Moriarty himself!"

"It is possible, but hardly likely," said Holmes laughing. "No, the Professor will be standing back, well out of the limelight. The next piece of the jigsaw is to find the person to whom Hayes sent the reply."

"Since he had had very little time in which to put the plan into execution, presumably he went to a post office in the vicinity of the Hotel?"

"Exactly, but which one, for there may be dozens. Dash it, I am unable to use to my normal method for flushing out our quarry from the covert; if only I had a detachment of the Irregulars, I could send them round to check at all the offices of *La Poste*. Still, we could narrow the field though, could we not? Yes, I believe so. Le Villard told us that Hayes went out to buy a newspaper—at least, that was the pretext. I have here the 1895 Paris Directory; now be good enough pass me that map."

Holmes studied them briefly, "This Directory gives me two offices within about 10 minutes walking distance: one in Le Marais, and one on Boulevard Saint-Germain. Since Le Villard says his man lost Hayes on Rue Maître-Albert, it is a perfectly reasonable assumption that he went to the latter. Let us waste no further time in speculation: to the Gare du Nord, then Boulevard Saint-Germain."

"But how on Earth are you going to get into a locker for which you have no key or ticket?"

"I should prefer not to enlist the regular force unless it is absolutely necessary, so it comes down to a plain choice between brute force or subterfuge."

As it turned out, there was little difficulty in obtaining the entry to the locker in the Gare du Nord. Holmes played to perfection the part of the absent-minded and eccentric Englishman so well that the railway official in charge could scarcely have been more helpful. Following Holmes's lengthy and apologetic monologue in very bad and broken French about lost tickets, missed trains, and difficulties in handling French currency, he produced a key and handed over the contents of the locker, a dark brown suitcase, with a look of relief.

Once out of the station, we retired to a café in a quiet back street and applied ourselves to discovering the contents of the suitcase. We found a suit of clothes of unmistakable French cut, a man's blond wig, a pair of spectacles with plain glass, and a large buff envelope which Holmes tore open at once.

"Well, what have we here? Identification papers in the name of Pieter Van De Hout, some Belgian currency—rather a lot to carry around—and a railway ticket and a seat reservation in the name of Van De Hout from Paris to Antwerp."

"Antwerp—the diamond capital of Europe?"

"Precisely, Watson! The reservation was dated for the 06:10 train from Gare du Nord on Tuesday. Well, well, the clouds begin to clear at last don't you think?"

"Indeed, this was surely Hayes' escape plan with the Nebrodi Sapphire?"

"In the guise of *Mijnheer* Pieter Van De Hout. There was enough currency to keep him going for weeks. Well, whoever it was, they made a good job of improvisation. Unfortunately, someone seems to have been one step ahead of them."

A short cab ride took us to the Boulevard Saint-Germain, where Holmes explained to the clerk that he had sent a telegram a couple of days ago which seemed to have gone missing. He added that he had sent one of the hotel staff to dispatch it, but perhaps the boy had got the address wrong.

"The telegram was to a business acquaintance of mine and should have been sent in the name of Michael Carter, on the afternoon of Monday, 21 October."

The clerk got up from his stool and went to a desk behind him. He fished about in a drawer for a moment or two, then returned to the counter.

"Yes, I have the counterfoil here," he said. "To James Jennings, Hotel Lambert, eighteenth arrondissement. Is that the one?"

"Yes. You don't retain copies of the actual telegrams sent?"

"No, I am afraid not. If it has been lost or mislaid, you may make a claim if you wish."

"Not at all, it was a trivial matter. I merely wanted to make sure it had been delivered in the first place."

"It has not been returned; therefore it must have been delivered."

"Oh, well," said Holmes, in an offhand manner, "he must have lost interest in the deal."

Leaving the office, Holmes hailed a cab and gave the address of the Préfecture.

"I thought we would have gone straight to the Hotel Lambert?"

"No. My reasoning is this: Jennings, if that is indeed his real name, has no reason to be particularly cautious; neither will he want to vanish suddenly, lest it draw attention. Indeed, if my theory is correct, he may still have work to do in Paris."

Le Villard and Dubuque were astounded when Holmes arrived at the Préfecture with the suitcase. Holmes explained how he had managed to decode the messages in the postcard, but said nothing, however, about the man Jennings.

"Well, Monsieur Holmes, once again you have astonished us," said Le Villard. "I must confess that I did not ascribe the least importance to those postcards. I did consider they might have been some sort of a coded message but, although my English is not of the first order, I knew enough to see that the contents were innocuous. The intended flight to Antwerp, as you suggest, proves beyond doubt that Hayes had intended to steal the Sapphire and either sell it, or have it cut there."

"I believe it would have been sold in one piece," replied Holmes, "and that the buyer would have been awaiting its delivery. It would then have been a simple matter for Hayes to disappear with the proceeds, or more likely, hand them over to Moriarty in Antwerp, and then skip back to England on the next ferry."

"Monsieur Holmes, I am greatly indebted to you. I do not wish to sound ungrateful, but until I have my hand on the murderer, the question of who intended to steal the Sapphire is secondary one."

"I give you my guarantee that, very soon indeed, I hope to be able to clear up all that is presently shrouded in mystery. I hope to produce both the Peretti brothers and their abductors. As to the person responsible for the death of Hayes, that may take just a bit longer. I still have a number of facts to check regarding that aspect of the case, and until that is done, it is useless to speculate."

"You would not like to give us even the smallest hint as to who could possibly have murdered Hayes?"

"Eliminate that which is impossible, and you will be left with the truth," replied Holmes. "Now, I trust you have communicated my version of the abduction to the Press?"

"Indeed. I expect that the evening editions should carry the story."

"Well, then, we have set up the first part of our trap, though we can hardly expect immediate success. There is little for us do at present. In the meantime, we can only play what the hunting fraternity calls 'the waiting game.' "

Chapter VIII
The Bassin de La Villette

Sherlock Holmes did not, as it transpired, have very long to wait: the morning papers, which arrived with breakfast, brought news of an unexpected dramatic event, albeit one that was not directly related to the case. Nevertheless, it threatened to upset our plan and sever the slender thread which we held.

"A stroke of bad luck Holmes," I said.

"In what sense Watson?"

"It is one of those whimsical little incidents which has nothing whatsoever to do with our business, but which has caused a completely unforeseen train of events, if you will pardon my entirely unconscious pun. There was a train crash yesterday at one of the main railway stations in the city."

"Which one?"

"The Gare de l'Ouest.[11] A train coming in from Normandy seems to have overrun the buffers, and the engine crashed through the station wall into the street below, tender and all."

The accident itself was no great catastrophe, but speculation was rife in the press that it had been the work of the same Anarchists who had assassinated President Sadi Carnot the previous year. Suspicion was that the saboteurs had either greased the rails on the approach to the station, or that they had interfered with the braking mechanisms on the engine. Some passengers had been

---

[11] Later renamed Gare Montparnasse. The accident mentioned here really happened, on 22 October 1895.

injured and a woman in the Rue de Rennes killed by falling masonry, but the damage could have been much worse.

Le Figaro observed that as such outrages were becoming more common under the moderate republican government, and that a complete change of direction in public policy was now not only clearly necessary, but long overdue. The leader attacked the Prime Minister personally for his close sympathies with English institutions and predicted (as it turned out, correctly) his imminent downfall; the article alluded to a number of secret Anarchist organizations and concluded by advocating that the Police keep a much closer watch over Italian immigrants.

La Croix also drew attention to the increased frequency and audacity of such attacks on under the present administration. Referring to the bombing of the Chamber of Deputies, the assassination of the President, and the Trial of the Thirty, it claimed that the Anarchists had now become so emboldened that they deemed it acceptable to attack public targets. Clearly, the paper argued, the *Lois Scélérates* were not harsh enough and the Anarchist movement needed to be suppressed by even more forceful and efficacious means.

Paris-Matin remarked that there was no doubt as to the event being politically motivated, but the recent repressive restrictions on the Press had had a counterproductive effect, driving otherwise moderate persons into sympathy with the Anarchists, and against further regulation. The outcome was, if anything, likely to be an increase in civil unrest until the laws were repealed. As it subsequently turned out, the engine driver had simply mismanaged the brakes, a misdemeanor for which he was fined a mere fifty francs.

"The point is, Holmes, that the sensational head-lines and photographs of the crash have kept Le Villard's story of the Perettis' disappearance off the front page."

"It is too bad, but we could hardly have anticipated that."

"The story is here all right, but it is buried at the bottom of the third page. What shall you do now?"

"Precisely what I had intended to do, Watson. Go to the scene, question people, look for further clues, immerse myself in the atmosphere."

"When?"

"Later today."

"Why not right away?"

"Because there is someone with whom I wish to speak, and who will only be there at a certain time."

"Who?"

"Apply my methods, Watson! You recall when Le Villard was recounting to us how Meurant failed to arrest his quarry? He said that his agent returned just as dusk fell. That's an interesting observation, is it not? What does dusk imply? Why, the lighting of lamps! And since lamps do not spontaneously self-illuminate, it implies lamplighters—they are never noticed by anyone, but they go everywhere and see everything! If I asked, did you see anyone in your street about six o'clock last night, you would be likely to reply in the negative. Yet, who lit the lamps? Why, a lamplighter, of course—and yet, you would claim not to have seen him; that is to say, you saw, but did not observe."

"Very well, I shall I order a cab to take us La Villette later."

"No, I think we shall walk. You know that I find it a valuable exercise to steep myself in the atmosphere of the place," he replied.

And he went off to make his preparations with the air of a man who has a pleasant task ahead of him.

A pleasant stroll along the Seine and up the Boulevard Richard Lenoir brought us to the chestnut shaded banks of the Canal St Martin, from where it was a short walk the Bassin de La Villette. The Bassin itself was an insalubrious part of the city, a district of docks and warehouses, shabby *guinguettes* and dingy working men's eateries. The stench from the slaughterhouses hung in the late afternoon air and the area around the *quais* was marked with the indelibly presence of boatmen in a way it that made me think of Smithfield and Wapping rolled into one.

The Flemish, the Corsicans, the Russian and Polish Jews, all seemed to have their own shops and cafés, though the Italians were by far the most numerous. The area to the north of the Bassin comprised tiny artisan dwellings of low-roofed two storied houses of yellow brick, granite doorsteps and dull, uncurtained windows. We found the workshop of the Perettis in one of these back streets, just off the Quai de l'Oise, behind the canal wharves. The premises had a narrow shop front with a window in the Rue de l'Argonne, with a workshop and small yard in the rear. The garish colors of the statuary and pictures on sale contrasted with the dreary surroundings. Holmes rang the bell on the counter and soon a rough-looking man appeared.

"Good afternoon," said Holmes. "May I speak to Ghjuvan or Petru please? I should like them to undertake a small commission for me."

118

"That will not be possible, I am afraid, they have not come in today. They've had a spot of bother," the man replied vaguely. "What sort of commission did you have in mind?"

"I have a small garden which, I think, would be greatly improved with a few carefully chosen pieces of statuary—I was especially recommended to come to the Perettis."

"If it's statues you're after, I won't be able to help..."

"No, you are the picture frame maker I assume?" I followed Holmes's inference as far as the blotches of glue between the man's fingers and the tiny splashes of gold leaf, used for the more expensive type of frames, on the cuffs of his dungarees.

"Yes, but how did you know that?" asked the man in surprise.

"It is my job to know these things. Have you any idea when Ghjuvan or Petru will return?"

"No, I can't say. I merely work for the brothers and occasionally mind the shop for a few hours when they are out. If you would like to leave your name, they will be in contact with you, I am sure."

"Oh, it is not urgent, and I can call in again. You have no objection to my friend and I taking a look around the shop?"

"None at all. There is more stock in the yard if you would like to take a look there. Just ring the bell if you want me again," said the man before disappearing into the workshop again.

Holmes wandered around the shop for a while, amongst the relics and the alabaster statuettes.

"What is it that you are looking for?" I asked.

"I am not entirely sure," he replied in an undertone. "It seems fairly obvious that this fellow has nothing to hide at any rate." Holmes had stopped in front of a shelf of prayer beads and Latin missals with gold leaf edging. "This looks promising," he said.

"My attention has been distracted by this fellow with this head in his hands," I replied, pointing to a statue. "*Sanctus Dionysius*—Saint Denis, if my church Latin does not fail me."

"The Patron Saint of Paris—he was martyred by beheading. The legend goes that he picked up his head and walked off afterwards. It is this section here which interests me," he said Holmes pointed to the shelf.

"The missals?"

"No, the rosary beads. Those black African hardwood ones with the gold chain are rather finely turned; these fellows seem to have a remarkably fine touch," he said, quite to my bemusement. Aside from the odd metaphysical speculation as to inconceivability of the universe being ruled by chance, I had never once known him to take the slightest interest in the study of divinity or the subject of religion. Indeed, he once recommended Winwood Reade to me on the subject, hardly an action liable to occur to a devout believer.

"Look closely at these," he continued, picking up another pair, "don't you think they are rather unusual? They're from Lourdes. It is the curious shade of very pale blue and the remarkable translucence which draws my attention. Yes, I think shall have a set of these."

I confess I was astonished at this, and thought that they must be a present for someone.

"A present?" he replied. "No, I mean to put them to quite practical use."

"Really, Holmes? I hadn't marked you down as…"

"Rather too Romish for your tastes, Watson?" he chuckled and rang the bell.

"Well I have no wish to… I mean to say, one's religious beliefs are private after all," I stammered in reply, wishing now that I had said nothing

Once Holmes had paid the picture framer, we went across to the café on the corner of the Quai de la Gironde for a glass of *blanc sec* at one of the outdoor tables. The *patron* was evidently a local man, for Holmes engaged him in a conversation about the area where he said he had lived all his life. In response to my friend's seemingly off-hand remarks as to the Peretti brothers, the man said he had read something in the papers about them, but as usual, the reporter had got the details all wrong, for he knew for a fact, he said, that the two brothers had gone missing.

"What do you think happened?" asked Holmes.

The man shrugged and raised his eyebrows, "Corsicans!" he said, as though that were an explanation in itself.

"Do they ever come in here?"

"No. They have their own haunts and keep to themselves—they go to the Café Paoli in the Rue Rouvet, just around the corner, where they gamble their money away to the early hours. Ah, here is the very fellow who may have been the last to see them," he said to Holmes, indicating a man coming along the *quai* with a pole and a short ladder.

The *patron* nodded to him and said, "We were just talking about the Corsicans, Étienne," and the man stopped. "You were the last to see them."

"To see them *alive*, you mean!" replied the lamplighter. "You know what they're like, that lot", he added, making a sign as though to signify the cutting of a throat.

He said that, on the night the Perettis had disappeared, he remembered passing up the Rue d'Argonne by the shop which was still open, as usual.

"You saw them?" asked Holmes.

"Oh yes, the lamps had been lit inside. First, a young woman and then a man went into the shop..." Holmes and I exchanged glances—that was the maid and Meurant surely.

"Then, the two Corsicans went through to the back shop with the girl, and left the man in the front."

"Did you see anyone else in the street?"

"No… well, no one of any importance."

"What do you mean?"

"There were two road menders working at the bottom of the street."

"Did you recognize them?"

"No, but they change all the time."

"How long did it take you to light the lamps in the Rue d'Argonne?"

"From the bottom to the top, about seven or eight minutes."

"And the Perettis did not pass you?"

"No."

"No one seems to have seen them going off," said the *patron*, "that's the queer thing. They didn't go to the café that night, for they would have had to pass this way, and I was standing outside talking to one of the *bateliers* for a while. No cab passed either."

"Could they have passed another way though?"

"Yes, they could have gone along the Quai de l'Oise" replied the *patron* nodding in that direction.

"Ah, wait!" said the lamplighter. "No, they couldn't have. Don't you remember, Gaston, there was an accident under the railway bridge? A cab hit a bicycle with no lights. The gendarmes were called and the road was closed there for a bit. At least, someone would have seen them, you'd think. Well, thank you, my friend!" said the lamplighter, draining the glass of beer which Holmes had procured for him

After the man had gone, Holmes said, "What do you make of it, Watson? Does something not strike you as odd about the road menders?"

"No."

"Really, when have you ever seen them working after dark, even in dusk? There is no doubt that it was Jennings and Parker, waiting for their chance. They may have recognized Meurant and struck when he left the shop to go for assistance. It will be just as well for the Perettis if their abductors do not come back here to check the veracity of the Press reports. But I am sure they will not want to excite suspicion."

"But what have they done with them?"

"We are able to narrow the scope of possibilities. According to the waiter and the lamplighter, they did not pass up the Rue d'Argonne, walked along the Quai de l'Oise or the Quai de la Gironde. They do not appear to have left by cab or on foot, therefore…"

"They went by water!"

"I have a vague premonition that they are *in* the water!" said Holmes as we drained our glasses. "After all, Moriarty did not send Parker here for a change of scenery."

We went inside to pay the *patron*. The *bateliers* mixed with the drovers from the slaughterhouses; men were standing at the bar with their drinks, or sitting in small groups playing *écarté* at the baize-topped tables. The *patron* was talking to one of the canal men perched on a stool.

"Not much moving at this time night," said Holmes as he placed the coins on the counter.

"No, very little; they usually stop before dusk and the *éclusiers* knock off for the night," replied the *batelier* affably.

Holmes mentioned the case of a corpse found in the canal the previous year.

"Oh yes, they fish out about half a dozen a year, mostly murders, a few suicides... Occasionally a *batelier* falls in drunk by accident," said Gaston, with a sly wink at Holmes.

"More likely a drover or a meat packer!" the *batelier* interrupted animatedly, with a gesture of bending his elbow and raising a glass to his lips, "they'd drink it out of a latrine."

Gaston and the *batelier* both laughed.

"How soon do they find them?" Holmes.

"Very quickly, for the canal is quite shallow; they can't really sink very far and the mud at the bottom is constantly churned up," answered the *batelier*.

"If a body was in dumped in the Bassin here, how long would it take to find its way to the Seine from here?" Holmes asked.

"That's impossible I should say—don't you think, Gérard?" Gaston said to the man on the stool.

"Oh, quite impossible, yes," replied Gérard. "They'd get trapped in the locks, you see—there's quite a few between here and the river. More likely, they'd get stuck the tunnel section. We had a pretty awful mess in there a while ago—last summer it was, the body got cut up by a few of the barges' propellers. They suspected it was a Greek who had murdered his girlfriend. She had gone missing. But they couldn't tell whether it was a man or a woman. The Greek disappeared a while afterwards too."

"Not thinking of doing someone in, are you?" asked Gaston, laughing as we left.

"Well, at least that will save me the trouble of calculating the rate of water flowing into the Seine at Quai de l'Arsenal," Holmes said as we retraced our steps along the canal.

"The rate of water?"

"Yes, to see how quickly a body would turn up there."

"You think they have been done away with and their bodies dumped?"

"That was one of my suspicions. The other was that they had been taken off on a barge, but there are difficulties for the movement of a barge at that time of night, even on such a busy stretch of the Bassin. It might excite comment and draw unwanted attention. After what we have heard, I am not so sure. You see how quiet the waterway is; yet, I feel we are quite warm."

"They may, of course, have left in a barge the next morning," I suggested.

"In that case, the possibilities are innumerable, but my instincts are against that. You see, things had gone very badly wrong for them—their accomplice was dead, and the Sapphire was, by then, on its way to a bank vault. There was little time to draw up a plan and they were having to extemporize."

Not a vessel was moving on the canal as we walked along by the little pools of light thrown from lamps the deserted *quais*. We looked at the long lines of barges moored in the basin, most with little squares of light in the windows as the families aboard settled down to dinner.

"A precarious living," I said "and an odd one too. Home and work combined."

"Yet, you see most of them are neat and tidy, and the living quarters are kept in a state of cleanliness and order that would surprise a landsman."

We walked right to the end of the *quai* and then stopped to turn back. In an inshot where the wharf made an angle to the main waterway, there was a sorry looking, rusting and dingy heap of a disused barge by the water column whose decks were strewn with old tackle, the warps in sad disarray. Most of the letters had fallen from the name leaving only: *t**le P*l*i *e*.

"I think we have seen enough, Watson," Holmes said.

Chapter IX
Two Slender Threads

"No, Watson, I do not think I am exactly guilty of the charge of withholding information from our French colleagues," Holmes had said in reply to my reproach. "After all, if they had followed up the hints which I gave them, and applied the methods which I have occasionally taken pains to explain to them, they would have made the same discoveries as we have. They had time enough to examine the postcards, and I made them a present of the suitcase. Their problem stems from a self-inflicted belief in a theory, which is supported not by the data but by something amounting to prejudice: the Corsican background of the Perettis, their previous convictions for burglary, and their suspected membership of the *Habits Noirs*."

"But if Jennings should escape…"

"Jennings will not escape, because he has no reason to. On the contrary, if my theory is correct, he has unfinished business here, and will not want to leave until his task is completed. Do not forget that the Contessa is to visit the *Exposition* on Friday evening where she will be wearing the Sapphire; no doubt, Jennings has a plan prepared for that eventuality. Le Villard is not a bad fellow, and while I believe he has much to learn in the field, I should not like to do anything to injure his reputation or damage his self-assurance. But, for the present, it is a question of timing."

He blew out a few coils of smoke from his pipe. "When it comes to following established processes and applying techniques, Le Villard and his men are very assiduous, better even than Scotland Yard, as I discovered last year. But my reason for not telling him of Jennings' hideout is this: it is an incontrovertible fact, Watson, that Police forces, whether good, bad or indifferent, whether French, English, or Russian, all suffer from the same inclination to use the greatest of sledgehammers to crack the smallest of nuts. There are few exceptions, and, given the opportunity, they will simply throw men at the problem, when they ought to be throwing brains at it. I am concerned that even Le Villard would adopt a heavy-handed method, which will cause our bird, or birds, to fly the nest.

"For example, he would have had some flat-footed plainclothes man scuffling along after Jennings, or he would send the local gendarmerie around there on the pretext of a routine check for the identity papers of foreigners. Either way, Jennings would give him the slip, then he and Parker would be on the first train back to Calais and our opportunity to take them would be gone for good. By diligence and attention to minutiae, we have two slender threads, which lead in different directions. I suggest that we take one each and divide forces. If you would be so kind as to take this sample along to Peltier's laboratory, just by the Porte d'Italie in the thirteenth arrondissement. The precise address is on the front."

"What is it?"

"It is a work of chemical analysis," he replied evasively, handing me a small package. "It may turn out to be important, or it may not. I have been pondering this for some time, and am quite certain of the answer, but I simply need a second opinion. If my calculations are correct, it should turn to be a perfectly simple job and it should take very little time. The instructions I wish Peltier to follow are contained in this also," he said pointing to a buff envelope. "Please convey to him my very best wishes and also my apology that I was not able to come in person."

"He is expecting this, then?"

"No, not exactly. Perhaps I ought to have explained that Peltier is a former associate of mine. I made his acquaintance in Montpellier in '94 when I was working my way back to England from Khartoum. He ran a small one man business at the time. Whilst engaged there in research into various organic compounds, I was instrumental in assisting him in discovering some novel industrial uses for naphthalene, including the process for synthesizing a certain compound which he later patented. He made a substantial amount on it and later moved to Paris, where he has now set up shop on the Boulevard Massena. I am sure he will be more than happy to do me this small favor. I think you had better take a cab, for it is a fair distance, and it may be worthwhile to ask the jarvey to wait, for the job that should not take very long."

"And you?"

"I intend to do a spot of dog-walking, Watson."

"Dog-walking!" I replied incredulously.

"Yes, I really need to stretch my legs, so I may be gone for a few hours," he replied with a mysterious smile.

From Holmes's description, I had imagined the premises to be some out of the way place in the back streets, for I was used to the laboratories in London: dank, ill-lit, lofty chambers, crammed with numerous bottles, bristling with retorts and test-tubes, cold as the grave and permeated with the faintly nauseating smell of the gas from Bunsen burners. Instead, I was astonished to find a sizeable and very modern-looking manufactory.

I had to ask at the reception desk for Monsieur Peltier, but once he understood upon whose errand I had been sent, he lost no time in summoning a young, white-coated assistant and gave him orders. He was plainly disappointed not to see Holmes in person; nevertheless, he prevailed on me to return Holmes's good wishes, and expressed the hope that my friend would visit him before he left Paris. Holmes had been correct in his assumptions; within a few minutes, the assistant reappeared from the corridor with the results of the analysis written down on a slip of paper.

"It is exactly as Monsieur Holmes expected," the laboratory assistant said, handing me the paper. I had not seen the original note from Holmes, but when I looked at the note I saw what the man had written:

1. Neurotoxin; 2. C_6H_5OH and CH_2O; 3. Yes, quite certainly.

As Holmes had indicated that he would be gone for some time, I delayed my return to the Hotel des Mamelouks by asking the cabman to drop me off at the Jardin des Plantes. For an hour or two, I wandered through the gardens and galleries, admiring the exhibits. It was the middle of the afternoon when I returned to find Holmes struggling out of a dark, ruddy-tinted tweed suit with a loud check. A wide brimmed hat of the fedora type lay discarded on the sofa. To complete the masquerade, he appeared to be sporting a large false moustache.

"Good Lord, Holmes, you appear to have been auditioning for a spot in the Music Hall!" I remarked. Even Holmes laughed. "Where on Earth have you been?" I asked.

"Well, as it is entirely possible that this hotel is being watched by some of the Moriarty crew, I thought that if I presented myself in the foyer and departed in the guise of an American tourist, I might stave off any undue curiosity. To have been followed on this occasion would have ruined the plan completely. It has been a tiring afternoon for I was compelled to try to take almost a foot off my height just to make sure. Once I am out of this ridiculous garb, I shall tell you my story."

Five minutes later, he reappeared in the smoking room and proceeded to enlighten me.

"As I did not have my London resources to fall back on, I had to ask a somewhat astonished Le Villard to supply me with the costume, without giving away too much. I resolved to become an occasional patron of the terrace café of the Hotel Lambert."

"Jenning's hotel?"

"Yes."

"I wanted to discover where this Parker fellow is holed up too. I thought it might be useful to know in case things do not turn out quite the way I expect, and we need to lay hands on both of them quickly. I had assumed that, as neither Jennings nor Parker have any reason to believe themselves to be under any suspicion, the likelihood was that, although they may not be completely off guard, they might nevertheless associate quite openly."

"But if that is so," I asked, "why would they not simply reside at the same hotel?"

"That would be just a bit too careless. Two Englishmen in a small hotel or a *pension* might draw too much attention. I conjectured that, if I could follow Jennings, he would eventually lead me to Parker's lair, which I was sure wouldn't be very far off. Alternatively,

I could have waited until he had vacated his room and then burgled it; a rather more risky proposition and, in any case, success would be dependent upon Jennings having written down the address of his accomplice. On the whole, I thought the probability was marginally against this. Therefore, I used a more direct and simple method, a hoary old ruse. Fortunately, Montmartre is overrun by tourists of all nationalities, even at this time of year, so I did not stick out too much. First, I called round to Le Villard's office and picked up Beyrand..."

"Beyrand?"

"Yes, I had sent a telegram in advance requesting some assistance."

I was rather piqued at having been left out of this adventure and I ventured to ask Holmes testily what particular qualities Beyrand possessed that I did not.

"His sense of smell, for one thing," Holmes remarked gleefully, ignoring my petulance.

"*What?!*"

"It is a hundred times more powerful than yours, because, you see, Beyrand is a short-haired *Malinois*. A clever breed of hound, much more docile than its German cousin. The breed is very popular in the United States and Canada, which was of no small significance under the circumstances." Holmes chuckled again. "I am bound to say that, after this episode, Le Villard and Dubuque are more convinced than ever that the English are a race of lunatics. Nevertheless, they procured the dog for me and, after a brief introduction, we both went off on our hunt.

"At the Hotel Lambert, I sat down and ordered a small *café noir* and a glass of *pastis* after the French fashion. The *garçon* was particularly uncommunicative in that manner which the French have perfected and, at first, I had the Devil's own job to engage the fellow in some form of badinage. I remarked to him that his English was very good and, sensing an opening, I asked if he had learnt it from English-speaking tourists he had met in the hotel.

" 'No,' he replied, 'we do not get many of them.'

" 'Really, don't you have any at the moment?' I replied affecting no great interest."

" 'One or two,' he said, and he rattled off a few names, including that of Jennings. To cut a long story short, I managed to establish that the man had taken a room on the upper floor in the name of James Jennings, posing as a London artist, supposedly studying aspects of French art, particularly sculpture."

"And the Contessa is interested in sculpture."

"Exactly so, and it is just such an exhibition she will attend on Friday evening. The professor has certainly done his homework. I told the *garçon* how interested I was in the subject and was about to ask him tactfully for Jennings' description when, looking round, he said, 'In fact, there is the gentleman coming through the foyer now.' I thanked him, gave him a decent tip, and off he went. After stopping very briefly at the reception desk, Jennings then came out on to the terrace. I recognized him immediately—this Jennings is none other than Gabriel Ferriter, one of Moriarty's most trusted lieutenants."

"Gabriel Ferriter? The son of Sir Gervaise Ferriter, the eminent barrister? Why, he defended Goldmeier in the Carrington-Palmer fraud case, did he not?"

"Very successfully, and saved an innocent man from public opprobrium, not to mention a long spell in jail. But then, Watson, the criminal tendency is no respecter of social class. I happen to know that young

Ferriter was involved in the famous shooting in Stepney Green where Moriarty's crew eliminated the Strutton Boys; he was the man who lured Badeczosky and Perkoff to their fatal rendezvous outside the Mile End Empire. He is, perhaps, the third most dangerous man in England.

"As he passed my table, I stood up and, as we collided, I managed to spill the residue of my glass of *pastis* over his shoes. I apologized in that exaggerated and profusely irritating way that Americans have, but he waved away my apology quite coolly, and it was all I could do to let him allow me to wipe his shoes with my table napkin; then, he was off, quite unsuspecting I am sure. There are few odors stronger than *anis,* so I let old Beyrand have a whiff of the napkin and off we went after a suitable interval.

"I kept Ferriter in view most of the way and not once did he give as much as a look round, nor did he behave in any way that could be described as furtive. I think it unlikely that he even considered the possibility that he may have been followed. We turned out of the Rue Nicolet, crossed the main road and walked down for a few blocks; finally, we turned into warren of narrow streets. It must have been the easiest job the old boy was ever asked to do for, within five minutes, we reached the door of the Pension Boissieu just in time to see Ferriter disappear inside. I then hailed a cab, dropped the dog off with Le Villard, and here I am. At least, we now know where our foes are ensconced, should we have the need to rush them."

I handed Holmes the slip of paper containing the result of the analysis from Peltier.

"Phenol and formaldehyde, if my memory serves me correctly," I said.

"It does indeed, Watson. Yet, I recall you said that chemistry was never one of your best subjects."

"No, but you will have heard of parkesite." Holmes's knowledge of chemistry was astounding for one who had never systematically studied the subject. "It was invented by Parkes of Birmingham—I once happened to attend lecture by his more famous brother. The details somehow stuck, and saw that this must be a similar substance."

"Yes, a relatively simple compound, but much more soluble."

"What is its connection with the case?"

"Oh, it merely means that I have solved the mystery of Hayes's death," he replied airily, "insofar as there *was* any mystery."

"*What?!* You know who the murderer is?"

"Oh, there was never much doubt as to the person directly responsible for Hayes's death was, but I am now in a position to reconstruct exactly how it happened down to the finest detail."

"Who..."

"All in good time, Watson, all in good time. You know I like to present the finished article in one piece rather than in installments. I must say, though, it was a remarkable brain which conceived this: shrewd, subtle and audacious at the same time. Such a person would be a worthy foe or a precious ally; I am not sure that I would have come up with something as clever myself. Considering how little time there was to think it up and put it into execution. But for one infinitesimal error..."

"Holmes, surely this is unfair of you! After all, you are here at Le Villard's request and it would be irresponsible if the murderer should strike again..."

"There will be no repetition, that is certain, and the person whom I believe to be responsible has no reason to escape, of that I can also assure you. But as the case is almost complete…"

"Complete?!" I repeated in astonishment.

"Yes. Now it is time to draw the matter to a close."

"Do you intend to go after Ferriter and Parker yourself? If so, I mean to be with you if there is to be any…"

"Good old Watson!" he said, clapping me on the shoulder. "I know there is one person I can rely upon to be beside me in the gap of danger. Yes, Sherlock Holmes and Doctor Watson will be in at the kill, but not quite yet. Rather, I hope that Ferriter and Parker will come to me, and if my plan works out, then to Le Villard and Dubuque will go the ultimate privilege of arresting them. You must remember that, at this moment, our principal difficulty is that we have little proof against them."

"But the postcards, surely?"

"A decent lawyer could explain the postcards away. No, we must deceive them into incriminating themselves. We shall wait until it is time lay the final trap and, unless my instincts are all wrong, they will walk straight into it."

Chapter X
At the Porte de Bagnolet

Holmes and I were about to go down to breakfast, when we heard a heavy tread outside in the corridor, followed by series of loud raps on our door. A gendarme appeared and handed Holmes an envelope, which he tore open immediately.

"Well, Watson, events are moving in our favor at last, for our little stratagem appears to have worked," he mused. Then turning to the uniformed official, he said, "Thank you, you may advise Messieurs Le Villard and Dubuque that we shall call round at ten o'clock this morning."

He handed me the note from Dubuque which informed us that the two Peretti brothers had been arrested at five o'clock that morning when they had reappeared at their apartment in the suburbs. Dubuque added that they would not normally be able to hold suspects *without charge* indefinitely; officially, the Perettis were considered to be guilty of Hayes' murder; nevertheless, they would wait until Holmes had had the opportunity to discuss the matter further before they pressed any charges.

"It is as well to have your difficulties at the outset of a case and we certainly did not lack those," said Holmes briskly, "but I believe the matter will be cleared up by tomorrow morning. And then, as the Contessa leaves for Sicily on Saturday, we may begin to make our own plans to return to London."

Le Villard and Dubuque were waiting to welcome us at the Préfecture. "Monsieur Holmes" said the Préfet as he waved us both to our chairs, "it seems that your view has been the correct one. The two men have been knocked about quite badly by their captors, but they will survive. Of course, they refused to reveal anything concerning their disappearance; by whom they had been abducted; or to where they were taken. I had great difficulty in explaining to them that they had had a close shave. Still, they would not talk."

"Well, they are safe enough for the moment," replied Holmes. "I have a good idea as to where they were taken, but that is unimportant at present. I believe I can produce their abductors for you. One is Parker, the man I told you about; the other is Gabriel Ferriter—the man who sent Hayes the postcards. No doubt, they have been sent to exact revenge and post a warning to anyone in the Parisian criminal underworld not to meddle with the plans of a certain master criminal."

"How did you discover this Ferriter?"

"That is rather too long a story for the present. Incidentally, our ruse worked only because Ferriter and Parker did not know the two Corsicans by sight. However, they will not make the same mistake a second time, but will take pains to find out where the Perettis live and will go after them there. I think it is a hundred to one that they will do this during the hours of darkness."

"Surely, they will act immediately."

"No, I think they will be more careful this time. By day, an apartment building has many witnesses: the concierge misses nothing, the neighbors are inquisitive, there is the postman, the milkman, and so on... No, they will come during the night."

"We are in your hands, Monsieur Holmes," replied Le Villard. "Presumably, you know where they are, and

I would prefer it if we simply sent a detachment up to arrest them."

"On precisely what charge?"

"Abduction, assault, conspiracy to commit robbery."

"The Perettis will not testify, so there go your first two charges; on what evidence would you press the third charge? A few vague references on a postcard, some forged identification papers? Moriarty would have the best lawyer in Paris on the case within an hour. No, I have thought over every possible course of action, and this is the best. What is the precise address of the Perettis?"

"Their apartment is in a *cul de sac* off the Rue Des Lyanes," replied Dubuque.

"Excellent, this is a large scale plan of Paris with details of all the residential and commercial properties," said Holmes, unrolling and spreading it out upon the table. "It shows all the alleyways, courts and paths. Here is the Porte de Bagnolet area. As you can see, the street is closed off at the eastern end. For the last six months, as you know, the Compagnie Générale Parisienne de Tramways has been laying new tramlines along the greater part of the Rue de Bagnolet night and day, and all wheeled traffic and pedestrians have been diverted along other routes. To take a cab would be to put themselves in the cabman's power, so it is likely that Ferriter and Parker will come on foot. There is only one way in and out—from Rue Pelleport. Once our assailants enter from there, they shall be caught like rats in a trap.

"We four will go to Bagnolet before dark and take up our stations inside the apartment. I would suggest placing a police marksman on the roof opposite, but our aim must be to forestall, rather than to avenge any violence."

"I will have a contingent of armed men concealed in the main route and have them seal off the *cul de sac* as soon as they see the men entering the street," said Le Villard.

"We can replace the concierge with a plainclothes policewoman for the night. She will be armed too," added Dubuque.

Holmes nodded in agreement, "These are desperate fellows who would not for a second hesitate to shoot down any policeman who stood in the way of their escape, far less any amateur auxiliary force. Although they will take the usual precautions, they will not be expecting any opposition. It is up to us to use the advantage of the attacker."

We reached the narrow thoroughfare at about ten o'clock in the evening, having dismissed our cabs six or seven blocks away. We made our way to the apartment in groups of two, in order to avoid drawing undue attention.

The policewoman who was acting as the concierge motioned Holmes and I up a narrow flight of winding steps. At the end of a dark, musty smelling passage, we found the dingy, cramped apartment, then went through another door to the bedroom. It was agreed that Holmes and I would take up positions behind a chest, whilst the two Frenchmen elected for the space behind the curtains. Le Villard and Dubuque suggested leaving the apartment door unlocked, but Holmes took the view that this might have the effect raising suspicions in the two men.

"I can assure you that a standard door lock will present no obstruction to men of Ferriter's or Parker's caliber," Holmes said, "they will be through it in no time."

We had fixed the nets in place, a task which brought with it something of that thrill of anticipation which we had often experienced in many such adventures. Then, our excitement ebbed away as we began the long, dreary vigil. The small room managed to be cold and stuffy at the same time as we crouched in the darkness. For an hour or two after the bistros and cafés began to empty, we heard the unsteady steps of a straggling home-going drunkard, or the sound of raised raucous voices from the nearby apartments breaking the silence, but as the night wore on, these intrusions died gradually away, until an eerie stillness fell upon us. My limbs began to ache after a few hours, and I nodded off intermittently. The hours crept by ever more slowly, punctuated only by chimes of Saint-Germain-de-Charonne's bell tower nearby, which beat slow time through the half-hours of the night, or by the hiss of an occasional fall of rain upon the pavements outside and against the windows.

At about three o'clock in the morning, we heard the first stirrings: a metallic click as the intruders picked the door lock.

"Ready, Watson?" Holmes whispered to me.

"Yes."

"Good. I will take Ferriter—he is the taller and more dangerous of the two. If I know Parker, he will throw in the towel once he realizes the odds are against him. But if the other tries to fight it out, I shall not hesitate to shoot him dead."

We heard the sounds of the two men creeping stealthily through the house; the steps in the hallway became closer, and, by now, the eyes of the intruders would have adjusted to the dark.

Le Villard's man had set up two bundles, one in each bed, with a dark wig on the pillow. From where we had taken cover, they looked for all the world like two sleeping men. Then, the bedroom door inched noiselessly ajar and two figures eased in silently and steadily. The lightest of sleepers would not have heard a thing. Each man held in his hand a long thin blade which flashed sinisterly in the darkness. We had supposed they would have come armed with guns; though, no doubt, any pistols they may have carried were out of sight. This would make their capture all the easier. The taller man motioned to the other man to approach the bed which was farthest away. The two men poised, crouching, above their intended victims for a second, until, at a sign from Jennings, they pounced like tigers upon the supposed occupants.

There was a muffled cry of surprise; then, Holmes cried fiercely:

"Drop the knife on the floor this instant, Ferriter! Parker, drop yours too and step away. Don't make a move for your guns for you are outnumbered inside here by two to one, and the building is surrounded by armed police. The concierge is a police detective and there is a police marksman on the roof opposite. If you try to shoot your way out of this..."

"Through the window Parker! He daren't shoot!" shouted Ferriter, as he reeled round with a snarl of rage.

But, in an instant, Le Villard and Dubuque had stepped from behind the curtains and a pistol was clapped to the garrotter's head. The two gendarmes who had followed the men into the building now came crashing through the door and flattened Jennings to the floor before he could reach for his pistol. Parker had dropped his knife and had thrown his hands up in surrender; he was standing, white-faced with fear and disbelief with his back to the window.

"Holmes! Sherlock Holmes!" repeated Ferriter in astonishment.

"Really, Ferriter," said Holmes walking over to the bed and coolly turning over the bed sheets to reveal the decoys, "I'm surprised that you were fooled by a bundle of rags and a couple of stage properties. You know, you really ought to pay more attention to detail."

"You cunning swine!"

"I thought it would be courtesy to be here to welcome you here after all the trouble you have gone to. Well, the charge against you would have been merely conspiracy to robbery, and perhaps abduction. But I am afraid that now, it is attempted murder. Of course, that is nothing new to you."

The man stared at Holmes with hatred burning in his eyes.

"And you, Parker, I warned you off only last year, but you refused to take my advice. Well, as an accessory, you will go down for some time, too. You see, the French judiciary have a particular prejudice against foreigners coming here with their dangerous toys, trying to murder their citizens; they have quite enough scoundrels of the home-grown variety. It may be the guillotine for you, Ferriter, for there are a number of unsolved murders in Paris and I recognize a few of your hallmarks."

"Well, the guillotine is quicker and cleaner than a rope," replied Ferriter insouciantly, "but do not concern yourself with my end, Holmes, for your own may not be so far away once a certain person discovers the part you have played here. He missed you once in Switzerland; he won't miss you a second time."

"No, I think it is you who ought to be careful, Ferriter. After all, you failed to take the Nebrodi Sapphire at the cost of Charley Hayes; now, you have failed to get at those whom you thought murdered him. Moriarty does not tolerate failure."

Ferriter looked surprised as the gendarmes pulled him to his feet. "Oh, yes, we know who Michael Carter was; he made a great mistake when he gave up the stage for a life of crime. Our paths had first crossed in '87 and he went from bad to worse. Well, Monsieur Le Villard, you heard it from this man's own lips—did I not tell you that Moriarty was behind this, and our friend Ferriter has as good as admitted as much. I wonder if he will be bold enough to repeat it in front of a judge," said Holmes.

"You are mistaken, Holmes, I will face neither guillotine nor judges," replied Ferriter with quiet dignity.

"Ah, suicide in prison, will it be?" asked Holmes mischievously. "Well, perhaps they had better keep a special watch on you in La Santé."

The man looked as if he would kill Holmes.

"May I?" asked Holmes, inserting his hand into an inside pocket of Ferriter's and pulling out a gun. "I believe this is the one you used to kill Rothière outside the Auberge du Marais. I think you will find it matches perfectly," said Holmes passing the weapon to Le Villard.

"To be fair, I think I owe you an apology too, Ferriter."

Ferriter looked puzzled, but remained silent.

"Yes, for making such a mess of your shoes, so that my dog could trail to you to the Pension Boissieu where your accomplice was hiding out. And I'm sure you will also forgive my ruse in getting the Press to believe that you had abducted the wrong people. It was a well-justified one, for I ought to tell you quite honestly, these two men had no more to do with Hayes' death than I did. Well, I'm afraid that you are going to miss the *Exposition* on Friday evening. Where did you hide the men, Ferriter, on the *Étoile Polaire*?"

Ferriter, pale with rage, said nothing.

"That will do for the record, Watson, for I see the merest flicker in his eye that tells me I am correct. Well, Monsieur Le Villard, to you and to Monsieur Dubuque belongs the undisputed credit for the arrest of these two. No doubt, the Press will be ringing with your praises."

At a nod from Le Villard the gendarmes led the two men out of the apartment.

"I am greatly indebted Monsieur Holmes. As our nation has already conferred upon you the greatest honor that any foreigner can obtain, I do not know how we can properly reward you now," said Le Villard.

"It was an honor in itself to be asked. As you know, I have made my admiration of the methods of Sûreté quite plain. And as to the question of a reward, I shall be adequately materially compensated by the Contessa."

Le Villard smiled, "It has been most instructive to work alongside you and observe your methods, and your results." He continued more hesitantly, "I have no wish to seem ungrateful; indeed, I feel almost apologetic in having to raise this but… I am still short of a murderer."

"Yes, of course," replied Holmes in his most off-hand manner. "Let's meet again at the Hotel des Mamelouks five hours from now. I promise I will produce for you the person responsible for the death of Charlie Hayes."

"I would rather have his name and address for I fear that if we hesitate further, he may escape."

"There is not the slightest likelihood that this person will leave Paris," said Holmes, "you have my solemn word on that."

"I would rather have the handcuffs on him, than your word," replied Le Villard in comic resignation.

Holmes was not prone to egotism in the ordinary sense, but he loved nothing better than to hold an audience in his power, having no doubt picked up the rudiments of stagecraft in his undergraduate days in student theatricals. I recalled an encounter earlier in his career when Baron Dowson was so taken in by Holmes's disguise that he declared that, what criminal detection had gained, the stage had lost, and there was little doubt that, had Holmes desired to do so, he could have emulated Mr. Henry Irving as the foremost thespian of his age.

Despite the intellectual stimulation which his chosen profession afforded, he exulted in those moments when his more theatrical instincts could be allowed full rein. This occasion was no exception, containing as it did one of those little enigmatic flourishes, so characteristic of his nature.

"Handcuffs?" he smiled mysteriously. "You may leave your handcuffs at the Préfecture, Monsieur; you shall have no need for them," was all he would say.

Chapter XI
A Murderer Unmasked

Holmes and I were at the Hotel des Mamelouks at the appointed time. First, we had a long, private discussion with the Contessa, where she told us that she had engaged a new secretary from one of the agencies which Holmes had recommended. Holmes then gave detailed instructions for the visit to the Galeries Jonquin, and reminded her that Moriarty was not the sort of person to be baulked by his initial failure.

"I do not believe there will be another attempt on the jewel whilst you remain in France," he said, "nevertheless, Watson and I will travel with you by train as far as the Italian border. After that, you will need to take the utmost care until you arrive back in Sicily. However, this new fellow you have appointed must be prepared to act as your guard during that period."

There was a knock at the door, and the two French detectives were ushered in, followed a few minutes later by the maid.

"I have asked you here," began Holmes, "in order to clear up the mystery surrounding the death of Michael Carter, alias Charley Hayes, and the attempt to steal the Nebrodi Sapphire. I confess that, when I arrived, I was rather taken aback to find, so to speak, that the first act in the drama had already been acted out. The obvious explanation was that someone had gained entry to the room in an attempt to steal the Sapphire and had murdered Carter in the process—a lesson in the power of assumption—and a wrong-headed assumption at that! The chief difficulty in this case was that there seemed to be almost too much evidence, and most of it contradictory. The fact that the jewel case been taken out of the safe could possibly be explained away—perhaps, the thief or thieves had been disturbed and fled? But it was the discovery that Carter's pistol had not been loaded which put me on the right scent. What could one make of this? Having received a warning that one of the most ruthless international criminals was after the Sapphire, the person charged with its protection couldn't fail to take the most rudimentary precautions. It immediately suggested to me that he had feared no intrusion, because he *was* the thief. My investigatory telegram to London elicited the fact this Carter was none other than Charlie Hayes, one of Moriarty's men, with a record of robbery and murder.

"In that case, the most likely explanation for his apparent murder was that he had been killed by a competitor, possibly a rival organization—the *Habits Noirs*, for instance. There was suspicion that the Peretti brothers, and indeed Mademoiselle Peretti herself, may have been implicated in this; their Corsican background, the brothers' previous record for burglary, their former exploits on the high wire, and their suspected membership of the *Habits Noirs*, made them all perfect suspects. Mademoiselle Peretti had even been entrusted with the key to the jewel case, and she would have known all of the movements of the people in the Contessa's party. *Monsieur Le Préfet* theorized that the two former acrobats had come through the window and committed the murderers, but I was forced to rule this out after I had examined the window and the balcony. Though by no means impossible—it has been done before—there was no trace whatever of entry.

"Most intriguingly, there was not the slightest indication that there had been anyone in the bedroom other than Hayes himself: he had been alone all night, yet someone had managed to poison him though they *had not taken the jewel*. It was immediately obvious that no ordinary explanation could explain all the facts.

"At about seven o'clock on Monday evening, Giulianna Peretti was sent along to deposit the jewel for safe-keeping. Mademoiselle Peretti, I give you the opportunity to tell us why, between leaving the Contessa's room and Hayes's room, you took the Nebrodi Sapphire from its case, and concealed it in your pocket?"

There was a gasp of surprise around the room and all eyes looked at the maid whose features blazed with guilt and defiance.

"I did not steal the jewel," she spat out. "You know that the genuine Sapphire is safe in the bank, so why do you falsely accuse me of stealing it?"

Holmes smiled, "You misunderstand me, Mademoiselle, the only thing I accuse you of is acting very quickly, very bravely, and very cleverly to protect your mistress's property. But you give yourself away, do you not? You said the *genuine* Sapphire."

The maid looked confused, but remained silent.

"There was another Sapphire, was there not?" continued Holmes.

A spasm of fear scored the girl's face. The Contessa looked startled. "Another Sapphire?" she asked incredulously.

"Yes, there was another Sapphire, of sorts," replied Holmes. "If Mademoiselle is disinclined to tell the story in her own words, I shall do it on her behalf. Once the message had come through warning of the robbery, Mademoiselle Peretti's suspicions as to the integrity of this man Hayes were confirmed, were they not?"

The girl nodded.

"She had suspected him from the outset for some reason, and now, she put two and two together. As a newcomer to the party, she knew well that her suspicions would carry no weight. As the Contessa would never hear a word against Hayes, she set about protecting the jewel as best she could. I will tell you precisely how she did that. I was struck by the fact that the girl had gone to visit her cousins at the workshop, not at their apartment. This could only mean that there was something which she wanted at La Villette which was not in Bagnolet. Very strong circumstantial evidence from the *post mortem*, beyond the bounds of coincidence, pointed straight to the Peretti family. How was the poison administered? There was no indication that it had been had not been forced on Hayes. In fact, it was not."

"But, Monsieur Holmes," interrupted Le Villard, "you know of the conversation which Meurant overheard in which the entire family practically admitted to the murder."

"There was never any intention to do any harm, but something went fatally wrong, and I shall attempt an explanation of the words Meurant overheard. I visited the workshop in La Villette and saw immediately how the whole thing had been done as clearly as if I had been there. I shall attempt to describe that, and perhaps Mademoiselle Peretti will take the trouble to point out to me whatever details I may get wrong.

"She went to the workshop to ask Ghuvan and Petru if they could make a copy of the jewel. Her purpose was to substitute the fake jewel for the real one at some point, and that is what happened. On a previous visit, she had seen the brothers using a pale, bluish transparent substance to fashion a set of rosary beads. It was very similar to the color of the Sapphire and would probably pass muster under the circumstances, providing Hayes did not look too closely. So, she made the switch on Monday night on her way to hand over the Sapphire. She believed that Hayes would probably disappear during the night with the fake jewel, and, at that point, she would be able to hand over the genuine Sapphire to the woman to whom she had pledged her loyalty."

The Contessa sprang to her feet and hugged the girl ardently. "I knew you would not have done anything against me. Did I not tell you, Signore Le Villard?"

"Unfortunately, it was at this point that the plan started to go fatally wrong," Holmes continued. "You see, Hayes, had also thought a few steps ahead. Although he had intended to steal the jewel and had made plans to leave Paris by the earliest train on the following morning, he had considered the possibility that the train might be stopped and searched before he got to the Belgian border. He had not had time to find a suitcase with false bottom, or something with a hidden compartment, so he used a much simpler method and hid the jewel where a search would never find it."

"Where exactly?" asked Le Villard.

"In a canal," replied Holmes with a mischievous glimmer.

"The Canal St Martin?" said Dubuque.

"The alimentary canal! He swallowed it, intending to retrieve it in the usual manner a day or so later after he had arrived at Antwerp under a new identity. Unfortunately, Giulianna had already substituted the fake jewel in the case, and the blue substance, containing phenol and formaldehyde, acted as a slow poison and killed Hayes during the night. When in the morning, Giulianna found the key was still in the inside of Hayes's bedroom door, she was very puzzled; then, the full horror of the situation came home to her. She realized that she must say nothing; she surreptitiously replaced the Sapphire in the jewel case when Giuseppe Gazzano's attention was distracted, and she pretended that the Sapphire had never left the case. How well she recovered from what must have been a petrifying shock when she found that Hayes had been killed as a result of her innocent plot to fool him, and with extraordinary quickness she reasoned that her credit in saving the jewel would have to be sacrificed in order to avoid being arrested on a murder charge, is truly admirable."

"But, surely, there can be no charge of murder," cried the Contessa in agitation. "I will find the best lawyer in France if…"

Le Villard waved away the suggestion, "If there was no intent to murder or to do harm, then there is no question of any charges. You could not possibly have foreseen the consequences of your actions, Mademoiselle. I shall speak to the Magistrate personally."

"Now, you accept my interpretation of the conversation which Meurant overheard?" asked Holmes.

"Unreservedly. 'Death by misadventure' I think you would call it in England, Monsieur Holmes?"

"Undoubtedly. Have I told the story accurately, Mademoiselle Peretti?"

The girl nodded. "This man Hayes had told us that he knew no one in Paris," she said quietly and calmly. "When he received a postcard only hours after we had had the warning about the robbery, I became suspicious. When his attention was diverted, I took the postcard and read it. I do not understand English very well but I saw that it had been posted in Paris and I *knew* it must be a secret message connected to the robbery. I watched him closely and when he left, suddenly my suspicions were confirmed—I knew he must be going to send a reply. I decided to follow him, then realized that I could not prove anything against him. An idea came into my head that I could find a substitute for the jewel and so I went to see Ghuvan and Petru to ask them to make a counterfeit."

"They almost paid for it with their life," said Le Villard. "Had it not been for Sherlock Holmes, their bodies would probably be floating in the Bassin de La Villette at the moment."

"They will be very grateful to you when I explain this, Monsieur Holmes, as I am too," said the girl.

"You have acted throughout with exceptional cleverness, bravery and spirit, Mademoiselle Peretti. You have qualities in abundance to make a splendid associate. As to the abduction of your cousins, I believe that Hayes and Parker took them to a disused barge called the *Étoile Polaire* near the Quai de l'Oise which Doctor Watson and I found moored in a quiet corner of the canal wharf. I noticed that the gritty dust on the decks had been disturbed, and I observed amongst the debris four set of footprints going to the deck hatch, and only two returning. I knew there was a possibility that we were being watched by one of Moriarty's men and, as I have in the past betrayed myself by an indiscreet eagerness, on this occasion, I merely noted the name of the barge and turned away, walking in the other direction.

"I imagine they were bound and gagged and threatened with all sorts, but I calculated that they would refuse to cooperate with to their captors. By a simple ruse—which was almost undone by the railway accident on Tuesday— Hayes and Parker were misled by the newspaper report into thinking they had captured the wrong men. We lured them to Bagnolet the following night and they walked straight into the trap we had laid for them.

"As Messieurs Le Villard and Dubuque are aware, I followed up the trail of the postcards which had been sent to Hayes, and these led me to Ferriter's and Parker's hideouts. Ferriter was posing as a sculptor by the name of Jennings; I have not the slightest doubt that, left to his own devices, he would have made this evening's *Exposition* a rather more lively and memorable affair than it may turn out to be."

"Wonderful, Signore Holmes," said the Contessa. "You have certainly lived up to your reputation. I shall recompense Giulianna's relations very well for any injury they have received, for they have also rendered me a service. As to Giulianna herself, I do not know how best to show my gratitude, but you know that I never doubted your integrity for one moment."

"Well, I think that rather explains everything, and we may now look forward to an interlude of quiet calm until it is time to leave Paris. There remains only one thing puzzling me."

"What is that, Monsieur Holmes?"

"Concerning another Corsican."

"Another Corsican! Which one?"

"According to his will, the Emperor Napoleon recorded his wish to be buried on the banks of the Seine. I often wondered why the great man's request had never been granted."

Chapter XII
Virtue Rules the Heights

Our excursion to the *Exposition* passed entirely without incident. The following day, we picked up the Contessa's new secretary, Harrison Elliott, and then traveled, as Holmes had promised, with the party to Menton. There, at the station, we watched the tail lamp of the Contessa's train disappear towards the Italian border in the early hours of a misty Mediterranean dawn.

As it turned out, Giulianna Peretti did not return to Sicily with her employer, but decided to stay behind and make her own way in Paris. The parting, albeit a poignant one, was more than amicable for the Contessa. In gratitude for the girl's part in preventing the theft of the Sapphire, she presented her with a substantial reward with which the young woman was determined to use to set herself up in some business or other. The Peretti brothers, having recently found Paris to be rather too exciting to be enjoyable, returned to Bastia.

So it was that Holmes and I eventually left France in the last week of October. By the time we returned to London, the city was in the grip of an unseasonable spell of freezing cold, and it was a dark, foggy, and inhospitable place that we found when we alighted from the boat train in Victoria that early morning.

The streets were just beginning to resound to the unmistakable sights and sounds of stirring and coming awake: the jingle of horses being harnessed; the tramping feet of laborers and carters as they emerged one by one on the streets; the shuffling of red-eyed, rough-looking men, spitting and coughing over a cigarette or a

155

pipe on their way for the first drink of the day—an "eye-opener" as it was called—for the publicans seemed to keep early hours in the rougher districts around the railway terminus.

The night had been full of drizzling haze, and now a half-moon peeped through the cloud intermittently, bathing the damp streets in which broad bars of light were beginning to appear in the windows of the buildings. I was cold and hungry, and my limbs were beginning to feel stiff and sore from three consecutive overnight journeys, for it had been a long slog back from the frontier to Calais, Dover, and finally London. I was suffering from the accumulated mental exhaustion brought on by the case itself and by the long journey. Despite my desire to see the Contessa's check safely deposited at the Capital and Counties Bank in Charing Cross Road, I went off upstairs to try to get a few hours of desperately needed sleep leaving Holmes to pursue Mrs. Hudson for breakfast.

I could see that something was at work in his mind, and I knew him well enough to know that he would take no sleep until he had made some resolution to the problem. A few minutes later, I could hear him scraping away on the violin; first, a set of melancholy chords, followed by what sounded more like an unconnected series of dreary, cheerless resonances than actual music.

It turned out to be a broken and fitful sleep for me, for I found I could not shut out the diurnal sounds of the street outside, and Holmes's own restlessness nagged at my unconscious mind through the gloom of the curtained room. It was, in any case, a sleep which was destined to be interrupted by the arrival of Sergeant Hill around midday, who had hastened to Baker Street with some news from the continent.

Through my torpid but sleepless state, I could dimly hear them conversing below: Hill, rueful and gloomy; Holmes, irritated and impatiently questioning. I knew that there was nothing for it but to rouse myself and go down to find what had happened. As soon as I entered the sitting room, I could see that all was far from well; indeed, I read disappointment instantly from Holmes's expression, and I felt a premonition of what was to come.

"Well, Watson, you will be dismayed to know that, despite our carefully planned arrangements for the Contessa's journey back home to Sicily, we have completely failed to prevent Moriarty from striking again."

"The Nebrodi Sapphire has been stolen?"

"Yes, on the ferry from San Giovanni to Messina, and Harrison Elliott has disappeared."

"Disappeared?"

"Yes, presumably murdered and his body thrown overboard, but there remains the doubt that, despite all the precautions which we had taken, he may have been yet another accomplice of Moriarty's who managed to infiltrate the agency."

"Yes, it is certainly possible and cannot be ruled out," said Hill.

"And no one saw or heard anything, I presume?" asked Holmes.

"No, the party stepped on the boat at San Giovanni in broad daylight, and neither Elliott nor the Sapphire was ever seen again," replied Hill.

"If Moriarty is behind this, as I have no doubt, then it is gone for good. I had been uneasy on the journey home and began to wish that we had gone all the way to Sicily, but as you recall, the Contessa would have none of it." Holmes shook his head. "Satan's toys, Watson, Satan's toys."

There was at least one consoling footnote to the episode of the Nebrodi Sapphire. A day or two after Hill's visit, Holmes was surprised to receive a communication from Giulianna Peretti. Amongst other things, she expressed her thanks for all he had done in the case, particularly in saving the life of her two cousins after they had fallen into the murderous hands of the Moriarty crew, and in clearing their name and hers in connection with the attempted robbery. She had, she said, pondered for a while as to how best to invest the money she had received from the Contessa. She had initially considered whether to set up an agency business in supplying maids and traveling companions to the idle rich, for it was something she had experience of. But recalling Holmes's words of approbation at her part in averting the robbery, she had come up with the quite bold idea of setting up her own private detective agency, *L'Agence Peretti,* and was writing to Holmes to ask his advice in the matter—which he was more than happy to give freely. It was to be the only agency in Europe run by a woman, and even Holmes, the eternal misogynist, clapped his hands delightedly, and admitted that there was every prospect that this exceptional young woman would achieve success in the field.

Holmes was still nursing his vague disappointment, however, over the outcome of the case when, a few weeks later, an even greater blow fell; not a physical blow, but a psychological one. We were cocooned in the cozily stuffy sitting room one moist foggy morning over breakfast as a roaring fire crackled in the grate, and had been discussing the case which he had temporarily abandoned in order to go on our Parisian adventure.

It was the loss of the ancient Athanasian scroll in which he had been advising His Holiness Pope Kyrillos, and which had necessitated Holmes's intercession with a cabal of the international antique thieves, the bargaining for which entailed translation in three languages whilst striving to maintain the secrecy of the matter. After the plates were cleared, Holmes lounged by the green shaded lamp reading the agony and social columns of the time *The Times*, whilst I had remained at the breakfast table poring over the card at Doncaster in the pages of *The Sporting Life*. Billy the page arrived with the post which contained a letter for Holmes.

I noticed that his features sharpened as he picked up the envelope; it bore an American postmark, which immediately seemed to me unusual, for Holmes, to my knowledge, had no regular transatlantic correspondents. Moreover it was addressed to "Sherlock P. Holmes," which purported to indicate that the sender was Porlock.

Holmes stared at the envelope for a while in puzzlement, turning it over a few times, then on opening the letter, he was struck quite pale with shock by its contents. His brow grew more furrowed and he continued to stare at the single sheet of paper in bleak empty silence with such a look of foreboding that I was loath to interrupt his train of thought.

"Dear, oh dear, Watson," he said at last, "we are not out of this one yet, and I fear we shall hear no more of our friend in Camberwell."

"Another message from Porlock?"

"No, Watson, we have had our last message from the man who calls himself Fred Porlock. The American postmark concerned me as soon as I saw it. I said before that I could tell an old master by the sweep of his brush; I detect the same stroke here."

I looked in puzzlement at the sheet of paper, it contained only four letters: *V I E R*.

"Very strange Holmes—what do you make of it? Surely *vier* is German for four. What can it have to do with the Nebrodi Sapphire?"

"It has everything to do with it, but the meaning of *V I E R* is not four, at least not in this context. I should have expected this of course, I should have known that having been baulked in Paris his infernal pride, the pride of Lucifer, would have driven him to deliver this final thrust of his sword. He knows I will understand the significance of the postmark: Pottsville, Pennsylvania—for it is none other than the Vermissa Valley of evil memory. You see, I had thought that when Ferriter got the message saying *'Holmes has left London,'* it signified nothing more than that we had been watched. On the contrary, a certain Professor must somehow have discovered the communication from our friend in Camberwell, and he has evidently now deciphered and counterfeited the protocol with, I fear, fatal consequences for the man Porlock."

"Is it another code, then?"

"No, Watson, it is an animal cry; a feral howl of pure triumph which wounds me more than any weapon has the power to."

"Then what does it mean?"

"It stands for *Virtus In Excelsis Regnat.*"

"*Virtue Rules The Heights?*" I asked, still puzzled.

"Precisely Watson, *Virtue Rules The Heights*—the motto of the Irish clan, Moriarty."

The Adventure of the Bognor Prestidigitation Circle

In considering some of the singular encounters and remarkable events which my friend Sherlock Holmes has experienced during the last decade, there are a certain number of which I have been forced to conceal from the public gaze. In some cases the reason for this has been to avoid scandal or opprobrium falling upon innocent persons; in other cases, such as in Holmes's success in bringing to justice the conspirators of the Diamond Jubilee assassination attempt, grave issues of national importance hung upon on the outcome of the case, and it was not hyperbole to suggest that the destiny of certain small nations swung in the balance; in yet other cases again, where we had to take due cognizance of the laws of libel, silence was the only course of action open to me. There was another category of cases: those for which I had written up the notes, but had then simply failed—through forgetfulness, or from pressures of work, or due to sundry other quotidian considerations—to bring the matter into the public realm.

I have had, from time to time, also to contend with Holmes's own deep-seated personal aversion to publicity, and it was due only to my persistent urgings that he agreed to bring the matter into the public realm. Happily, on this particular occasion, however, he was the one to instigate the publication of the strange affair of the Bognor Prestidigitation Circle.

We had been relaxing comfortably in the Baker Street sitting room after one of Mrs. Hudson's excellent breakfasts when Holmes broke in on the silence.

"My dear Watson, I seem to recall that, when you published your account of the Tregennis affair last spring, you tantalized your readership somewhat by alluding briefly to the remarkable case of Dr. Haylie-Foster. I see no reason why this should not now enter the public realm—unless you have a disinclination to wash the dirty linen of your own profession?"

"Not at all, Holmes, on the contrary, I believe the profession can best uphold its well-earned reputation for integrity, and defend its patients' general interests, by chastising its members in the most open manner for irregular or substandard practice, and for insisting that justice be done wherever and whenever its members are found engaging in criminal activity. You will recall very recently how the testimony of our reigning monarch's very own physician was instrumental in helping to hang the doctor involved in the Lambeth poisoning case. I shall delve into my dispatch box and hunt out the notes of the case."

On consulting the records which I had made at the time, I found that it was on the Friday, October 7, that we received a visit from the eminent Harley Street physician, Dr. Moore Agar. We had been sitting over a pot of coffee one afternoon when we were interrupted by Billy the Page who advised us that we had a visitor. I was delighted to make the personal acquaintance of the man who had, some years previously, consented to become Holmes's physician, for hitherto I had known only the great man's name and his reputation from the reading of various medical journals. Although he had called in order to speak privately to Holmes, he was diplomatic enough to assent to Holmes's request that I remain in order to hear the remarkable account which he had to tell.

"I have been placed in a very delicate situation, gentlemen," our visitor began, "concerning a colleague of mine—*of ours*, I should say, Doctor Watson—a Dr. Gabriel Haylie-Foster, who currently practices in Upper Brook Street. Haylie-Foster is thirty-eight years of age and unmarried. He is a brilliant young man in many ways, perhaps a degree more impulsive and impatient than one would expect or desire from a member of the medical profession, but no doubt, he will mature with experience and, as one of our rising specialists in neurology, he has truly great prospects. It is not impossible to imagine him attaining the highest peaks in our profession, wouldn't you agree, Doctor Watson?"

I concurred without hesitation for I had only the previous year read one of his treatises in the *Lancet*. Moore Agar continued, "I have a personal interest in that, some years ago, I had to a certain extent taken Haylie-Foster under my wing, for it was clear to me that this young man represented one of the most interesting and valuable discoveries in the field for many a decade. He was diligent, clever, quick witted and could describe both his theories and results of his experiments in the most transparent prose—an uncommon trait in our profession as anyone will know who has had the misfortune of having to plough through the turgid prose in medical journals by some of our more plodding and lugubrious practitioners. He had few personal faults or besetting vices: he neither drank, nor smoked, nor gambled; he was not a gregarious young man and he had no club to speak of. The only trait which came to my notice was that he had a keener interest in monetary rewards than is common amongst those who see medicine as a vocation.

He once said to me, quite seriously, that he desired to make enough money to retire comfortably at forty years of age! But as the young man came from an impoverished background—his father was a Billingsgate porter—I felt that could easily be forgiven."

"The son of a Billingsgate porter with a double barreled name?" asked Holmes incredulously.

"Ah, no. That was a slight affectation; he added his mother's maiden name to his own surname, and changed his Christian name from George. Lately, he seems to have been drawn to the slightly more esoteric regions of his chosen subject but, without wishing to seem to cast aspersions, that is often the inherent bias of the medical man whose subject is *mens sana* rather than *corpore sano*. One of the occupational disadvantages of practicing neurology in this country is that there is a quintessentially English prejudice against that which cannot be seen and touched, which is why the French, the Germans, the Austrians, and even the Americans, tend to lead the field.

"But I fear I weary you with shop talk, Mr. Holmes. To come to the point, it was with some surprise that I found Haylie-Foster's assistant in his general practice, Bernard Coram, in my consulting room yesterday morning. He had come to tell me that Haylie-Foster had suddenly disappeared. He had gone out for a newspaper on Wednesday evening, and simply never returned. As you may imagine, this caused chaos as well as astonishment. Coram reported the matter to the Police obviously, but he was faced with the sudden and slightly embarrassing problem of having to arrange at very short notice for a locum to attend Haylie-Foster's practice for the next few days, whilst maintaining a pretense to the patients that the reason for the doctor's absence was that he had merely taken unwell. The matter was reported to the Police. who did not exactly move Heaven and Earth to find Haylie-Foster and, apart from a brief visit from an Inspector Lestrade, who did not even bother to question the servants, they have done very little."

"I see," replied Holmes, "and you have come to me in order to ask me to find the missing doctor?"

"It is far more complicated than that, Mr. Holmes. You see, after the doctor's disappearance, Coram—who is a very intelligent young man—went through some of Haylie-Foster's private papers in order to ascertain if there was anything which would give some suggestion as to the reason for his disappearance, or some hint as to where he may have gone. I am afraid to say that he unearthed some troubling concerns about the behavior and professional conduct of his senior colleague, who is also, of course, his employer. In fact, he came to see me straight away, partly because I am a member of the General Medical Council, and partly because I was a former mentor of Haylie-Foster's. To put it bluntly, Mr. Holmes, if the suggestions with which Coram has presented me can be proven to have some foundation, it may, at the very least, result in Dr Haylie-Foster being stuck off the Register."

"Struck off the Register!" Holmes exclaimed. "But, why?"

"Well, according to Coram, he seems to have taken a fancy to predicting the very hour and date of the deaths of some of his patients. One can see how this might be rather unsettling to the clients."

"And to the GMC, no doubt, yes, though it scarcely seems grounds for striking one from the Register."

Dr. Moore Agar looked from one to the other of us, and then he answered, "It does when he got it perfectly correct to the hour three times in a row."

"Ah, I see," said Holmes, leaning forward with interest. "Perhaps you had better give me more details."

"In addition to his fine personal attributes, I must point out that Dr. Haylie-Foster has had an unblemished record in the profession thus far. But, within the last three weeks, three of his elderly patients have died suddenly of apparently natural—but, in truth, medically unknown—causes. There is nothing unusual in this, of course: doctors are not infallible, they make mistakes, and they cannot cure every ailment or condition. Providing there is no negligence involved, such as misdiagnosis or misapplication of treatment, there is no cause for concern.

"Something in the recent course of events, however, seems to have set off Coram's suspicions. You, gentlemen, will presumably well understand how it is when two persons work together very closely; there is an area of unspoken exchange which often allows one to read the other's intention, and, occasionally, to predict that the other will, or will not, take a certain course of action. Coram is a very thoughtful young man, and as a student of a subject which treats more of the mind than the body, he is perhaps—if you will excuse my generalization, Doctor—more perceptive than one whose field of study relates solely to the physical. Haylie-Foster has perhaps one small professional shortcoming: he is impatient towards what he regards as outdated theories and practices, which is, by no means, necessarily a bad thing in an age of discovery such as ours, when the frontier of science are continually being pushed forward; unfortunately, he is also disparaging towards those who uphold such outdated ideas and, as is commonplace with clever, quick witted young men, he has ruffled a few feathers amongst the traditionalists—none of which, you will understand, would stand him in very good stead should he come up in front of the GMC—assuming, of course, that he re-appears. In addition to his specialist work, as I have said, Haylie-Foster runs a general practice: this is what brings in most of the income, and it is this which has presented Coram with the severely practical question of what to do with the patients if the doctor does not return."

"What exactly did Coram discover? Please be specific," said Holmes.

"When it began to look unlikely that Haylie-Foster would return soon, Coram, on his own initiative, entered without authority his private room and, searching through his papers, discovered what might be described as his mentor's private daybook. There, he found the names of the three patients who had recently died, and against these were the times and dates of their death. The names had been ticked off, as it were, and the inexorable circumstantial effect is that it appears that Haylie-Foster had successfully predicted, not just the day, but the very hour of these three patients' deaths. Apparently, all three patients were elderly and were fading away—recovery from their condition was, to say the least, unlikely. Professionally, Coram is concerned that there may have been some degree of malpractice, and as Haylie-Foster's personal assistant, he does not wish to see his own name dragged through the mud if there has been any wrongdoing. This suspicion appears to lend a motive to Haylie-Foster's otherwise inexplicable disappearance."

Holmes considered for a moment, then said, "I am not entirely sure what it is you are asking me to do. Presumably, if you consider that there is evidence that

Haylie-Foster is unfit to practice, then you must do what you consider to be your duty, raise the matter with the GMC, and have him struck from the Register. Surely, you neither need, nor want, my judgment on that. Why, Doctor Watson here would be far better placed than I am to render a judgment on whether the very strict guidelines applying to your profession have been transgressed when dealing with allegations of professional malpractice."

"That is correct, Mr. Holmes, however I would put it rather more strongly than that. I have not come to you in order to determine to whether Haylie-Foster is fit to practice or not. I am concerned as to whether the matter should be reported to the Police, not as a disappearance but—and I am not a man given to self-dramatizing—as to whether a murder has been committed. Or rather, three murders."

"Murder?" asked Holmes.

"Yes, consider: three patients have died, and there is evidence to suggest that Haylie-Foster may have had a hand in this."

"But, surely, a doctor has a perfect right to draw up some forecast of how long a patient is likely to last under the given circumstances of any malady, especially if this is written up in his private notes."

"Yes, assuredly so, but the missive which contains this information bears no resemblance to either the form or content of written medical records, which would normally be available for colleagues to read. It is contained in a private diary, which was quite frankly hidden away."

"And you suspect these three patients were murdered—poisoned perhaps?"

"I am not certain. All three deaths were reported as being from natural causes, but, of course, there was no suspicion at the time."

"Did any of these patients leave anything to Haylie-Foster in their wills?"

"Nothing, not a penny. Coram has since checked the details and found that all three were elderly and in fairly modest circumstances."

"And the legatees of the deceased?"

"Received very little, to Coram's knowledge."

"Then, there is a complete absence of any material motive."

"So there was too with the Lambeth poisoner," I interjected. "He did away with many out of sheer sadistic pleasure."

"You will understand that I am, on the one hand, extremely reluctant to take that first step on what may seem an unfounded allegation without solid evidence to support it," said Dr. Moore Agar. "On the other hand, I have a certain degree of guilty knowledge which does not justify me doing absolutely nothing."

"Yes, I perceive your dilemma," replied Holmes.

"If you would be so good as to look at the case, Mr. Holmes, your diplomacy and tact are as well known as your intellectual brilliance and so..."

"You wish me to keep the matter as secret as possible."

"Yes."

"That puts me at an enormous disadvantage, but it is by no means impossible, although I will possibly have recourse to speak with my colleagues at Scotland Yard. Well, thank you for bringing me such an intriguing case, Dr. Agar, I shall be delighted to look into it."

Holmes lit his pipe, "Well, Watson, what do you make of it?" he asked as the door closed behind our visitor.

"On the face of it, Moore Agar's suspicions seem rather far-fetched."

"Let us conjecture for a moment. There are many things which motivate men to dramatic steps, to take chances against great odds: there is material gain, which I think we have ruled out here; the love of a woman, which I think we can possibly exclude in this case too; let us also for the moment discount sheer malice or, as you put it, sadism; then, there is the exercise of absolute power... Ah, now there is something which might appeal to the scientific mind, especially that of a doctor who, as you know, often seems to hold the power of the Almighty in his hands; then, perhaps the foremost, is the pursuit of knowledge, especially scientific knowledge. If this were not so, if men were not so inspired, then science would never progress.

"Let us assume that Haylie-Foster had made some discovery—a form of treatment or something novel in pharmacopeia—which he thought may extend the boundaries of medical science. It is not too much so suppose that this clever and arrogant young man might well be the very type who would be tempted to experiment upon a live human subject—his patients? The justification, at least to the cold rational mind, would be that those subjects were nearing the end of their natural lifespan, and as no prospect of recovery was anticipated, that greater good would be done if others should benefit in future. Thus, the motivation would not be a malevolent one, but rather undertaken in the spirit of scientific inquiry. In fact, he may have felt that he was, to some extent, putting these incurables out of their misery."

"It is possible, Holmes, but the ethics are entirely questionable; neither the law, nor the medical profession recognizes the distinction between murder and euthanasia. Leaving that aside, where are the fruits of his research? A few scribbled lines in a private diary? Where is the description of the treatment, the conditions of application, the anticipated results, the notes of observations, and so on? You would expect Coram to have found these too, would you not?"

"There may be other secret, or at least private, documents which Coram has not managed to lay his hands on. Perhaps Haylie-Foster took them with him?"

"But, surely, if Haylie-Foster had made some discovery, he would have shared it with Coram, who was his collaborator, taken him into his confidence, so to speak?"

"Not if the experiment was unethical."

"What is to say that Coram hasn't done away with his mentor, and has simply forged these notes? Or that he found the diary, tried to blackmail Haylie-Foster who refused to pay, and, in the fall out, the younger man murdered the elder one?"

"Excellent, Watson! Those were the most obvious explanations which occurred to me too. Perhaps we ought not to theorize further until we have spoken to Bernard Coram."

A note from Holmes brought the young man to Baker Street the next morning. He was a tall, dark-haired, striking looking fellow in his early thirties, sharply dressed for a doctor. There was something in his manner which suggested the studiousness of a pupil ra-

171

ther than the confident bearing of a medical man. He looked from one to the other of us, then addressed Holmes. "Dr. Agar has told you of our little mystery then?"

"Yes, he has appraised Doctor Watson and I of the basic facts of the matter; however, as the doctor's professional assistant, and to some extent his protégé, I believe you may be better placed to provide us with an insight into the man's character. I should like to hear the account of the doctor's disappearance in your own words.

"Well, it is very true, Mr. Holmes, that I am, to some extent, both his protégé and his amanuensis. Professionally, I had always felt that I had enjoyed the doctor's confidence; indeed, I could not have found a better mentor. I handled every piece of professional paperwork which was addressed to him, and he left the running of the general practice entirely in my hands. It is fair to say that, over the last few weeks or so, I had begun to detect something rather strange about the doctor's manner. Not unfriendly, I may add; furtive, I suppose, is how I would describe it. I developed a definite impression that he was hiding something from me, and yet, as I handled all the correspondence, I could not fathom what it might be. I hope I am no more self-conscious or insecure than the average fellow but..." and here the young man hesitated, "...I also felt that there was something at which he was secretly delighted or amused.

"Following the deaths of the three patients in such a short period, I became suspicious—nothing tangible, you understand, just a vague feeling of unease. A man of science hesitates to place himself in the position of appearing to endorse the metaphysical, but, on the night he disappeared, something told me that he was not coming

172

back. I determined at once to find out what was behind this, for I was convinced that his vanishing and the deaths of the patients were related. Then, I discovered the list with patients' names, and that was what had brought me straight to Dr. Moore Agar."

"May I ask what may seem a rather obvious question: were Haylie-Foster's powers in any way detrimentally affected by this recent change of character?" said Holmes.

"I should say they weren't. He was as lucid as ever."

"And his performance?"

"The very same. I suppose you think he may have developed some drug habit? Neither his physical abilities, nor his mental faculties, seemed to be affected."

"Is it possible that he could have discovered or devised some new method of treatment? One possible theory Doctor Watson and I discussed was that he may have used these patients as experimental subjects without their knowledge?"

"And tested it with fatal consequences? Why, yes, in the absence of any other motive, that is precisely what I was concerned about, bearing in mind that I am seen to hold some responsibility as his professional assistant. I felt that the private notes which I discovered bore out that very supposition to some extent, though I can find no other records of any kind. And yet, it would have been very difficult for him to conceal anything like that from me, for in the past, there have been no professional secrets between us."

"But it is not impossible?"

"Knowing Haylie-Foster, I would rule nothing as impossible or improbable. He is a remarkable man and could be a very impetuous character when the mood was upon him."

"Did you observe any change in his private mail?"

"Absolutely none, although I do not actually open his private mail, nor do I have any knowledge of his personal finances. It did occur to me to double-check the books, but the business side of the practice has never been better, and we have no shortage of patients. I pay all the bills, and therefore I know."

"Where do you bank the business's money?"

"I bank all the money from the general practice at the Chiltern Bank in Soho. I have no idea what happens with his specialist consultation fees."

"In the purely hypothetical instance that Haylie-Foster may have been murdered, did he make a will?"

"Yes. He has no living family and apparently he has left everything to me in a will which he made out about three months ago. I only discovered that after he disappeared; he never mentioned it to me."

"Ah!"

"Yes, Mr. Holmes," the young man said resignedly, "you may as well say it plainly: it must seem as though I have every motive for murdering Haylie-Foster and blackening his character."

"It would not be the first time that one partner in a business, especially a junior partner, had made away with the other, nor would it be the first time that some guilty party had the audacity to call upon on my services as a means of shielding his own guilt—as though to say, 'I have reported the matter to the police, and have even consulted the great Sherlock Holmes.' But let us leave that aside for the present. What are the domestic arrangements?"

"Haylie-Foster had a lease on the house paid until the end of the year, so at least, if he does not reappear, I shall not be turned out of doors. All bills are paid up to date, and there is no debt outstanding. I have complete authority over the financial side appertaining to the practice; there is no question of joint signatures or anything like that. As to the domestic servants, there is a cook, a cleaning lady, and a general help; there is also a coachman and a stable boy. The latter, I always felt, was a rather extravagant expense considering the three thousand a year or so that we take in, but as Doctor Watson will tell you, it is important for an aspiring and ambitious young medical man to keep up appearances. All of the servants live out, except the stable boy who sleeps over in the loft. To tell the truth, I have already begun to make alternative arrangements, both for my career and my domicile. I am proud enough to believe that I have a good reputation, and that I should have no trouble finding a post as an assistant in some practice, providing, of course, that the mess which Haylie-Foster has left behind imparts no stain on my professional reputation."

"I think that is very wise, Dr. Coram."

"Then, like myself, you hold out no hopes of his returning."

"Frankly, I do not."

"Then I have not panicked unnecessarily?"

"No, certainly not, and you have done very well from the outset."

"You do not think you will be able to find him, alive or dead?"

"That is a different matter."

"Then where has he gone?"

"You must leave that question entirely in my hands for the moment. I should like you to furnish me with a detailed description of Haylie-Foster, and also a copy of this private diary in which he kept the details of his patients' deaths."

"I have brought the diary with me and a photograph. He was just over middle height, thick set, fair hair, clean shaven, brown eyes; the rest you can see."

"Did he ever wear spectacles?"

"No."

"Excellent, you are a model client. Do the servants know about his disappearance?"

"No, I told the servants and the patients that the doctor had been taken suddenly ill with a seizure and was taken to a private hospital in Surrey where he may not be visited. But it is only a matter of time before they work out what has happened, and I really feel that they, too, ought to be given the opportunity to find work elsewhere as soon as possible. If you believe that Haylie-Foster is not likely to return, I think they should be told the truth."

"I think that would be advisable, although I would ask you to allow me forty-eight hours to confirm a few details before you do so. Beyond that, I cannot think that any further concealment will advance the case, nor as you say, would it be fair. To return to the deaths of the patients, who signed the death certificates?"

"They were signed by an independent doctor, Clark Maxwell."

"What makes you think that this doctor could have erred in three consecutive cases, or do you consider that he is part of some possible conspiracy?"

"No, Dr. Maxwell is entirely above suspicion. The deaths of the patients seemed to bear all the hallmarks of natural causes. But afterwards, I realized that there was almost exactly the same time elapsed between the patients' last consultation with Haylie-Foster and their death. He visited them in their own homes exactly two days before they died in each case; look, here is the record, you may judge for yourself," he said, drawing out a small notebook from his briefcase.

Holmes took it and flicked through the pages with interest. "I congratulate you on your observation. Now, let us see... This shows that the doctor visited his first patient on September 12, and this patient died on the September 14; then a consultation on the 20th, followed by the death of patient number two, in this case a woman, on the 22nd; finally, in the third case, the corresponding dates are September 26 and 28."

"Two days between the consultation and the death of the patients seems rather too short a time for poison not to have been detected as the cause," I said.

"Yes, at least for known poisons," Coram agreed. "To begin with, I had my own muddleheaded idea that these patients may have left something to Haylie-Foster in their wills, but afterwards, I discovered that to be wrong."

"And have you found anything else?"

"Absolutely nothing. However, recently, I noticed that he was spending more and more time away from the practice, and he had started to go out more regularly in the evening, something which he never used to do."

"Where did he go on these occasions?"

"I have no idea."

"Then, we shall make it our point to find out. Did he go by foot?"

"No, he usually took the coach."

"And you have not asked the coachman, presumably as you did not wish to arouse any suspicion?"

"Yes, I have said nothing."

"I believe the doctor went out for newspaper last Wednesday evening and did not return?"

"That is correct."

"Did he normally collect his own newspaper, rather than have them delivered?"

"No, he rarely read the evening newspapers."

"I see… And where is this newsagent."

"I have no idea."

"Good lord, you mean no one has checked?"

"No. I assume he went to Galton's in Park Street, which is around the corner."

"Very well, we shall be in touch if we require further information."

"Well, Watson, you will be pleased to know that, should I ever fail in my chosen profession of consulting detective, I should have at least one alternative career to fall back upon," Holmes chuckled.

"Only one? You mean, of course, in addition to those of pugilist, violinist, actor, and master burglar," I replied.

"Good, Watson, very good! Yes, another in addition to those four. Last night, following our instructive interview with Dr. Coram, I went in the guise of an unemployed and slightly disreputable looking groom, to the Haylie-Foster stables at Upper Brook Street, or rather in Wood's Mews. Horsey folk are, as a rule, a clubbable lot, and my spell a few years ago as a jarvey in Paris stood me in good stead, so it was not long before I was gossiping away affably with Haylie-Foster's coachman, a fellow in late middle age by the name of John Faulkner, with respect to a possible vacancy. Of course, there was nothing in the way of employment to be had, though he felt aggrieved for having only two staff, he said, which was cutting it a bit fine. However, he put me in touch with a few of his cronies, whose governors were looking for stable hands. He mentioned that he was very quiet at the moment, as his governor had been taken suddenly ill. I managed to guide the conversation round so that he happened to mention taking his governor out Tuesday and Thursday evenings. 'Some posh club, I'll wager,' I said to him; 'No,' he replied, 'to the Sion Tabernacle in Northumberland Square,' which I afterwards discovered was the place of worship of some small millenarian sect."

"Haylie-Foster did not strike me as that sort."

"Nor me. He did not, however, go there on Sundays, which I had found odd at the time, or at least Faulkner did not take him there."

"Perhaps he is a strict sabbatarian, in which case he would not travel in his coach on the Sabbath, even to the church."

"That would have been a very likely explanation— but your theory has one fault."

"What is that?"

"When I spoke to the Pastor of the tabernacle, a Dr. Acland, he said he knew the young man concerned thoroughly through medical and normal professional channels, and that not only had he never crossed the door, but that he considered Haylie-Foster an unlikely candidate for salvation!"

"Then the excursions to the Sion Tabernacle were a blind."

"Unless you know of any reason to disbelieve Dr. Acland?"

"Well, Holmes, Acland certainly has the reputation of being a very strict puritan. I recall hearing as much from my old tutor, Kingsley, who shared bachelor's quarters with him in Finsbury during their undergraduate days, and who found Acland's particular brand of self-righteous chiliasm somewhat alarming and rather distasteful. But I cannot imagine him telling a blatant lie. If he said he knew nothing of Haylie-Foster, I think that would be the literal truth."

"I then went to the newsagent in Park Street where Haylie-Foster had gone on the night of his disappearance. I happened to say that I was looking for a good book for a neighbor who had been taken ill recently, and happened to mention his name. He said he knew Haylie-Foster by sight, as some of the house servants collect newspapers and tobacco there and had heard of the Doctor's illness. He was surprised, he said, for the man had looked the very picture of health when had come into the shop last week. He had bought a copy of the *St James Gazette*, then left and whistled up a cab right outside the door. My ears pricked up at this, for if a cab had picked him up, then I knew someone who would find that cab for me. Ah, in fact that will be Wiggins now."

The doorbell rang and we were interrupted by the arrival of the young captain of the Baker Street Irregulars.

"Wiggins, will you go down to the Public Carriage office in Scotland Yard?"

"The one they call 'The Bungalow,' sir?"

"Yes, that's the one. Ask for a list of all cab depots and call at each of them in turn; split them up between yourself and Simpson. You are looking for the number of a cab which was in Park Street at about seven-thirty on the evening of October 5—that was last Wednesday—and which picked up a professional gentlemen." He handed his young lieutenant a pile of coins. "The usual rates, plus an extra sovereign for the boy who can bring me the number of the cab."

We had not long to wait, for within the hour Billy the Page arrived with a telegram for Holmes which read: *"Cab No 1798, out of Brewhouse Yard, Red Lion Street, Clerkenwell. Cabman John Benjamin will call tonight at 8—Wiggins."*

Soon after eight o'clock, a rough-looking, heavily whiskered fellow in ill-kempt clothes was led up to the sitting room by Mrs. Hudson.

"Now then, Benjamin, my good man, I have a sovereign here if you can tell me about the fare you picked up last Wednesday night outside the newsagents in Park Street," said Holmes to the man's surprise.

"There no mystery about that, sir. The gennelman 'ad come out without 'is coat, 'e said, an' as it were gettin' very chilly about then 'e 'ad decided to take a cab as 'e 'ad a long way to go."

"Can you describe him?"

" 'E was about a middle height, well built, I'd put him at about forty years of age, fair hair—'e'd come out without 'is 'at as well as 'is coat, that's 'ow I know. Dressed like a toff, but didn't talk like one."

"Yes, you said it was a long way to go; I should like to know where you dropped him."

"Let me see now... Yes, it was an address in the City."

"Where exactly?"

"Northumb'land Square, he was going to, what was it now... some furren' soundin' name... Ah, yes, the Zionist tabernacle or sumthin' like that. I dropped him right outside of it."

Holmes and I exchanged glances.

"I see. And you saw him go inside?" asked Holmes.

"Lor' no, sir, I didn't wait to see. But if a gennelman gives me an address, I assume that's where he's goin'. I don't suppose he went there just to take a pitcher of it"

"Yes, of course. Here's your money."

"Thank you, sir, and goo'night"

Holmes shrugged. "A dead end," he said. "He had calculated that he might be followed, or that someone might ask his coachman where he had gone, and has deliberately left a false trail. I should say, this disposes of any theory that there may have been any foul play on Dr. Coram's part."

Holmes had sent a note to Scotland Yard, asking Inspector Gregory Lestrade to pay him a visit at his earliest convenience. Knowing Lestrade, I was sure that it would not be long before we saw him, for the Scotland Yarders were ever in need of Holmes's professional guidance.

My friend had been standing gazing out of the window after lunch when we were abruptly distracted by the loud ringing of the front doorbell, followed by the sound of voices in the hallway downstairs. Presently, we heard footsteps tramping upon the stairs, and then a knock on the door. Mrs. Hudson had arrived with our post-prandial coffee, which she laid out for us upon the table; the lean, sallow, dark-eyed figure of Inspector Lestrade in his check suit and bowler hat trailed in her wake. Accompanying him was a short gentleman of heavy build, dark-haired and hazel-eyed, with a fresh complexion and mutton-chops moustache, whom I took to be, from his appearance and demeanor, a successful lawyer or bank manager.

The stranger bade both us a brief good afternoon and we shook hands; then I began to hand round the coffee cups.

Holmes waved both men to a chair; turning to the stranger, he said, "And this, surely, must be one of your fellow Inspectors, Lestrade?"

"I was just about to introduce Frederick Abberline to you, Mr. Holmes. He was indeed my fellow Inspector for many years, but he retired a few years ago now," replied Lestrade, somewhat puzzled. "How on Earth could you possibly know that?" he asked. "Did Mr. Gregson tell you, or perhaps you gentlemen have already met?"

"Neither. In fact, until I observed from the window your arrival here in the hansom across the street, I can assure you that I had never seen Mr. Abberline before in my life. Apart from the fact that your former colleague hails from Dorsetshire, is a Freemason, has spent a long time on the beat, held the rank of Inspector, has done some horse-riding in his day, and was formerly involved in an occupation which entailed the handling of delicate instruments, I know absolutely nothing of him."

Lestrade burst into a fit of laughing, much amused at his colleague's palpable astonishment. "I did warn you, Abberline, about Mr. Holmes's little habits. I suppose you deduced all this as usual."

"Indeed, it was hardly difficult," replied Holmes in his most offhand manner.

"Mr. Holmes, you are quite correct in each of those particulars," said the stranger, betraying a slight dismay as though he felt himself to be the victim of some prank, "but would you mind explaining to me how you worked that out?"

"In truth, I was barely conscious of the chain of reasoning, and arrived at my conclusions almost mechanically. However, it goes something like this. Firstly, although you do not dress in the usual manner of a policeman, you have a certain unmistakable gait which is common to peelers who have spent half a lifetime on the beat. Secondly, your demeanor has something about it which plainly suggests the man-in-charge, and since I observed, albeit briefly on your entry, that neither you, nor Lestrade, defers to the other, the suggestion is that your are his peer, rather than his subordinate or superior—hence an Inspector."

"Very good, Mr. Holmes! As Mr. Lestrade said, I held the rank of Inspector alongside him for many years."

"Your Dorsetshire origin, I determined from your accent which, despite being eroded by what I would estimate as probably twenty years contact with the estuarial dialect, nevertheless retains subtle, yet distinct, rhotic and retroflex qualities: not so pronounced as the Devonian or Cornish, and without the lengthened vowels and forward-shifted diphthongs of Somerset—hence Dorsetshire—in fact, I should say, the east of the county."

"Astounding! I was born in Blandford Forum in fact, and yet, I have been in London for fully twenty-five years. Quite incredible, Mr. Holmes."

Holmes waved away the compliment and continued, "Doctor Watson will tell you that I am engaged in research at the moment with the aim of producing a small monograph on the regional accents of the English language. I also observed that you have the erect upper torso bearing of someone who has spent some time on horseback..."

"Yes, my father, peace to his soul, was a saddler. I was never out of a saddle as a youngster, for we had horses of our own."

"I could not help but notice that your tie has a subtle weaving of the letters *AVT* corresponding to the motto of your order, *Audi, Vide, Tace*; and on shaking hands with you as you entered the room, I noticed the delicate touch which you have retained in your slender fingers, this was confirmed by the manner in which your small, artistic hands elegantly manipulated your coffee cup and teaspoon—hence, the delicate instruments. A lapidarist, perhaps?"

"A clockmaker, Mr. Holmes, but nevertheless, very similar in many respects. What remarkable powers you have, sir! My colleague, Mr. Lestrade, certainly did not exaggerate. Are you always able to deduce such things from the instant someone walks through your door?"

"Very often I am able to infer much of a client's background, particularly with regard to occupation or station in life, as this is perhaps the feature most amenable to inference; in this respect, I can tell you that the most instructive indications are to be gained from a woman's sleeve, and then perhaps from the hands; in a man, I would particularly observe the knee of the trousers, then the shirt cuffs, and of course, the shoes or boots. For peculiarities of personality, the principal indications are probably a man's hat and a woman's gloves or her umbrella. Yes, Inspector, a most instructive day could be spent wandering around the streets of London studying the minute details of one's fellow travelers, working out just these very practical questions."

"I should like to spend many such days in your company, Mr. Holmes," Abberline said.

"In addition, I am generally able to judge almost instantly whether a client has come to consult me over the safety of their own skin, about a business matter, or with regards to an *affaire de coeur*—though, in the latter case, the symptoms vary widely between men and women, and even between married and unmarried women. In your case, the deductions were quite commonplace really."

Holmes continued, "Well, Lestrade, your timing is impeccable in more than one sense. The coffee is poured, pray help yourself to the cigars in the box. Watson and I were just discussing a subject which we feel may come to be of some professional interest to you."

"First of all, I had better ask if you have any objection to me bringing Mr. Abberline along," said Lestrade. "He is now working as a private inquiry agent for Pinkerton's, and, as such, he may be considered one of your rivals."

"Oh no, not at all! The field is quite large enough for many more practitioners—providing they be of a sufficient standard as to ennoble the reputation of the profession. As you know, I am forever turning business away. Mr. Abberline will be the third Pinkerton's man whom I shall have had to pleasure to meet."

"The third?" asked Abberline. "As far as I am aware, I am the only one in London."

"Yes, the others were Americans you see: the late Birdy Edwards from Pennsylvania and Humphrey Leverton of Long Island fame, whom I met a few years ago. I am sure I have heard your name before." Holmes pondered for a moment, "Yes, let me see, it was Whitechapel was it not?"

"Yes, I was sent in by the Yard to take over the murder investigations in H division nearly ten years ago—I suppose I should say sent *back* there, for I had been promoted from there only the year before and had a great deal of intimate knowledge of the locality and its, er, more colorful inhabitants."

"You never took the man, Mr. Abberline. As I recall, there was a plethora of theories at the time, each more outré than the last, as to the identity of the murderer. But the killer must have been a local man who had a good working knowledge of the female anatomy, a preponderance towards violent misogyny, and ready access to some very specialized knives or razors."

"Indeed, Mr. Holmes; with hindsight, we ought to have asked for your assistance."

"It was Klosowski, of course."

"That is absolutely correct, Mr. Holmes. He had been trained as a surgeon in Poland, made his living as a barber, and lived above his shop in Cable Street," replied Abberline.

"Then why didn't you arrest him?"

"We hadn't the evidence to go before jury. We, or rather *they*, still don't. He fled to America and has never been seen since."

"You don't believe the story about him being dead then?"

"Oh no, he'll turn up again I'm sure."[12].

"No doubt; now, what drives a Pinkerton's man to Baker Street today?"

Lestrade said, "When I got your message, I guessed you must be looking for information and I thought that

---

[12] He did: in 1903, Klosowski's triple murder became front page news. By then he had changed his name to George Chapman.

perhaps a *quid pro quo* would not be out of the question."

"By all means," said Holmes, "and what is the *quo* in this case?"

"Pinkerton's have been engaged by one of the large insurance companies with respect to a recent spate of robberies at the small banks in the city," Abberline said. "After the third one, they started to become very, very, suspicious that it was an inside job."

"Ah, yes, of course. Tut, tut, Lestrade, three bank jobs in as many weeks. You will have to pull your socks up."

"Don't I know it, Mr. Holmes," Lestrade said ruefully. "Problem is, we can't make head or tail of it. We couldn't work out how the intruders made entry in the first place without leaving any signs of disturbance. Then, it became obvious that they must have been using keys."

"Yes, I confess I did have my suspicions as to that," replied Holmes. "I also noticed that the first two banks which were robbed shared one singular trait; when I looked at the street plan, which shows both the surface railways and the underground railways, it jumped out at me." Holmes took down the plan from one of the shelves and spread it out.

"Look here," he said, "the Metropolitan railway line runs under part of the Minories as it curves away from Aldgate station, then under part of Seething Lane before straightening out as it heads towards the intersection with the City and South London line. I had thought they had got in to the banks through the basement level from the railway tunnel."

Abberline and Lestrade looked in admiration at Holmes, who continued, "Of course, then the third bank which was robbed, at the corner of Mitre Square, is a considerable distance from any railway, but it did occur to me that there might be an access tunnel nearby. Perhaps, you had better let me have more details, Mr. Abberline."

"On the morning of September 18, the manager of the Metropolitan and Suburban Bank opened up to find that he had been robbed of twenty thousand pounds during the previous night or during the day when the bank was closed."

"One moment," said Holmes glancing at the calendar above the fireplace, "the bank was closed on a Monday?"

"Yes, it is owned by a Hebrew gentleman, or at least he holds the controlling interest—all the banks are—and they close on all the Jewish holy days. As Mr. Lestrade said, there was no sign of forced entry and the safe was completely undamaged; indeed, it had been locked again after the theft. A similar fate befell the manager of the London and Home Counties Bank on Tuesday, September 27. Again, the bank had been closed the previous day, and again the Police found no signs of forced entry and no damage to the safe. Due to the value of the money and bullion in the banks as well as in the jewelers' stores in the area, these streets in the vicinity are all heavily patrolled at night, but after the second robbery, the patrols were stepped up even further. The Police were sure that they had the entire area around the City fairly well staked out. There wasn't a street or alleyway that didn't have a regular copper's beat every fifteen minutes or so, quite apart from the men on fixed point duty. Every constable had an instruction to report anything remotely suspicious on his beat and to challenge anyone acting suspiciously in the area after dark. If there were more than one person, or if he thought the man might be armed, he was to summon help from the neighboring beat. Then, the third bank was done—in an absolutely identical manner to the first two—in the early hours of Monday, October 3."

"And you believe," said Holmes, "that the intruders had used copies of the keys?"

"Or the originals," replied Abberline darkly.

"Which would imply at least the connivance of senior officials?" asked Holmes.

"It wouldn't be the first time."

"No, but there are far more subtle and less risky methods available to bank officials who wish to cheat their shareholders and investors. It is rather too obvious, I think, therefore we will assume in each case the keys must have been extracted and copies made."

"There is only a handful of staff at each bank," said Lestrade, "we've been through the list of employees, including the managers and directors, but every one of them seems quite beyond reproach. We've had them followed, we've searched their houses, and in some cases, their mistresses' houses, we've checked their bank accounts. And yet, it seems obvious that it *must* be an inside job," said Lestrade.

"If I were to argue the Devil's Advocate position," said Holmes, "I should say perhaps *too* obvious, for as you say, it seems that the thief merely walked in the front door, helped himself to the money, and walked straight back out again, very considerately locking up behind himself."

"Yes, Mr. Holmes," replied Lestrade, "it is exactly that. But if it isn't an inside job, how the deuce did they lay their hands on the keys? And the thief seems to be invisible too!"

"In what way?"

"Because despite the precautions that Mr. Abberline has just described, no one seems to have seen anything. On the night of the third robbery, Constable Watkins of the City force had been patrolling the area all night. His is a single beat, which is to say one that's normally safe enough for one copper to do on his own, which is quite usual in the City. It covers this area here," he said pointing to the plan, "around Duke Street, Aldgate, Bury Street, Cree Lane, Leadenhall Street, Mitre Street, and Mitre Square. A quiet area generally, a few houses, but mostly offices and banks with a few warehouses; the beat would normally take fifteen minutes, though it's a lonely job and now and again a copper meets a colleague from another beat and has a jaw with him, so it takes a bit longer. On this occasion, Watkins saw no-one all night, he didn't meet Cocker, his neighbor on the next patch, and his own beat had been completely uneventful all night; he passed the Square roughly every fifteen minutes and checked every door with his lantern."

"And all these other alleys or lanes leading to the square?" Holmes asked.

"Yes. Watkins's patrol would normally lead him in to the square from Mitre Street, but there are two other possible routes as you can see, one into St James's place, and one into Duke Street. Constable Cocker was on the adjacent beat, and it was his duty to check the passage leading off Duke Street, but not to actually enter the Square—that was Watkins' patrol. If either needed to raise the alarm, he would use a rattle—City Police do not carry whistles at night, but neither of them saw anyone suspicious, although Constable Cocker on the adjacent beat did mention that he thought he saw someone moving about in the fog at the bottom of Houndsditch, just prior to his turning into Stoney Lane, but couldn't remember at what time exactly. He saw nothing suspicious about it and he didn't follow the man," Lestrade added somewhat weakly, "he says, it would have taken him outside his own beat."

"Come, Lestrade," said Holmes, "nothing suspicious about a man walking about the deserted City at what o'clock of a morning? In the middle of a spate of bank robberies!"

"Well, in truth, Mr. Holmes, just between you and me, some of the City men believe that part of street, by the old deserted churchyard, to be haunted and they avoid it if possible when they are alone."

Holmes hissed with impatience.

"Frankly if it were me, I should have rebuked the man on the spot; we would have none of this nonsense at the Yard, but Cocker is a City man and he and his colleagues are beyond my jurisdiction. To tell the truth, they have it rather too easy there," said Lestrade as Abberline nodded in agreement. "It's hardly proper behavior for a police-constable, and I should certainly have put a black mark against him."

"Then the paths of Cocker and Watkins crossed and re-crossed on either side of the Square repeatedly during the night. And you say neither Cocker nor Watkins saw anything near Mitre Square?" asked Holmes.

"That's right. I did ask Watkins myself, though, if he thought anyone could have concealed themselves in the square when he was passing. He answered no, but after visiting it myself, it would have been possible that, in the misty dark, someone could have hidden in a doorway and then, there are the two narrow, dark passages which lead away from the square in any case."

"Yet, the thief must have passed near to one or other of the two uniformed constables within fifty yards of the Square. Can we be sure that they actually *were* on the beat all night?"

"Watkins is an old hand and is one of the City's most reliable men, with a number of commendations to his name; besides, the night-watchman at one of the warehouses remembers speaking to him at several points during the night," Lestrade said doggedly.

"I happen to believe Watkins is telling the truth," added Abberline.

Holmes shrugged. "The person who carried out these robberies must have an exact knowledge of the back streets and alleyways of the East End and a familiarity with the habits of its denizens, as well as either a bolt-hole in the immediate locale, or a means of getting in and out of the area unrecognized. A person living alone, I assume—certainly not in a boarding or lodging house—so that he could come and go at all hours of the night without questions being asked. It seems that this enterprising fellow has an intimate knowledge of each policeman's beat. If this Watkins is telling the truth, he had about eleven minutes to get into the bank, commit the robbery, and then disappear unseen into the fog."

"Yes."

"Do any of the banks' staff live near here?"

"No, they are all suburbanites."

"Are there any other suspects?"

"No serious suspects," replied Lestrade. "But I looked at the problem from every angle. The three banks were all closed on Jewish holidays, and I had contemplated the possible significance of the dates. The first robbery was committed on Rosh Hashanah—the Day of Judgment, which is really two days; the second on Yom

Kippur—the Day of Atonement. Anyone who knew that the banks were closed on these days, knew they were unlikely to be disturbed if they chose that time. We half-expected the next robbery to be on the first of Sukkot, which would have been the next non-working day on the first of October, but it was two days later, so the pattern falls apart completely."

"You seem to have left no stone unturned," Holmes remarked.

"To do him justice, my colleague, Mr. Gregson, must have had similar ideas. Possibly reading the pattern of events as I had done, he arrested someone in Jewish religious dress who was behaving suspiciously on the eve of Yom Kippur just outside the Aldgate Underground," said Lestrade. "However, the fellow turned out to be a harmless Irishman called McKenna, perennially drunk and a complete crank, who is well-known locally for such ridiculous antics."

"I recall the name McKenna from the newspaper reports," I said. "Was he not arrested previously in connection with a murder?"

"Yes, at the Adelphi case last year," said Abberline. "But he was released as he had an unshakable alibi: he resides, when not in some form of custody that is, in the boarding house run by a Mrs. Wheeler, who confirmed he had been at home on the night that the murder took place. I knew him when I was in H Division. He once famously, and to the great amusement of the local populace, walked down the Whitechapel Road on All Hallows' Eve dressed as the Ace of Spades, barefoot and stark naked underneath his paper costume. On the day he was arrested by Mr. Gregson, he had somehow managed to produce a skull cap and long black robe, no doubt purloined from the wardrobe of some pious unsuspecting

194

neighbor who was at that point solemnly chanting *Kol Nidre* at the synagogue. For some reason, his pockets were stuffed with cloves of garlic."

"To ward off evils spirits no doubt!" I said.

"Ah well, such whimsical incidents lighten our burden, Doctor Watson," chuckled Lestrade, "but we haven't turned up a single lead, so the insurance companies got together and turned it over to the private boys and that was where Mr. Abberline came in."

"Well, I shall certainly take a closer look at it. As it happened, I had asked you here to discuss the Haylie-Foster case."

"Oh, the disappearing doctor?" said Lestrade. "It was brought to our attention, Mr. Holmes; discreetly, of course. We looked at it, but found nothing to excite our suspicions. He hasn't left any debts and it is no crime to disappear—not yet, at any rate. Perhaps he has simply run off with the wife of some rich patient?"

"I think that is unlikely. My attention has been drawn to the case," Holmes said diplomatically, "by the fact that three of his patients died within a three week period—does that not strike you as a coincidence?"

"We can't arrest anyone on coincidence, Mr. Holmes, but there was not the slightest motive. No personal gain. Another doctor, quite independent, signed the death certificates, everything seemed above board."

"No, but if fresh evidence were to be unearthed…"

"Do you have such evidence?"

"Not at present, but I am certainly warming to the idea that there may have been foul play. Say, if it were to be found that there had been poisoning for example…"

"*Poisoned?!* We'd need to exhume the corpses to prove that. Good Lord, Mr. Holmes, we'd look a right bunch of fools if we started digging them up and then found nothing. If the papers got a hold of it, they'd be calling Gregson and I the Burke and Hare of the Yard!"

"No. I was merely using the possibility of poison as an example."

Lestrade looked dubious. "Well, if you come up with something more solid, we will certainly investigate it. In the meantime, we have noted his status as a missing person and are obliged to take the usual steps, but no more than that."

"As to your problem, I'll call round and speak to the managers of the banks. But I do warn you, Mr. Abberline, that I do not hold out much hope."

"But there must be some link, however tenuous, between these three banks. And there must be some directing mind behind the robberies—if it exists, I have no doubt you could find it," said Abberline.

"Yes, but if the culprit has already decided that he has enough money, he will already have laid plans to disappear with it, possibly under a false identity, and it could be very difficult to track him down," replied Holmes.

"But, if he plans to do more…"

"Then, he may become careless and start to make mistakes—in that case we will have your man."

"All the same, I'm very obliged to you, Mr. Holmes, for agreeing to take a look at it," said Abberline. "This is my first really big commission and I am keen to show results. I have great faith in you; from what I have heard, you can penetrate deeper into such mysteries than anyone I have ever met."

"Thank you. Lestrade here will confirm that my methods are irregular, and if there I make any progress, I shall say very little until I have the case practically complete."

Whether Holmes had taken something of a shine to the Pinkerton's man from Dorset, or whether he was simply jealous of his own reputation, or whether he was more susceptible to flattery than he imagined, whatever the reason, we lost no time in setting out on a rather weary trudge round each of the banks in the City, asking the same questions of each of the managers: had there been any recent recruits to the bank? had they had any unusual or unexpected visitors? did they suspect anyone? and so on.

We alighted at Mark Lane underground station, which was virtually next door to the premises of the Metropolitan and Suburban Bank, where we were welcomed by Mr. Glaser, the manager. He had nothing unusual to report, he said, other than that he had had the locks changed immediately after the robbery; yes, he was only too well aware that he was shutting the door after the horse had bolted, but if there were a repetition, what would the shareholders say. No, he did not suspect anyone in the bank, and he was sure, despite the circumstantial evidence, that it was not an inside job; he was sorry that he could not be more help, but personally he found it a complete mystery.

We then walked the short distance to the London and Home Counties Bank. The manager was attending a board meeting when we arrived and it was his assistant, a Mr. Falk, who answered our questions. Neither he, nor the manager, suspected anyone in the bank, the young man said, but they had recently, at the beginning of September, taken on a new junior clerk.

"I have not really got to know the man yet," said Falk, "however he came to us with excellent testimonials and lives with parents in Blackheath. I believe his house has been searched—which has happened to all of us—

and he has been shadowed by the police who have discovered nothing."

"No, it is quite inconceivable that a junior clerk with a few weeks' service would be in a position to copy several sets of keys—I myself would have the greatest difficulty in doing so," he answered in reply to Holmes's question.

Finally, in a mood of anticipatory disappointment, we called at the Whitechapel and East London bank at the corner of Mitre Street and the Square of the same name.

"Anything unusual?" the manager, Mr. Bergman repeated in answer to Holmes's question. "Well, I don't know if you would call it unusual, but as you may understand, after the incidents at the other banks in the area, I was perhaps rather more alert than the other managers who had been somewhat taken by surprise. We are a similar size of bank, located in a quiet part of the City, and so, therefore, I decided to take further precautions. We changed the locks and made a rule that only myself should hold all the keys. This caused a great deal of inconvenience, but there seemed no alternative; we also installed a stronger safe; we checked and double checked the associations of our employees—I am happy to say, we found nothing to alarm us; all to no avail. A few days before the robbery, a gentleman called Mr. Cyril Blackstone, who has had a savings account with us for some months, requested a loan to which I was more than happy to agree. As you can see, Mr. Holmes, we are a small outfit and we need every customer we can get; he was a professional man, in credit, with a decent address in the city—and so the sum was duly deposited in his account following the usual formalities. However, I recall that, when he visited us here, he insisted to the Chief Cashier,

Mr. Winter, that he thank me personally, even though, as I said, it was quite a modest sum. It was inconvenient since I was preparing for an important audit at the time, but the man said that he always liked to meet face to face the people with whom he was doing business, which I suppose is perfectly laudable. I must confess that, after he left, I had a strange feeling of unease which I could not explain; perhaps, I felt that he would abscond with the money. My apologies for digressing, for I can see you believe it quite trivial," said Mr. Bergman.

"I confess I can see no significance in the matter," replied Holmes.

"No, very likely not. But that incident stuck in my memory because he paid the money back very quickly."

"He did? Pray continue."

"Afterwards, the Chief Cashier mentioned to me that the loan had been paid back within a few days. He said, 'Mr. Bergman, you recall, that gentleman who made the fuss about thanking you personally? Well, he turned up three days later and cleared it off.' I thought it rather odd at the time, but, of course, there is nothing against borrowers paying off loans early. I suppose that I ought to be thankful that he did not default on the debt."

"All the same, I shall take a few details if you do not mind. On what date did you speak to this Blackstone?"

"I forget the actual date; do you think it significant?"

"Undoubtedly."

"Then allow me to call Mr. Winter; he will be only too happy to assist."

The bank manager rang a bell to summon the Cashier, who told us that Blackstone had called on September

30, three days before the robbery. Holmes noted this and then asked to look at Blackstone's account.

"I understand that you are acting on behalf of the insurance companies, sir; nevertheless, I am unable to do that as it is against the rules. I am only obliged to give this information to the official Police," he said with a glance to the manager for confirmation. "However, I may be able to answer any other questions you may wish to put."

"When this fellow Blackstone returned to pay off the loan, did he ask again to see the Manager?"

"He did not, sir."

"When was the account opened?"

"Four months ago, on June 19."

"Can you give me a description of the man?"

"Oh, just above medium height, well built, dark hair, a full beard; that's really all I can remember," Winter replied.

"What age?"

"Hm, difficult to say really; forties, I should think, perhaps mid forties."

"Did he wear spectacles?" Holmes asked.

"Yes," replied Winter.

"I seem to recall that he didn't," interjected Bergman with a shake of the head. "Odd, isn't it, how two people can witness exactly the same thing and still disagree as to particulars? No, wait, yes he did wear spectacles, but he took them off during our conversation, then replaced them when he stood up to leave."

"Very interesting. What did Mr. Blackstone give as his occupation or business?"

The Cashier flicked over a page, "General dealer, it says here, sir."

"Hm, not much to go on—what is his address?"

"13 Vine Street."

"Thank you gentlemen, I think that will be all," said Holmes. I could see he had that excited air when he had picked up a scent.

Before we left the City, Holmes stopped off at the District Messenger's office in Lombard Street to send off a couple of wires, with replies paid in advance. We enjoyed a quick sandwich and some coffee at Caxton's, and then we dropped in to Lestrade's office at Scotland Yard so that Holmes could report to him the bank manager's story.

"Well, Lestrade, what do you make of it?"

"Of this Blackstone character? A secret gambling habit perhaps. It may be horses? Equally, it may be a modest speculation in stocks or shares. He borrowed the money not wishing to touch his capital, makes his wager, then pays back the loan and keeps the rest of the winnings for a further plunge."

"Quite possibly, but it was his insistence on meeting the bank manager personally which struck me as singular."

"You think it may have been a pretext for casing the place?"

"In a sense, yes; though, I think he was more interested in the people rather than the place."

"But, surely, he could have done that without the fantastic rigmarole of borrowing money?"

"I think we will know soon enough," said Holmes as a uniformed constable arrived in Lestrade's office.

"For you in person, sir, District Messenger brought them," said the man briskly, presenting the two envelopes to a surprised Lestrade, who looked at Holmes suspiciously.

"Ah, yes, I took the liberty of, shall we say, acting on your behalf," said Holmes coolly, once the uniformed man had departed. "I discovered that there was a rule against banks divulging personal information to consulting detectives—but not, of course, to Police detectives. So I addressed the reply to yourself."

"I think the proper term is 'impersonating a policeman'," said Lestrade, shaking his head in comic resignation, "but I suppose I shall have to turn a blind eye as usual."

One reply was from Mr. Glaser, and read "September 15;" the second was from Mr. Falk, which said "September 23." "What does it mean, Mr. Holmes?" Lestrade asked.

"It means that the very same fantastic rigmarole has been repeated at two other banks in the city. My question to the manager of the other banks was whether someone named Blackstone had borrowed money within the last month, and if so, what date did he request a meeting with the manager. Things are turning in our favor at last, and we are making progress." Holmes smiled triumphantly.

"Excellent, Mr. Holmes! Yes, I think I understand now. It's what we call a 'long firm:' you borrow a small sum of money, pay it back quickly to build up your reputation as a safe borrower. Then, finally, with your testimonials from three other banks, you go for a few thousand and, this time, you disappear."

"I think it may go rather deeper than that, Lestrade. It is too much of a coincidence that these are the three banks that have all been robbed within the last few weeks."

"But what the Devil is the meaning of it all? What connection can there be between this man taking out loans that he doesn't need and the banks being robbed?"

"I cannot exactly say at this stage, but a vague suspicion is forming in my mind. In the meantime, I suppose you ought to warn the other small banks in the City, and suggest that if a Mr. Blackstone should request a loan, they must contact you immediately."

"Very wise, Mr. Holmes, I shall do that straight away."

"Perhaps you could also let Mr. Abberline know that we are making some progress."

"He will be most delighted, for he has been working very hard, day and night, trying to solve the case and has got nowhere. He did mention that if you were to call in, whether there was anything in particular you would point out to him?"

"Yes, I should refer him to *Ecclesiastes 1:9* and ask him if he remembers the affair of Silver Blaze."

"Silver Blaze? The racehorse that was lost on Dartmoor? Lord, that was nearly ten years ago!" said Lestrade, looking puzzled. "Do you mean the incident of the dog that didn't bark?"

"No, I mean the perplexing outbreak amongst the sheep," replied Holmes to a dumbfounded Lestrade as we left Scotland Yard.

"I must confess Holmes, I am at a loss to explain why Haylie-Foster should have disappeared, leaving all his worldly goods to his associate. Can there have been some collusion between them, and his disappearance is a mere sham?"

"No, not at all, just gratitude, Watson, genuine gratitude. Why should he not sympathize with the plight of a young doctor struggling to make his way in the world, a world in which he, Haylie-Foster, had already achieved recognition and some prosperity? After all, he had no family."

"He seems to have vanished into thin air," I mused.

"Oh, I should hardly say that, Watson."

"Do you mean to say that you know where he is?"

"Well, there is no great mystery."

"*What!* Then, where is he?"

"Surely, it is perfectly obvious. Apply yourself to the data Watson—there is only one possible conclusion that can be drawn. Now, as to this business of the banks: you know the Irregulars are presently watching our chief suspect in Vine Street, and reports reach me at regular intervals from Wiggins and Simpson. It is, perhaps, a strange consequence of our social system, Watson, but the struggle for existence seems to have made their wits far sharper than Gregson's or Lestrade's. Wiggins, in particular, is most diligent, a little terrier of a boy. On Tuesday evening, they followed Blackstone to the City of Hereford..."

"Upon my word, Holmes! The City of Hereford! How on Earth...?"

"...To a public house in Haydon Square in the shadow of the railway's goods depot," continued Holmes with an amused expression. "Being a public house, of course, it was one of the few places into which a child could not follow an adult easily, and Wiggins was concerned that he might lose his man. However, Blackstone took a turn into an alley off the square, which led him into Mansell Street. From there, he went through the gardens of Bognor Court and entered premises which bore the name of The Bognor Prestidigitation Circle."

"*Prestidigitation!* You mean, stage magicians?"

"Exactly so."

"But what possible connection…?"

"I confess I have no idea. Given our suspicions over Blackstone's involvement in this affair, I began to wonder if the circle was a front for something rather more sinister and gave my imagination full rein—I wondered, for example, if 'prestidigitation' was a euphemism for making things disappear, such as banknotes! Or perhaps, it was the fencing of stolen goods, or faked art. After the Cleveland Street business, I began to have even darker forebodings. Still, we shall soon be in a position to determine for ourselves, for unless you have made other arrangements, I suggest we take a turn down by Bognor Court this evening."

Holmes sent Billy to fetch a cab and, within half an hour, we presented ourselves at the door of the club which, from the outside, seemed no different from many of the other buildings of its type in the area. It was a narrow three-storied warehouse, and was set on a corner site in a quiet cobbled lane. It had been refurbished to meet the style and function of its present use; the entrance was well kept and the glow from the lamp illuminated a circular sign embellished with zodiacal symbols in silver against a background of indigo, which proclaimed *Nunquam Privata Loqui* and, more prosaically, "New Members Welcome."

We rang the bell and were led in, introducing ourselves as Mr. Jones and Dr. Price, to meet the President of the club, a Mr. Chapender, who welcomed us with a hearty greeting. It soon became obvious that he was one of those enthusiasts who delighted in sharing his private obsession.

"New members are always welcome," he said jovially. "We teach all of the branches of illusionism here, you know, everything from card tricks to levitation and escapology. Of course, not all of our members are active illusionists, only the full members; the vast majority are associate members, who come here simply to be entertained, and our guest nights are always packed out to the rafters. I am happy to say that we have the reputation of leading the field. Some of the very best practitioners have appeared here—Maskelyne and Cooke, Le Roy and Asrah, Devant and his Spirit Wife—they have all graced our boards. Is there any particular branch in which you are interested?"

"Our neighbor, Mr. Blackstone, recommended us," Holmes replied evasively. "I believe he is a regular attender here."

"So, that's how you found out about us!" said Chapender. "Word of mouth is always the best way. Well, Cyril is very well up in mesmerism, you know; such a quick learner, taken to it as though he'd studied the subject all his life. He has graduated—stage-ready within three months, Mr. Jones, quite a record!—and has a promising career ahead of him. Please feel free to have a wander around the club and examine the subjects as the estate agents say, before you make any decision about joining. On the ground floor, we have the Members' bar, which you are free to use, and the Robert-Houdin Theatre; on the first floor, we have the Instruction Rooms for each of the disciplines—there are no classes in progress tonight, unfortunately; on the top floor, you will see props, as we call them—feel free to experiment, but do please take care with the knives and swords; they have minds of their own, I always say, though I'm sure you shan't come to any harm. I would take you round the premises myself, but we are rather short-handed tonight and we are being treated to a display by the Junior Circle at eight-thirty in the Theatre, so I have to set things up."

I had thought it was a pretty fine distinction between the Diogenes Club and the Amateur Mendicant Society as to which was the strangest club in the city, but I must say that the Bognor Prestidigitation Circle ran both pretty close. Every aspect of the place seemed dedicated to the fantastic. It contained more Egyptian hieroglyphics than a Masonic Temple, or a Hawksmoor church. The Instruction Rooms were full of false walls, collapsible chairs, mirrors, corridors that led nowhere and sundry optical illusions: there was a staircase at the end of a passage which appeared to ascend but which deposited you back down on the floor below. One of the attic rooms was crammed with stage properties: cloaks, masks, gloves, elliptical billiard balls, fans, rabbits, doves, silk handkerchiefs, ropes and innumerable trick card packs—a veritable emporium of the bizarre. Each of the rooms was named after one of the famous exponents of that branch of the art.

As Holmes casually opened the door of the Fred Russell Room, he gave a sudden gasp of horror: I followed his gaze as far as the glazed lifeless eyes of a grotesque cadaver crumpled into a leather armchair, the neck of which seemed to be drawn out of its diminutive body at a monstrous angle.

"Good Lord!" I exclaimed.

"Yes, it gave me a bit of a turn, Watson. As you know, I am far from being a fanciful person," Holmes said, "but I can never look at one of those horrible ventriloquists' dummies without experiencing a creeping sensation."

"Automatonophobia," I replied coolly having now recovered my bravado. "I must confess, those hideous parodies of human figures make me flinch too. Even as a child, I could never stand to watch a Punch and Judy show."

"Well, I think we have seen enough." he said as we descended to the office.

"Now, forgive me my poor memory, but what was it you said you were interested in?" Chapender asked Holmes once we had returned.

"Dr. Price here is interested in card tricks," replied Holmes, "and Mr. Blackstone has certainly kindled my curiosity in hypnosis."

Chapender proceeded to give us a short discourse on both subjects, conducted very much in a spirit of fun, and explained a number of things to us without giving away any professional secrets.

"You have come at just the right time," he continued, "for Cyril will be on the bill next Thursday evening as The Amazing Blackstone, alongside the famous card magician, Neville, The Ace of Knaves. Let me present you gentlemen with two complimentary tickets," he said, reaching into a drawer.

"Excellent," replied Holmes enthusiastically, "we are obliged. Oh, and between us three, let it be a surprise that we are coming along to see our neighbor actually performing on stage."

"You may trust me," said Chapender, smiling conspiratorially, "not a word."

"We are not really going to see this Amazing Blackstone, are we?" I asked Holmes once we had arrived back in Baker Street.

"And why should we not?" he replied.

"There is something slightly strange about that place."

"Perhaps, but it is pretty obvious that it is all above board."

"All the same, Holmes, there is something positively outlandish, is there not, in pretending to be something which one is not, or pretending to have powers which one has not?"

"I don't know about that. Actors have done the former since the days of the Ancient Greeks, and a cynic might say that clergymen have done the latter since the dawn of time. The *legerdemain* of the conjuror may mystify the audience, but there is no attempt to insinuate that they have any mystical or supernatural power. As you saw, these fellows are happy to admit that it is all done in an atmosphere of showmanship."

"It is odd though, how it continues to attract audiences who *know* that it is all illusion; it is as though there is something in the human psyche which craves delusion and deception. I am afraid it is quite beyond me."

"Still, if my calculations are correct, I think we shall witness a more interesting performance from the Amazing Blackstone."

"When?"

"Tomorrow morning, Watson, to be precise, if Lestrade is to be believed," he said, handing me a note. "The Manager of the Trinity Bank in Cornhill has reported receiving a request from a Mr. Blackstone for a loan of fifty pounds. It is the view halloo, Watson, and when our quarry breaks cover, we three old hounds shall be there. In fact, no... I think I shall reply asking Lestrade to invite Abberline along too; he has every right not to miss the fun."

The next morning, after breakfast, I sat for a while on the sofa pondering the case, the details of which, it occurred to me, I must perforce begin to record very soon before some of the events became clouded in my memory. Eventually, my mind turned to the outing we had in prospect and I began to wonder what dangers we might face, and how best to anticipate and prepare for them. Rather suddenly, my friend, who had been pondering, for some reason, over the City Trade Directory, and was now leaning back in his armchair with his eyes apparently closed, broke in upon my thoughts.

"No, Watson, you are right, you shan't need it."

"Upon my word Holmes! What...?"

"Your revolver, of course."

"But how could you possibly know what I was thinking?"

"Very simple, Watson. I could see from your slightly puzzled expression and the seriousness of your frown that you were ruminating on the case. Then, after a while, you stole a glance the writing bureau—you were considering whether to begin writing up your notes of the case."

"Absolutely correct. But the revolver?"

"Then you looked at the window, taking a measure of the present weather and, observing a little cloud gathering aloft, thence to the barometer for a prognostication. Glancing at the coat-stand, you were presumably deciding upon this morning's attire in the event of rain; then your gaze shifted back to the shelf beside the mantelpiece where you keep the key to the chest in which your old service revolver is stored. I recall you mentioning that the late Mrs. Watson would not suffer you to have the article in the house; therefore, it has not left the chest since you ceased to be a permanent resident here, except for those odd occasions when it has been necessary for your own protection—the last case being when we took the homicidal harpooner Patrick Cairns, right in this very room. You thought for a moment, then broke off and your gaze shifted back to the cupboard under the stairs in which are contained your outdoor clothes—inference, Dr. Watson has decided that he wouldn't need his revolver."

"Astounding, Holmes, you are correct in every particular."

"Very commonplace, Watson; I have told you before what faithful servants your features are. Now let us be off to the City again, the cab is due in five minutes."

"You have made progress then, Mr. Holmes?" Abberline asked once we had boarded the cab taking the four of us to the City.

"Oh, yes, the case is practically complete," replied Holmes.

"Complete!" Abberline cried incredulously.

"Well, it was hardly difficult," said Holmes in his most offhand manner.

"I got your message about the, ahem, sheep, Mr. Holmes. I had a vague memory of the case, but there was never any crime committed as far as I know, and I'm afraid I could not make any sense of it."

"All shall be made clear very soon," said Holmes, looking at his watch. "Within the hour in fact."

Abberline looked unconvinced, but said nothing more until we alighted at Cornhill. Marshaled by Holmes, we took up our position at a window table in Birch's Coffee House directly overlooking the door of the Trinity Bank.

"I'm not quite sure what your plan of action is, Mr. Holmes," said Lestrade. "Whilst I admit this Blackstone's behavior is suspicious, if the pattern of events follows its usual course, I can hardly arrest him for applying for a loan."

"All in good time, Lestrade, all in good time. And that time is drawing near," said Holmes.

At five minutes to ten, a man appeared, striding purposefully along from the direction of Leadenhall Street and disappeared into the bank. He was of medium height, heavily built with dark hair, a beard and glasses, wearing a double-breasted chesterfield and bowler.

"That's him, no doubt about it," said Holmes. "Give it another five minutes or so."

"I imagine Blackstone is an assumed name?" said Lestrade.

"Yes."

"But who is he?"

"Someone," said Holmes judiciously, "whom you have been looking for some time."

"You don't think, Mr. Holmes, that the bank manager is in any danger?" Lestrade went on, with a hint of concern in his voice

"Oh, none at all, Lestrade! The manager is perfectly safe. On the contrary, I expect he will scarcely be aware of what is going on at the moment," he said in a mysterious manner.

A few more minutes passed, and then Blackstone re-appeared from the door of the bank.

"What now?" asked Lestrade.

"Follow me," replied Holmes briskly, "I think I know where he is going, but it is as well to take no chances."

We slipped out of the coffee house and followed the man along the busy street. By the time we had got to the first corner, we were barely twenty yards behind him. Without a look behind, Blackstone turned into a lane which led down towards the market, then a few doors along disappeared into a shop opposite the Lamb tavern with the sign *Manby Smith, Locksmith, Est. 1869* above it.

"Now then, after him, full speed ahead before he parts with the evidence!" said Holmes, racing ahead and diving through the shop doorway with us at his heels. The dazed locksmith, a small, thin bespectacled man in blue dungarees, glanced up at us we came rushing through the double doors into the narrow gloomy shop. Blackstone was in the act of putting his hand into his overcoat pocket and glanced up in alarm as Lestrade pounced on him.

"What the deuce do you think you are doing?" said the man who had just walked into the shop, flushing angrily. I am sure that, had Lestrade not flashed his warrant card at that point, the younger man would have made a respectable attempt at taking on all three of us.

"Inspector Lestrade has come to arrest you," said Holmes coolly.

"On what charge?" Blackstone thundered, still trying to shake himself free.

"On three counts of murder," replied Holmes.

The man looked astounded, but no more so than Lestrade, Abberline, and myself.

"...and on the charge of robbing three banks and the attempted robbery of a fourth," Holmes continued.

"You must be mad!" the man spluttered. "Murder and robbery? What do you think...?"

"It is no use blustering, Dr. Haylie-Foster."

"*Haylie-Foster?*" repeated Lestrade.

"Yes, to yourself goes the undivided credit in discovering the whereabouts of the missing doctor, the murderer of the three patients, and the perpetrator of the robberies. And, Mr. Abberline, I think you will be able to restore confidence to the insurance company that there will be no further robberies for a while. Yes, it was all very cleverly done, I'll grant you that, though you rather overdid your part as the Amazing Blackstone. You may as well dispense with the disguise now, doctor, you are deceiving no one but yourself."

The young man recovered with an effort. "There is nothing against the law in disappearing from one's home and taking a new identity. I was damned fed up with the stuffy life of a doctor," he said. "And what bloody proof do you think you have of these preposterous crimes of which you accuse me?"

"We could start with this I think," replied Holmes, and as he spoke, he slipped his hand into the young man's pocket and withdrew something which looked like a large bar of soap. "A wax tablet, very useful for taking the impression of a key. Isn't that so, Mr. Manby Smith?" The locksmith looked pale.

"If you check this with the manager of the Trinity Bank," said Holmes, "I think you will find that it matches exactly the master key to the bank and the safe key. The doctor was no doubt about to hand it over to have copies made by this enterprising gentleman. Yes, Mr. Manby Smith, I think you too may have some explaining to do. For example, as to how a locksmith of almost thirty years experience was unable to distinguish the keys of a bank safe. It is quite illegal to make copies, as you know, without the proper authorization, for there can be only one reason to do so without that authority. I should take particular care of your charge, Lestrade, for all we know he may have been added escapology to his other stage tricks..."

"And here is the young man who set it all in motion," said Holmes as Bernard Coram entered the Baker Street sitting-room. "I thought the least we could do by way of thanking you was explain how it all ended."

"The thanks are all on my part, Mr. Holmes, for my reputation may have been sullied by association with this man", said Coram.

"Yes, Mr. Holmes, and from myself and Mr. Abberline too," added Lestrade.

"I still cannot figure how you worked it out, Mr. Holmes, you really must enlighten me," said Abberline. "Thirty years in the force and six years with Pinkerton's and I've never seen anything quite like it."

"The difficulty from the outset was motive and I confess I was puzzled as to Dr. Haylie-Foster's sudden disappearance, notwithstanding Dr Coram's suspicions with respect to the death of the patients. When I discovered that both false trails led me to same place—Dr. Acland's tabernacle—I immediately became convinced that Haylie-Foster's disappearance was both voluntary and intended to be permanent, which suggested the need for him to adopt an alter ego. Of course, what had happened was that, as soon as his coachman, and, in one instance, the jarvey, had dropped him at Northumberland Square, he simply turned along the alley, which doubled back, crossed Jewry Street into Vine Street. He changed his identity there, and went to the Bognor Prestidigitation Circle in Haydon Square. Afterwards, he merely completed the operation in reverse and was waiting for his cab where he had been dropped off.

"As soon as I discovered that this Blackstone had begun to request loans from the banks around the same time as the doctor's disappearance, I wondered if there could be a connection. When I looked at the dates of both the patients' deaths and the robberies, the correspondence was remarkable. The description of the man, with some slight changes, tallied too. It was obvious that the loans were a clever pretext to get inside the banks—I even gave Inspector Lestrade a hint at one point. Each robbery was preceded by a visit from Haylie-Foster in person—why had he found this necessary? Mr. Bergman told me that his visitor removed his glasses, and I became very curious. Why do such a thing? Suddenly, the deaths of the patients all fell into place alongside the spate of bank robberies. The answer was astoundingly simple."

"Simple!" said Lestrade.

"Yes, when I discovered Haylie-Foster's new hobby through the Baker Street Irregulars…"

"The *who?*" cried Abberline in astonishment.

"Of course, I forgot that you know nothing about them. Well, I shall digress briefly: I speak of the Baker Street branch of the unofficial force. A dozen observant, yet unobtrusive, street urchins, whose eyes and ears are as sharp as tacks. I commend them to you, Mr. Abberline, should you ever have to look for a needle in a haystack. If one could curb the social atavism of that class, they would make excellent police detectives.

"Now to return to Haylie-Foster—the Irregulars led me to the Bognor Prestidigitation Circle, a perfectly legitimate club whose members practice harmless stage illusions, including mesmerism, as a hobby. When I found that, under the name of Blackstone, Haylie-Foster was learning mesmerism…"

"You mean, hypnosis?" asked Lestrade.

"Yes, of course, stage hypnosis."

"Ah, I think I see now—the deaths of the patients were experiments which went wrong?" asked Abberline.

"No, experiments which were completely successful, but I shall come back to that. It was Mr. Bergman's statement that Haylie-Foster had taken off his spectacles during the conversation that finally made me realize how the whole thing had been carried out. It was child's play to someone who practiced mesmerism. By then I had all the information I needed: the dates and times of Haylie-Foster's visits to the patients; the dates and times of their deaths; his visits to the banks to arrange the loans, and the dates of the robberies; Haylie-Foster's new address in the city: it all formed a distinct pattern. My difficulty was that it remained in the realm of circumstantial evidence. If we could take him red-handed at the locksmith's, that would be a different matter. As Haylie-Foster was a neurologist, it was no wonder that Chapender, the club president, said he had taken to mesmerism as though he had studied the subject all his life; he practically had."

"I looked up the passage from scripture that you quoted," said Abberline, "about nothing new under the sun—but I'm afraid I must ask you what you meant about the connection between the lame sheep and the bank robberies. I am still flummoxed."

"That makes two of us," said Lestrade.

"Straker, if you recall, nicked the tendons of the sheep in the field prior to attempting the same operation with the racehorse in the paddock. I reasoned that Haylie-Foster would not attempt anything too risky without some practice, hence he hypnotized his incurable patients into dying at a certain time on a certain date.

If he could do that, the next bit would be easy: to hypnotize the bank managers into handing him over the keys while he made an impression, which was why he insisted upon meeting them personally. Once he had put them over, they remembered nothing of the incident. All he had to do was avoid the night shift constables on the beat, open the bank door, help himself to the contents of the safe, and back out again. Having a domicile in the area—none of the banks was more than a block or two away from Vine Street—was icing on the cake. If you look at the pattern, on each occasion there was a death, followed by meeting the bank manager, then the robbery."

"But he killed three patients; yet there were four robberies, at least, the fourth one was not preceded by a murder."

"He was a careful man. He was merely learning the game at the outset and, no doubt, he felt that he had to be sure that his powers were still working. By the time he had singled out the Trinity Bank, he had become quite confident and decided to take a risk. Moore Agar did warn us that he was a rather venal young man; no doubt, he deliberately chose elderly patients with incurable diseases whose expected life span was short. He did not murder them out of malice, but he murdered them nevertheless, and though we may have trouble persuading hard headed jury men whose experience does not extend to the subtleties of the mind, we certainly have plenty of evidence to convict him over the bank robberies."

At the assizes, plain George Foster pled guilty to the murder of his three patients; therefore the court was ultimately spared the lengthy and ponderous deliberations of the twelve dull tradesmen. He also pled guilty to three counts of bank robbery, for which almost all of the proceeds were recovered. Although the law does not distinguish between what the medical profession terms euthanasia and willful murder, his sentence of death by hanging was commuted to life imprisonment.

"Well, that is another one to add to the collection," said Holmes after we had read the court proceedings one evening after dinner.

As the fire roared in the grate, and the first fogs of winter clung to the window panes, he poured out two large glasses of whiskey, then lit his pipe.

"Pritchard, Palmer, Cream, Roylott, Kent... Klosowski was trained as a surgeon, too, you recall, and now, Foster... I think, Watson, that the next time I am hunting a murderer, I shall eschew the dens of criminal underworld and search instead at the conference of the British Medical Association. I have said it before, when a doctor goes wrong, he goes very, very badly wrong."

"*Corruptio Optimi Pessima Est*," I replied, as I reached for the gazogene.

The Afflictions of Dom Agostinho Mendoça

"Have some Madeira, my dear Watson," said Sherlock Holmes, indicating the decanter on the shelf. "This is a fine nutty verdelho, with a few raisiny notes, and a little spicy too. 1867 is the date on the bottle—one of the very special years."

I poured myself a generous measure and sat down in the armchair at the other side of the fire. "More than thirty years old," I said taking a sip, "and rather choice. That reminds me, Holmes, one of these days, I should like you to consider the possibility of my publishing the story of your involvement with the gentleman who bestowed this excellent vintage upon us."

"Ah, my apologies, Watson. I have been so wrapped up in the Spitalfields haunting case that I completely forgot to tell you. I received a communication informing me that the dear old fellow has passed away. I believe you were off shooting with Thurston at the time, and it went right out of my mind. The letter is in the usual place," he said nodding towards a pile of letters spiked by a jack-knife to the mantelpiece.

"What happened?"

"Passed away in his sleep at seventy-two. He had retired to Brazil a few years ago, chiefly to please his good lady, Dona Hermínia, who was terribly homesick."

"Then, no harm can come of the publication of that adventure?"

"I should say not."

Although I had previously suppressed all references to the details of the case, I recalled the beginning of the affair very well for it had happened only a few years previously. Returning from a stroll in Hyde Park, one fine autumn morning in the year of 1898, my friend Sherlock Holmes and I had stopped at a small café near Portman Square for morning coffee and croissants. During the last few weeks, Holmes had begun to take a scholarly interest in the Eleusinian Mysteries of the Mycenean period. Characteristically, he had made such a close and special study of these that, I regret to say, much of his discourse on the subject was distinctly above my head; at one point, he airily informed me that today was the 17th of *Boedromion,* the third month in the ancient Attic calendar, and I was only too glad, once our waitress arrived with her tray, to turn the conversation back to more prosaic matters.

I recalled the episode of Hazelwood House, the celebrated umbrella-maker's in Bloomsbury, and informed my friend that I had written a short account of the case which I should like him to cast his gimlet eye over it. I also took the opportunity to remark how quiet he had been in recent weeks.

"Yes, apart from a few trifles, things have been rather dull since we put away that nasty piece of work at Lewisham and the excitement of the curious business of the two Coptic Patriarchs has abated. As you know, I simply abhor the dull quotidian routine and crave stimulation. I am afraid, Watson, that the London criminal has gone to ground. Perhaps it is to do with the present unseasonable heat wave? It is a strange thing, you know, but I have a theory that this fine weather makes the London criminal somewhat lethargic: they feed better in the cold, rather like English coarse fish."

"*Coarse fish?*" I stammered in surprise, "that is surely one of your more fanciful notions, Holmes."

"Well, I won't insist upon it, but, nevertheless, the parallels are obvious to those enlightened enough to perceive them."

"Perhaps he merely decants to the shingle of Brighton or the sands of Margate, where there are greater possibilities amongst the milling crowds there."

He shook his head, "Summer brings with it an increase in visitors to London, does it not, who come to view the glories of this great Empire of ours, and with it the opportunity for the pickpockets and the fraud merchants to practice upon an unsuspecting foreign populace. I confess I have not yet troubled myself to compare my theories against the data; therefore, it remains in the sphere of speculation. It is in my mind, however, to speak to Lestrade or Gregson on the matter."

"It is just the very sort of thing," I replied, "that we ought to be employing our civil service statisticians to study. After all, they can tell us all sorts of useless things such as how many pairs of boots were issued to the army last year, and how many casks of rum the navy consumed. And after all ..." I broke off in mid sentence for Holmes had been gazing out of the window at the busy traffic passing by, watching the steady procession of people bustling about their business. This invariably presaged an opportunity for him to carry out some clever deduction, based on the most minute aspects of appearances, that this fellow must be an ostler, or that chap must be a tallow chandler. On this occasion, however, his attention became distracted and he stood up sharply.

"What is it?" I asked

"Why I believe it is... no, it most *certainly is...* Brother Mycroft!"

"Where?" I asked.

"He passed in a cab just a moment ago, the one going up Baker Street, number 3749. It is ten to one he is heading to 221B."

We both dashed down the remainder of our coffee, hurriedly paid the serving girl, and set off up the street at a good pace. By the time we reached the sitting room, the vast bulk of Mycroft Holmes was already sprawled in the armchair like a grounded seal on a rock, tapping his fingers impatiently as he awaited our return.

"Ah, Sherlock... Good to see you, and Doctor Watson, too. I trust you enjoyed your stroll in the park," he said, with a glance at our feet, "and Monsieur Bernand's delicious pastries? His *café noir* is reputed to be quite the best in Marylebone, though I personally prefer Lemaire's in South Kensington for *patisserie.*"

"Ah, then you saw us as you passed?" Holmes asked.

"Not at all, I had no idea you had been there until you walked through the sitting room door," replied Mycroft with an eye on the crumbs adhering to Holmes's sleeve.

Holmes laughed, "Yes, we left rather hurriedly once we had spotted you in the cab."

"You deduced, then, that I was coming here. Excellent."

"Yes, and I am afraid we did not have time to avail ourselves of a proper brush down. I assume you have brought some problem you wish to discuss?"

"Yes, indeed. I have come to see you concerning an affair that may take you to France, if you have the time to look into the matter."

"What could possibly take me there, Mycroft?" Holmes asked with a hint of suspicion in his tone. "Surely not this ridiculous saber-rattling over Fashoda."

"Not at all," he waved the idea away. "I know you have no interest whatever in the political situation, whether at home or overseas. Although it is difficult not to believe that entire regrettable incident, which was perfectly avoidable in my opinion, may have set back the cause of Anglo-French relations by ten years.[13] No, I have come to see you concerning the affairs of a certain foreign nobleman. It is a rather odd business, which I think may be in your line, although it may yet turn out to be as much a case for Dr. Watson as for yourself."

"I have seen nothing in the newspapers, that is to say nothing of interest to one of my *métier*," replied Holmes, sitting down in the armchair and lighting his pipe.

"No, you wouldn't have, Sherlock; it has been kept out of the columns of the press. It concerns one Dom Agostinho Mendoça of Bragança, to give him his full title," said Mycroft.

"Portuguese?" asked Holmes.

"Yes, Portugal," said Mycroft enthusiastically applying himself to the contents of his tortoise-shell snuff box, "England's oldest ally."

"Oldest, but perhaps its most useless," replied Holmes acerbically as he puffed out billows of Ships' blend. The meerschaum pipe usually signaled a disputatious mood. "Why, the aristocracy scuttled off to Brazil like frightened rabbits the moment Napoleon set his foot in the Iberian peninsula."

---

[13] Mycroft was being too pessimistic: the *Entente Cordiale* was signed in 1904.

"That is historically correct, Sherlock, as far as a generalization holds, but I must point out that the Mendoças were amongst those few families who stayed behind and put up something of a fight. Had it not been for the general insurrection in the peninsula by *guerrillas* led by such men as the Mendoças, then Bonaparte would have simply walked in the front door. We must remember old allegiances."

"I know you haven't come all the way from Whitehall to read me a lecture in European history, so let me conjecture: some unfathomable crime been committed which, through this person, affects in some way the Foreign Office, and involves a degree of political intrigue, which is why it has been kept out of the papers?"

"Wrong on all four counts, Sherlock! I am not entirely sure whether any crime has been committed, the matter has nothing to do with anyone at the Foreign Office, and there is no political intrigue whatsoever. The reason the matter has not reached the columns of the press is that it has not been reported to the Police and remains a private matter—simply, a bizarre series of events, which has culminated in Dom Agostinho, a fellow member of the Diogenes Club, believing that he is being poisoned."

"Hmm, most, er, most interesting, Mycroft."

"Yes, I thought you would be intrigued. I say, fellow member of the Diogenes, when I really should say former member."

"Then Dom Agostinho has left the club?"

"Technically, he remains a member, I suppose. But he now lives in Paris; his wife, who is of Brazilian origin, could no longer stand our English climate and, I am sorry to say, pestered the Duke to move to France. He has taken a large apartment, a mansion almost, in *Le*

Marais district, mainly because of its aristocratic connections and, in part, due the proximity of the religious institutions there. He is a very pious individual, makes his devotions, or whatever one calls it, daily, and is attached to a number of confraternities in the local Jesuit church. He and I formed something of an occasional friendship; like myself, he was apt to be somewhat reclusive, but rather oddly; this only strengthened our bond. He is a man of great culture and learning, one of the few members on my own intellectual level; a man who has seen much of the world, and also a great admirer of many of our English institutions. It was with some regret that I learned of his imminent departure a few months ago in the Stranger's Room. I heard no more of him until a letter arrived last Wednesday."

"It can hardly, therefore, be an urgent case, if you could delay coming to see me for a week."

"That is so; however, Dom Agostinho's first letter contained only the briefest details and, knowing your methods, I endeavored to draw out more of the points of the case. So, I waited until his more fulsome reply reached me this morning. I have brought it with me in case you should wish to read it."

"Excellent. Pray let me have the particulars then."

"Since moving to Paris some three months ago, Dom Agostinho has suffered recurrent attacks of an unusual nature—seizures is perhaps a better description. These attacks take place irregularly, but are invariably accompanied by almost identical symptoms." Mycroft drew a paper from his case and reading it, continued: "He tells me in this letter that the symptoms of these attacks consist of nausea, a feeling of light-headedness, sweating, and acute feelings of anxiousness. The phase of anxiousness manifests itself in a sudden desire escape or to run away, which he describes as feeling akin to a kind of temporary madness; he normally dashes off to his own chambers and locks himself in the bathroom until the feelings abate. After half an hour or so, he returns to normal. He has been to see a number of doctors in Paris, including, I believe, a professor, but they can find nothing wrong with him. In reply to my query, he states that no doctor has ever been present when one of these seizures have taken place.

"A few weeks ago, the family doctor took his wife, Dona Hermínia, aside and requested her to make preparations in the event of another seizure. He asked that she make a note of certain symptoms: whether Dom Agostinho's pupils were dilated, the color of his tongue, to try to check his pulse, check his temperature, also the rigidity of his muscles; she readily agreed.

"The following week, an attack took place but as a laywoman, she found it very difficult to comply with the Doctor's request. She tried to do all that she was asked, but the outcome was inconclusive. Knowing your requirement for very precise information, I pressed Dom Agostinho on a number of questions. I have the dates of the attacks—here is the list—but I can find no discernible pattern. On most occasions, the attacks took place when the Duke was accompanied by his wife. The very worst seizure was at a big dinner—an unusually bad attack which included an alarming breathlessness and nausea. They were in the dining room when it occurred, but the strangest thing of all is that the guests at the party ate the same thing. The Duke excused himself, fled to his room, and returned to join his guests later in the drawing-room. Once restored, the evening proceeded as normal and, by the time the port had circulated a few times, it was as though nothing had happened."

"At what point in the evening did the seizure take place?"

"As the fruit and dessert was being served."

"Hm, that seems rather singular does it not?"

I could see that Holmes was intrigued by the problem.

"Well, Watson, what do you think of this strange aliment which strikes the Duke at his dinner table?"

"I must confess it has me completely astounded, I have heard nothing like it," I replied. "I assume from what you say, Mycroft, that the Duke returns completely to normal after these attacks?"

"In every respect."

"There is no cumulative damage or injury?"

"None whatsoever."

"And no intestinal discomfort of pain of any kind?"

"No."

"Then, I should say it can scarcely be a case of poisoning—certainly not by any of the usual methods such as arsenic or antimony, which are both painful. Other methods of poisoning, such as strychnine, are generally quickly fatal."

"Not necessarily so," said Holmes, "there is a class of ordeal poisons which have very powerful, indeed dramatic, effects, but their symptoms are entirely fleeting and often leave the victim unaffected; indeed, the primitive belief was that if the victim survived, it would make him stronger. Does Dom Agostinho suspect anyone?"

"In the household? Not at all."

"He thinks that he may be being poisoned, and yet trusts all of the domestic staff. How can this be?"

"That is what he wants you to finds out. Poisoning is only one possible explanation."

"What if one of these attacks should prove fatal—to whom does the estate descend?"

"The Duke is childless—the estate descends to the younger brother, Aloisio, in Portugal, who is, if anything, even more wealthy than the Duke. He is a spectacularly successful speculator and has no apparent financial problems."

"And the title?"

"Descends to the brother too."

"Ah."

"The brothers are very close, Sherlock, genuinely so. I rather think that an attempted fratricide can be ruled out."

"Well, we shall see. What does Dona Hermínia think?"

"That it is voodoo."

"Good Lord!" I exploded.

"Dona Hermínia is as superstitious as her husband is religious," continued Mycroft as Holmes sat with brows drawn. "Her advice to her husband is to return at once to Rio De Janeiro, where he will find a medicine man whom, as she put it, 'will know how to shake off this evil curse.' "

"Dona Hermínia did not like England," said Holmes. "It follows that she may not entirely be thrilled with Paris either. The climate is, in fact, for much of the year, scarcely different from London. It is possible, is it not, that she harbors a secret desire to return to the land of her birth? And in attempting to persuade her husband to return to Brazil, she has engaged, say, the maid and butler in a conspiracy to frighten her husband into leaving Paris by applying some exotic, but ultimately innocuous, poison, such as perhaps some ordeal poison which

she may have obtained from one of these voodoo medicine men?"

"I suppose that is what Dom Agostinho is engaging
you to find out."

"The ways of women are capricious and unpredict-
able and she had made no secret of her homesickness."

"In fact, though, Sherlock, the entire entourage returns every year to Brazil for a few months in order to
winter out, so to speak, and avoid the snows and frosts
of northern Europe."

"Apart from the Paris doctors, Dom Agostinho has
mentioned this to no one?"

"No. I should have consulted Von Hennigen, the
neurology specialist, but he is in Sweden at the moment."

"Ah, and so Watson and I are the second choices?"
Holmes replied with some asperity.

"Come, Sherlock, do not be so infantile!" said Mycroft looking at his watch. "No, I should have consulted
him *before* coming here, in order to rule out any medical
causes. I am convinced it is more complicated than that
in any case, and the Duke is coming to the conclusion
that the matter may be beyond the reach of medicine. I
believe there may be a human agency behind this,
though the motive is as yet perfectly inscrutable to me.
But it is not a case for reasoning from the armchair; rather one for a more active pursuit. Now, the Duke requests that you attend personally, entirely at his expense,
of course. I perceive that you are not presently engaged,
therefore…"

"What makes you think I am not busy at present?"

"My dear Sherlock," Mycroft replied witheringly,
"if you had a case in hand, would you be wandering
around Hyde Park contemplating the russet boughs of

autumn? Or leisurely sipping *café au lait* in the bourgeois comfort of Bernand's? No, you would be running around with a lens pressed to your nose, cross-questioning all and sundry. Come, what could be better than a trip to Paris at this time of year—and Doctor Watson too, if he is able to go?"

"Well, it is not impossible," replied Holmes, who seemed to be warming to the idea.

"I should be delighted, Mycroft," I said.

"Of course," Mycroft went on, "I did warn Dom Agostinho that all his riches would not be sufficient to entice you, only the prospect of unraveling some abstruse enigma, nothing less than a four-pipe problem as you might put it yourself. However, in anticipation, he has enclosed a check for five hundred pounds."

"The Duke is no doubt aware that, due to the very nature of the case, I will be required to delve quite deeply into his personal affairs, all his business affairs, his private correspondence, relations with his wife and, indeed, his relations with any women, including the household servants?"

"Absolutely. I guarantee that you will not find a single skeleton in the Dom Agostinho's cupboard. He is a venerable, almost saintly man, if I may use the term, and noted for his charity and philanthropy. He is prepared, nay, anxious, to lay all open to you in the hope of finding some resolution to the matter: no secrets, absolutely none."

"Well, that settles it, Mycroft. There is an overnight boat train; you may wire to Dom Agostinho to say that that we will be in attendance no later than Wednesday morning."

"Excellent, Sherlock. I knew the problem would intrigue you," said Mycroft handing Holmes the letter from Paris.

"You were rather churlish," I said by way of reproach, after Mycroft had left.

"I accept without rancor the fact that Mycroft is my intellectual superior, Watson. It is, however, somewhat galling for me to know that the field in which I have spent my life in attempting to make a living, indeed in which I may be said to have an international reputation, Mycroft considers to be the merest hobby. Being one of the most physically lethargic and downright lazy persons with whom I am acquainted, I know that he is positively amused at the thought of me running around with a magnifying glass, taking samples of tobacco ash, following trails of three day old clues, and interrogating hotel porters and station masters."

"But why did you postpone our departure until tomorrow evening, for it is unlike you not to strike while the iron is hot?"

"There are a couple of threads which I should wish to follow first," he replied. "It is possible, for instance, that this is some recurrent malady which Dom Agostinho has picked up in the tropics—one which is unknown to our European science. You know how malaria comes and goes, for instance. I may avail myself of one of the unofficial specialists in the subject before we leave."

"And the other?"

He drew down from the shelf a slim volume marked *P.* "I rather fancy you could call this *The Lives of the Great Poisoners*," he chuckled. "They are all here, listed and ranked, including some of your own former professional associates. I am sure that several hours' diligent study will be handsomely repaid."

Arrangements had been made for us to stay with the Duke at his residence on the western side of the Place des Vosges. It was a magnificent house, palatial in scale, classical—indeed, pre-revolutionary—in style, looking out on to truly wonderful, linden-lined fountained gardens. After an excellent breakfast of deviled kidneys, we went across to the square and sat on one of the benches, basking in the warm morning air.

"Yesterday, I spent an instructive afternoon in the company of some of our most famous poisoners," Holmes said. "Much more and much better research on the subject is urgently needed for the detection of murder by poison. It is at present, as I am sure you know, anything but an exact science;: many murderers get off scot free, and yet it is a relatively simple matter. It is as well for Scotland Yard that I am not the criminal type, for I fancy I could poison half of London and get away with it. Cases which appear, at least superficially, similar to that of Dom Agostinho's have already occurred in Lisbon, Eindhoven and Leicester. However, they all have one important difference, in that the effects of poisoning were either, as you suggested, either directly or cumulatively fatal, and, in each case, there was a clear motive on the part of the poisoner.

"I then went to see a gentleman in Limehouse near the West India Docks, Charles Godwin-Seymour; it is unlikely that you will be acquainted with him, for he is not a qualified, or even a trained doctor, but something of an authority on tropical diseases. He is to South American disorders and conditions what Culverton Smith to Asiatic ones, though without quite the same murderous tendencies. Like myself, he is an enthusiastic amateur in his subject, and would fairly astonish the British Medical Association with the exactness of his learning and accumulated knowledge of the West Indies—of the sorts of things which have been picked up in the plantations there, close enough to Brazil at any rate to be worthy of my consultation. I spent an interesting hour or two and, though he went through all his notes and records, he could find nothing which matched any of the symptoms we discussed. On the question of ordeal poisons, it turned out, he was no more knowledgeable than myself."

"You have drawn a blank?"

"Two blanks, and wasted one full day," he said cheerfully. "They were slim hopes. in any case, for I foresee that the case may turn out to be far more subtle than we had imagined, but I wished to be sure that I had not overlooked any obvious solution before I began to look for more abstruse ones."

Dom Agostinho was a tall, spare man, with a very erect bearing; his hair was completely white and, though now in his late sixties, to observe his carriage and demeanor, one would have guessed perhaps fifty at most. He cordially welcomed us into his elegant spacious study like long lost brothers.

"It is most gratifying to meet you both," he said wringing my hand with the strength and vigor of a man half his age. "I have read all of your stories, Doctor. Needless to say, the younger Holmes shines through them all." He looked at Holmes shrewdly, "Yes, I can definitely see the resemblance. Mycroft is obviously the quieter one of the family, for he seems to lack that ambition and drive which has so characterized your professional success; yet, he excels in purely cerebral effort, does he not?"

"Yes, and he is as content in his chosen field as I, without being so famous," Holmes replied.

"But then, he has no faithful chronicler like Doctor Watson! And so, you have come here to assist me in my hour of need. Well, I thank you sincerely and you shall find that I am not ungrateful. I received a communication from Mycroft concerning your methods, and I quite agree that it is only proper for you to go anywhere you consider necessary, ask any question of myself or of anyone in the household. I have only one wish—and that is that the Police are not involved. Policemen will only go charging about the place and upsetting the household and, in any case, I wish to keep this matter private."

"I have no intention of involving the Police," replied Holmes. "However, it may be necessary for me to engage some local assistance, purely for some of the routine tasks of inquiring into the personal habits and connections of the members of the household, the servants and so on." I noted that Holmes had omitted to mention the fact that it was his intention to include Dona Hermínia in this surveillance. "The *Agence Peretti* in the 1st arrondissement will undertake some of this work and I can assure you that the proprietor, Mademoiselle Peretti…"

"*Mademoiselle?!*", Dom Agostinho interjected, "No? Is there such a thing as a woman detective?"

"Yes; there is not only such a thing, but she is enormously successful, and I can assure you Mademoiselle Peretti is the very heart and soul of confidentiality. Our paths crossed some years ago and I was amply impressed, not only with her general shrewdness and intelligence, but also her discretion. I suggest that she is employed—incognito of course—by yourself ostensibly in some below stairs capacity in proximity to the kitchen."

"But is it strictly necessary for her to know the details of the case, that is to say of my private affairs?"

"For one thing, Dom Agostinho, she is bound by a professional code of silence, and for another, I should not myself undertake any case in which the facts were concealed from me, and therefore would not ask another to do so. It would be unreasonable, as well as self-defeating for us, to expect her to act without taking her fully into our confidence. As to her operatives, that would be a different matter; they merely act on instructions and will shadow the servants—in fact, anyone who is in a position to poison or adulterate your food—for a few weeks in order to ascertain whether there is anything irregular going on."

"I am sure you know best, Mr. Holmes."

"Thank you, Dom Agostinho. I should also like Doctor Watson to speak to your own physician."

"Of course."

"I believe you are strongly religious man, Dom Agostinho?"

"Yes, that is so. I am a devout Roman Catholic, attend holy mass every day, and am an active member of the Society of Saint Vincent de Paul, in addition to which I support a number of ecclesiastical charities and foreign missions."

"I see from your notepaper that you also bear the arms of the Cross of Malta on your letterhead?"

"How very observant of you, Mr. Holmes. Yes, I am a Knight of the Equestrian Order of the Holy Sepulcher."

"You keep a stable?"

"No," Dom Agostinho smiled, "the 'equestrian' part is purely a historical relic from the days of the Crusades. No one in the Order has mounted a horse in anger since the fall of Acre, but the Society tries to maintain the traditions and ideals of the Hospitaller Knights—propagation of the Faith, support of Christians in the Holy Land, and charity towards other human beings regardless of their creed."

"It occurs to me then that I should perhaps speak to your confessor."

Dom Agostinho seemed surprised, but assented, "Yes, by all means, feel free to do so. You will find Père Létin at the Église Saint-Paul-Saint-Louis, in the Rue Saint Antoine; it is a mere five minute walk from here; indeed, those are the church bells that you hear ringing out every hour. Though I cannot see how he will be of any assistance in resolving this."

"Please describe your household, Dom Agostinho."

"All of the servants were brought from Brazil by the Dona, except for my old retainer, Bento, who is, I suppose, what you would call a butler in England, though we do not use such formal titles. I say 'old,' but Bento is in his forties, and his family have been with us for several generations; he tends to all of my personal needs. Then, there is the housekeeper Assunção, her husband Eloi, the head cook, and two maids, Dores and Eulália, who are their nieces. They have all been with the Dona's family for years. We bring help in from an agency for special occasions, but there are no new additions to the household staff. No doubt, you will find the usual petty jealousies amongst the staff, but I should be surprised if you uncover any real, or even imagined, grievances."

"And you have no personal enemies Dom Agostinho?"

"None whatever; I scarcely know half a dozen people in Paris."

"No business rivals?"

"Not that I know of."

"Or… I am bound to ask, sir, no wronged or jealous husbands?"

Dom Agostinho smiled, "Yes, you were bound to ask, but I am not sure if I should feel insulted or complimented—at my age!"

"And the servants?"

"You obviously haven't met Assunção!" he burst into a peal of hearty laughter. "Even *I* am afraid of Assunção. As for her nieces, they are mere girls—I'm afraid that *le droit du seigneur* is a figment of the romantic, and barbarous, past. Do not take my word for it, ask Dona Hermínia—a woman always knows these things. I wish to get to the bottom of this mysterious business, and I believe if anyone can do that, it is you. I have every faith in you, Mr. Holmes, and faith is something which I hold in abundance."

Holmes appeared after breakfast the next morning like a general about to hold a council of war.

"Here is the plan of action, Watson," he said. "You shall visit Docteur Vigneron and inquire after Dom Agostinho's general health. Ask about anything which occurs to you, and go over every physical and mental symptom which has prefigured, accompanied, or followed the seizures, but particularly for any sign which may presage an attack.

"Mademoiselle Peretti has now been installed as an assistant to Eloi and will keep a close watch on everything which goes on in the kitchen. If she discovers anything suspicious which may relate to the adulteration of Dom Agostinho's food, she is will try to acquire a sample for analysis. She will also eavesdrop on the servants' chatter, though they are not to know that she understands them."

"And does she?"

"Yes, of course. You will recall from our little episode here a few years ago that she was fluent in most of the western Romance languages; that is one of the reasons why the Contessa employed her. She is not even to respond to a 'good morning' in Portuguese and to feign complete ignorance of anything except French. One of the agency operatives, Jean-Marc, will tail Bento, and her other two agents, Patrice and Brigitte, will follow the housekeeper and the cook."

I am afraid to say that I returned from Docteur Vigneron's practice in a mood of disappointment. We had gone over each aspect of Dom Agostinho's case with a fine tooth comb, but everything seemed to corroborate his physician's belief that the malady seemed not to be related to any physical cause. Apart from a slight breathlessness prior to the onset of these attacks, nothing unusual was recorded. Vigneron also confirmed that Dom Agostinho's eating habits had not changed radically since his arrival in Paris, and that he had examined Dom Agostinho's stools immediately after one of the attacks had occurred, but had found nothing alarming or suspicious in the chemical analysis.

"Naturally I thought at first it was some species of epilepsy," Vigneron said, "and so I referred Dom Agostinho to Professor Thevenin, who is perhaps the foremost authority on the condition in the city. He was forced to conclude that the symptoms do not form any pattern within the current definition of epileptic seizure; most conditions are set off by an event in the life of the sufferer, but he was aware of nothing which could be said to fall under this heading. A smaller number of conditions are recurrent and unprovoked. But the chief difficulty, of course, in Dom Agostinho's case, is the rareness of his attacks. Unless Dom Agostinho were actually in my presence when one of the seizures took place, it will be impossible to come to any conclusion."

In my absence, Holmes had spoken to Dona Hermínia. He had, he said, gone over all the familiar ground until he was fairly weary. "She was a strange mixture of the religious and the superstitious," he said, "and insists that someone has put a curse upon her husband, and that only by returning to Brazil would he be cured. It was Père Létin who was preventing her husband from doing this. She suggested that the priest did not understand the local customs at home—that is to say her home—and that he was only interested in her husband for the money he could get out of him for the Church."

After a delightful lunch at *Il Saraceno* in the Rue Jean-Jacques Rousseau, Holmes and I meandered round to the offices of Peretti's in the Rue Bailleul, behind the Rue Saint-Honoré. Mademoiselle Peretti was having an afternoon off from the kitchen in the Place des Vosges. She had little to report, other than to say that she was delighted with the improvement in her knowledge of Portuguese and Brazilian cuisine.

"I have heard that there are about two hundred ways to cook *bacalhau*," she said, "and have just begun to master the Brazilian dialect of Portuguese, but apart from that, I have seen or heard nothing which gives rise to any misgivings."

"You are sure that the staff do not suspect you?" asked Holmes.

"I am quite certain about that. They resent my presence, but only in the way that people do with outsiders. I overheard one of the maids say, 'What do you think of the new French girl?' The other replied, 'She's not French, she's Corsican—they're all bandits and gangsters. She must be a bandit's girl,' and they both laughed. The first one said, 'She seems quite nice, but these French girls are all *galinhas*. She has old Bento swooning after her already.' Assunção is a fierce character who completely dominates her little mouse of a husband, but is really very kindly underneath. She and Eloi are childless and they dote on the nieces, whom I gather were orphaned when they were quite young. They never let the girls out of their sight for they believe Paris is an immoral place. All of the staff complain constantly that they are homesick for their families, but there is no animosity towards their employers, and it is quite impossible to imagine them doing anything disloyal, far less harmful."

"What have you discovered about the rest of the household?" asked Holmes.

"We have trailed around after the butler, the housekeeper and the cook for the best part of the week. Again, there is nothing suspicious to report: the cook makes routine trips with the maids to the big market in the Rue des Halles, the housekeeper has collected a parcel or two of religious books for Dom Agostinho at La Poste—in fact, they have barely left the fourth arrondissement; apart from these errands, they have gone no further than the gardens in the square. Jean-Marc has had an easy time of it for Bento has been doing the usual excursions to see the sights of Paris on an afternoon or an evening off; he has obviously done all the major ones already and has recently been to the Champ de Mars, the Trocadéro and a few others. He also paid a visit to a rather seedy club on the Place Cauchois, though he only stayed for about twenty minutes, before leaving. Jean-Marc says he thinks he was shocked by the decadence of it all."

"We shall maintain our surveillance for a few more weeks yet. At least until another of these attacks take place or until we find a solution."

Holmes and I walked the few blocks to the Église Saint Paul-Saint Louis in the Quartier Saint Antoine. Holmes looked at the letters above the gnomon: *A.M.D.G.*

"Jesuits," he said. "If anyone can penetrate the secrets of Dom Agostinho's mind, it will be one of this order."

Holmes insisted on wandering first through the lucent high-domed church, pausing occasionally to view this painting or that feature of the architecture, stopping once he pointed to an inscription on a pillar in the nave: *République française ou la mort.*

Père Létin was a short, dark-skinned, sinewy man with iron grey hair and piercing brown eyes, who looked to be in his forties. After we had introduced ourselves, he brought us into the dark wood-paneled sacristy, redolent of incense, altar wine and candle wax, seated us at a sparse green baize-covered table, and removed his biretta.

"I suspect that I shall not be of much assistance to you, Monsieur Holmes, although I shall do my best. I had heard from the Superior General himself about your efforts on behalf of our *pontifex maximus*, Leo, in the affair of the Marian cameos and, more recently, in your investigation into the strange circumstances surrounding the untimely death of Cardinal Tosca…"

"Yes, I was not only honored to be asked, but delighted to be able to bring both matters to a successful conclusion," replied Holmes. "Indeed, His Holiness holds the unique distinction of, thus far, being the only client to have consulted me twice."

"Then, you were, in some respects, able to make some thanksgiving to the Church for the very special gift which God has given you, for I have also read of some of your other cases. I assume the purpose of this visit is to catechize me on the subject of the afflictions of Dom Agostinho?" the priest asked. "I must point out to you that, as his confessor, I am not at liberty—nor am I obliged, even in a court of law—to say what passes between the priest and the penitent in the confessional."

"I understand that, Père Létin, but I reasoned that you might be able to assure me that there can be nothing on his conscience which could cause any unrest."

"I assume as you are, respectively, a logician and a doctor, that you have come to me as a final court of appeal, a last resort, in other words; that the doctor has sought the cause of Dom Agostinho's disturbance in the domain of the body, and perhaps the mind, and found nothing; and that you, Monsieur Holmes, have sought the cause in some maleficent individual whose aim would be to harm the man and, likewise, have found no cause."

"I would not put it so glibly," replied Holmes, "as to designate your reverence as a 'last resort,' but it is true to say that we appear to have exhausted all conventional explanations. There appears to be nothing physically or mentally wrong with Dom Agostinho, and I am convinced there is no hand against him in his household."

"And so, you wish me to look into something which is invisible to you: a man's immortal soul?"

"I did not exactly say that…"

"Because you do not believe in the existence of such a thing?"

"Doctor Watson will tell you that my knowledge of divinity is as close to being nil as to make no difference."

"That is to avoid the question. I was aware of your singular limitations in the matter of theology when I read some time ago Doctor Watson's account of the attempted theft of some military treaty—the details did not concern me—but your epistemological misunderstanding in postulating religion as being as accessible to deduction as an exact science struck me as injudicious in one so intelligent. Positivist science only deals with what it can see and touch; how comforting that must be, a world where there is no good and no evil, no wickedness or iniquity, only cause and effect, proven or refuted hypotheses; where everything may be placed under a microscope and observed, labeled and catalogued. It can examine the heart and the brain, but does not recognize the existence of the human soul, far less have the capacity to look into it."

"I am not in a position to dispute that but, you seem to imply that the cause is beyond medicine," said Holmes.

"I am not a medical doctor, but I have exercised my brain in an attempt to understand the causes and possible remedies. And although my own studies have at times brought me into contact with theories which try to give temporal explanations to such phenomena, and have taken in such diverse ideas as Bleuler's research at Rheinau, and the Abbé Faria's discoveries in this very city, I have found nothing in the field to explain Dom Agostinho's condition. You know that Dona Hermínia believes it to be voodoo, or *macumba* as it is known in her homeland?" the old priest smiled. "What do you think of that?"

"Yes, I have spoken to the Duchess," Holmes replied. "She believes that you are preventing Dom Agostinho's cure by your counsel."

"Then she is wrong."

"You would not?"

"No."

"But surely," I said in exasperation, "you, of all people, cannot possibly countenance this primitive nonsense."

"Of course not, but one must not ignore the fact that, if the believer has faith in the power of the curse, or the remedy for the curse, then it may work. Faith, even the perverted faith of a tree worshipping heathen, can move mountains. 'Everything is possible for him who believes.' No doubt, you would regard medical science as superior to voodoo, but you would be astonished, as well as offended, to learn that the sacrifice of a chicken or a kid had the same healing power as anything in your pharmacopeia. And at least, this savage creed recognizes evil in all of it manifestations and influences, and how the miasma of evil may attach itself to certain places, and certain people..."

"You mean, a haunting, like a ghost?" I asked.

"Ghosts? No, not ghosts. People who come back to life to haunt their enemies—that is the stuff of theater and pantomime. No, I mean the incarnation of the spirit of evil. The swine possessed by demons in Gadarea; the man possessed by an unclean spirit in Capaernum."

"And you believe that Dom Agostinho is afflicted in this way?" said Holmes.

"I cannot say so, for I am bound by the *Rituale Romanum* to determine absolutely beyond human doubt

245

that the nature of his affliction is neither physiological nor psychological, before I may proceed with an examination of that sort. I believe I have ruled out any physical cause; it remains only to rule out a mental one. He hotly denies that he is mad, or anything approaching it, and refuses to submit to what might be called a psychiatric examination. 'I am no lunatic," he said, 'nor is my soul possessed.' And yet, you know, it may happen to the best of men, which Dom Agostinho certainly is. But the Dom is afraid and proud: afraid that I shall find something, and too proud to admit his fear.

"All the same, I believe it is unlikely, because when I have visited the house, I have felt no presence. Ah, I see you disbelieve this too, Monsieur Holmes, and that you are skeptical as well, Doctor Watson. When you go out to entrap a criminal, no doubt you will visit the scene of the crime. You do this because you believe that this criminal has left behind some evidence, some infinitesimal but tangible imprint of his presence, from which you can divine his identity. So it is too with the powers of darkness, but I have found no trace of these in his home. I wish you the blessings of God in discovering the source of this saintly man's disturbance," the priest concluded, as he led us out through the cloister and shook our hands. "I trust your trip here has not been wasted."

"Not at all, Père Létin, I have seen the magnificent works of Delacroix and Pilon in the church, and am glad to have had the opportunity to appreciate some of the finer points of the French Gothic style."

"Utterly confounded, Watson, utterly so," said Holmes. "Which is perhaps a more common condition to me than anyone who reads your accounts of my adventures might imagine. Nevertheless, that is the situation. I have turned the matter over and over, postulating explanation after explanation, each more outrageous than the last. We have tried every avenue, followed up every thread; we have turned Dom Agostinho and his household inside out—all to no avail. I have given Peretti until the end of the week, then we must call off our dogs."

We were sitting again in the bench in the fountained square. "I can scarcely remember a case when things have gone so badly," I replied. "You know, I think we shall have to turn to the Dona's *macumba* for our solution after all," I added jocularly. "Perhaps we should order a black cock to sacrifice from the market."

Holmes mused ruefully for a moment, then sat bolt upright on the bench. "By Jove, Watson, that's it!"

"What! You are not actually going to sacrifice a chicken?"

"No," he spluttered impetuously, "of course not. You take things far too literally at times, Watson. But you have given me an inkling, just the merest inkling."

"Voodoo? But surely…"

"There is no time to explain," he stood up with the air of a man about to depart on some urgent errand.

"Before you dash off, Holmes, is there anything I can do in order to assist? Any avenue of inquiry that I may be able to undertake? After all, the entire investigation is becoming rather dull, despite the very agreeable surroundings."

"Nothing that is vitally important."

"Are you certain?"

"Absolutely."

"Then, where are you going?"

"I shall have to speak to Bento" he said.

"But why Bento?"

"This is neither the time nor the place for complicated explanations. Is it possible for you to procure and have ready a small vial of nitrate in the event of a seizure in order to suppress the symptoms, should one occur?"

"I have some in my case."

"Then withdraw it immediately and remain as close to the Dom as possible."

"But how?"

"Engage him in some small talk about his family origin, tell him you are a student of genealogy. What nobleman, saintly or otherwise, can resist engaging in glorious ancestor worship, especially to a foreigner? If that fails, ask him about his vintage Madeira collection, of which he is justly proud. Stick to him as a burr sticks to wool. But whatever you do, do not draw his attention to his ailment."

I must confess that Dom Agostinho managed to make the subject of his forebears a moderately interesting one, though there is a limit to one's tolerance to hagiography. His wine collection was different matter. The cellar was quite magnificent and justified his reputation as a connoisseur. We spent fully two hours there amongst the barrels and bottles, sipping this Sercial or that Lourinhã, so that, by the time the gong rang for dinner, I felt no need for an aperitif. He very generously suggested that, when Holmes and I departed for London, we should take back with us a very special memento or two.

I had noticed, as we went back upstairs to the flower-filled dining room, a quite discernible intensification of Holmes's manner. He was in the sitting-room reading a telegram, and as we went in to dinner, I whispered very quietly to him, asking him who the telegram was from.

"Oh, it was just Mycroft inquiring after progress and suggesting a few lines of development," he said dismissively with a characteristic flick of the wrist.

I had no doubt that he was, in some way, rankled by what he viewed as the meddling of the elder Holmes.

Dinner was, on this occasion as every other, a quite grandiose affair, but without that formal frigidity which one finds in similar situations in England. Throughout the evening, I kept my eyes on our host: his attention appeared to wander at times and, once or twice, he stared away out of the window for what seemed an unconscionable time. Finally, the dessert plates were laid out, and an extravagant fruit tray brought in, bearing, in addition to the usual produce, many types of exotic fruits, the names of which I never knew, but which I assumed were of South American origin. During this lull, I seemed to observe that the Dom's condition was worsening slightly.

A few minutes later, I noticed that Dom Agostinho was sitting rigid in his chair, gripping the table; he stared blankly ahead and began to take deeper and deeper breaths. At a sign from Holmes, I withdrew the vial and applied it to his nostrils as Dona Hermínia stood up and began to fuss around him.

"A few moments and it will pass," Holmes said to the Dona.

"It usually takes about half an hour," she replied.

"No, we shall have him restored very soon," I replied.

"Dona Hermínia, please ring for Bento," said Holmes.

When the man arrived Holmes said, "Please remove the fruit tray at once."

The Dom released his grip and seemed to be coming back to normal. I advised him to take a sip or two from a glass of water which had been poured from the carafe.

"How are you now, Dom Agostinho?" I asked.

"Feeling much better. That was the quickest recovery. What did you do?"

"I merely suppressed the symptoms," I replied.

"But unless I am very much mistaken, that will be your last attack," said Holmes to the utter astonishment of those present, including myself.

"My last attack! But how do you know?" asked Dom Agostinho.

"Because I removed the cause."

"The cause?"

"Indeed, the culprit has just left the room."

The Dom and his wife looked aghast "You mean Bento? But he has…"

Holmes held up his hand. "No, Dom Agostinho, not Bento."

"Then who?" Dona Hermínia demanded hotly.

"Please allow me to explain. The source of your affliction, I may assure you, was to be found amongst the contents of the fruit tray." Holmes continued, "I now have the incontrovertible evidence which proves to me that Dom Agostinho is suffering from an advanced form of *Phobos Musacae Sapientum,* or bananaphobia."

There was a confused silence in the room.

"I have never heard of such a thing, Holmes," I said in surprise.

"Very possibly, but then, if I recall, you had never heard of black Formosa corruption, or Tapanuli fever," said Holmes acerbically. "*Phobos Musacae Sapientum* is better known in the Malay Archipelago where it was discovered by one of the shamans, but it has spread wherever the genus has been cultivated to the West Indies and parts of South America. I happened to ask Bento this morning whether he could remember in detail the circumstances of each of the attack you have had. I had, by that point, eliminated all other possible causes. I asked him if a fruit tray or bowl containing bananas were present on each occasion of your seizures and he replied, as I expected, in the affirmative."

Dom Agostinho looked greatly relieved, "But is there a cure?" he asked.

"A cure is unnecessary," Holmes replied confidently, "providing the sufferer avoids close contact with the genus. Once the plant is cooked, happily the irritant is dissipated, for the attacks are set off by enzymes which are contained in the skin, which propagate and disseminate in the environs of a warm confined room. Simply ensure that the house servants do not to bring the fruit into close contact with you, and you shall be spared any further trouble."

"Astounding, Mr. Holmes, quite astounding," said our host, "I am incredibly grateful to you. Only a very fine and subtle mind, I am sure, could have uncovered this singular phenomenon."

"Oh, I can hardly claim too much credit, Dom Agostinho. It was, in the end, a simple matter and I was fortunate to receive assistance in pursuing the source of your affliction from a number of quarters. The main thing is that you may look forward to living a normal life from now on."

Dom Agostinho certainly confirmed that the reputation for philanthropy which he had established was entirely deserved, for, when Holmes and I departed Paris, we bore with us a most handsome emolument and two cases of the very best Madeira from his press. Holmes, ever kind and chivalrous where women were concerned, stopped off at the Rue Bailleul before we left, in order to bid *adieu,* and to convey his gratitude, to Mademoiselle Peretti for her assistance. We had agreed beforehand to leave behind a sizeable portion of our own share of the proceeds of the case, and Holmes now presented the girl with one of the cases of the 1867 vintage as a token.

I had come from the British Medical Association's Library in the Strand some days after our return from Paris. I walked, or rather stamped, into the sitting-room at Baker Street in considerable annoyance. Holmes had taxed my patience and forbearance to the limit many times, but on this occasion, I felt he had gone beyond the bounds not merely of reason, but of friendship too.

"Holmes, I believe I have a bone to pick with you."

"It is unlike you, Watson," he said looking up from his paper in some surprise, and putting aside his pipe. "As it happens, I was about to go out; the British Museum is exhibiting a facsimile of the Ninnion Tablet and…"

"Damn the Ninnion tablet!" I replied, "I desire to speak with you and I desire to do that *now!*"

"Good Lord, Watson, what has come over you? Are you feeling…?"

"Really, Holmes," I interrupted, for I was not to be deflected from my purpose by any of his soft soap, "*Phobos Musacae Sapientum*—what possessed you to come up with such a pathetic farrago of nonsense? *Bananaphobia* indeed! How long did you think you could deceive me?"

"Long enough for the cure to take effect; or at least long enough for the sufferer to believe that we had indentified the source of his malady, which could be easily enough removed, which was equivalent of a cure."

"I have spent all morning at…"

"At the Library of the BMA, no doubt, where you learned that there was, in fact, no such condition, and therefore, there could be no cure. Well, I must applaud your tenacity, at least, and your refusal to take things at face value."

"What? So you confess?"

"I'm not sure I would use the word confess, Watson."

"Holmes this is entirely unworthy—you are in danger of becoming a charlatan!"

"Not at all," he replied coolly. "I think I can easily defend myself against the charge of charlatanism. Let me explain. We spent a great deal of time and Dom Agostinho's money eliminating every conceivable cause—physical and, if you include our interview with Père Létin, metaphysical; in short, we were beaten. I had become convinced that the only person who could effect a cure was the man himself. You have read the work of Émile Coué? No? Then I commend him to you. Coué has developed the theories of Abbé Faria whom Père Létin mentioned to us; he also mentioned the power of faith, even in such a perverted form as voodoo. That gave me just the shade of an idea, and when you mentioned sacrificing the chicken, it recalled to me what Père Létin had said.

"I happened to meet Coué when he was an apothecary at Troyes, where he had begun to develop his theories of what he called auto-suggestion, which intrigued me. I must say I was skeptical at first, but he taught me a lesson in the therapeutic use of willpower and imagination. As all our efforts had uncovered no cause, I reasoned that if I could persuade Dom Agostinho to believe that we had found, and removed, the source of his malady, then his unshakeable faith would do the rest. I was compelled, nevertheless, to provide an explanation which would satisfy a man who was considered to be Mycroft's intellectual equal. On the whole, Watson, you must allow that this is no more than the imaginative use of what your own profession terms a *placebo*."

"Well, I suppose you may have discovered a novel application of the concept," I replied, though my feelings were still raw after the deception which had been practiced upon me.

"I have discovered nothing about the human psyche which was not already known: forgotten perhaps, ignored indubitably, but hardly unknown. It remains an open field, Watson, and after all, did Rousseau not say that provided a man is not mad, he can be cured of every folly but vanity?"

"Then, perhaps, you can tell me what *was* wrong with Dom Agostinho?"

"I am unable to say. He seems to have been oppressed by some anxiety of his own imagining, the origin of which medical science is as yet unable to discern."

"Perhaps some *hyperaesthesia*, compounded by mild hypochondria..." I tailed off in uncertainty.

"Perhaps we shall never know Watson, for there is a shadowy region of the human soul which, as Père Létin suggested, is not accessible to scientific analysis, and remains ever beyond our comprehension."

We sat for a few moments in an uncomfortable silence, until Holmes said, "Of course, I was obliged to take Bento into the conspiracy." This merely riled my sensibilities once again.

"But why not me?" I persisted.

"Because I have the most utter respect for your professional integrity. If Sherlock Holmes plays tricks with questionable ethics and is called a charlatan or a mountebank, what does it matter? I have no governor to confer or withdraw my right to practice, but you are a licensed practitioner, and I could hardly expect you to collude. Incidentally, you nearly blew the entire thing apart when you said that you had never heard of the condition." He picked up his pipe and relit it. "Now, Watson, let us put all discord behind us, ramble down to Great Russell Street, and attempt to unravel yet another category of mystery: those of ancient Eleusis which inspired Aristeides the Just to describe as 'the source of the most bloodcurdling sensations of horror and the most enthusiastic ecstasy of joy.' "

I grudgingly assented for my irritation was anything but assuaged; yet another objection came into my head, "What will Mycroft think when he finds out?" I demanded, "or had you intended to conceal this deception from him too?"

Holmes looked at me strangely through the blue tobacco haze for a moment or two, and then, he said nonchalantly:

"It was Mycroft's idea."

SF & FANTASY

Henri Allorge. *The Great Cataclysm*
Guy d'Armen. *Doc Ardan: The City of Gold and Lepers*
G.-J. Arnaud. *The Ice Company*
Charles Asselineau. *The Double Life*
Cyprien Bérard. *The Vampire Lord Ruthwen*
Aloysius Bertrand. *Gaspard de la Nuit*
Richard Bessière. *The Gardens of the Apocalypse*
Albert Bleunard. *Ever Smaller*
Félix Bodin. *The Novel of the Future*
Alphonse Brown. *City of Glass; The Conquest of the Air*
André Caroff. *The Terror of Madame Atomos; Miss Atomos; The Return of Madame Atomos; The Mistake of Madame Atomos; The Monsters of Madame Atomos; The Revenge of Madame Atomos*
Félicien Champsaur. *The Human Arrow; Ouha*
Didier de Chousy. *Ignis*
Captain Danrit. *Undersea Odyssey*
C. I. Defontenay. *Star (Psi Cassiopeia)*
Charles Derennes. *The People of the Pole*
Georges Dodds (anthologist). *The Missing Link*
Harry Dickson. *The Heir of Dracula*
Jules Dornay. *Lord Ruthven Begins*
Alfred Driou. *The Adventures of a Parisian Aeronaut*
Sâr Dubnotal *vs. Jack the Ripper*
Alexandre Dumas. *The Return of Lord Ruthven*
Renée Dunan. *Baal*
J.-C. Dunyach. *The Night Orchid; The Thieves of Silence*
Henri Duvernois. *The Man Who Found Himself*
Achille Eyraud. *Voyage to Venus*
Henri Falk. *The Age of Lead*
Paul Féval. *Anne of the Isles; Knightshade; Revenants; Vampire City; The Vampire Countess; The Wandering Jew's Daughter*
Paul Féval, *fils. Felifax, the Tiger-Man*
Charles de Fieux. *Lamékis*
Arnould Galopin. *Doctor Omega; Doctor Omega & The Shadowmen*
Judith Gautier. *Isoline and the Serpent-Flower*
Léon Gozlan. *The Vampire of the Val-de-Grâce*
G.L. Gick. *Harry Dickson and the Werewolf of Rutherford Grange*
Edmond Haraucourt. *Illusions of Immortality*

Nathalie Henneberg. *The Green Gods*
V. Hugo, P. Foucher & P. Meurice. *The Hunchback of Notre-Dame*
Michel Jeury. *Chronolysis*
Gustave Kahn. *The Tale of Gold and Silence*
Gérard Klein. *The Mote in Time's Eye*
Louis-Guillaume de La Follie. *The Unpretentious Philosopher*
Jean de La Hire. *Enter the Nyctalope; The Nyctalope on Mars; The Nyctalope vs. Lucifer; The Nyctalope Steps In; Night of the Nyctalope*
Etienne-Léon de Lamothe-Langon. *The Virgin Vampire*
André Laurie. *Spiridon*
Gabriel de Lautrec. *The Vengeance of the Oval Portrait*
Alain le Drimeur. *The Future City*
Georges Le Faure & Henri de Graffigny. *The Extraordinary Adventures of a Russian Scientist Across the Solar System* (2 vols.)
Gustave Le Rouge. *The Vampires of Mars The Dominion of the World* (w/Gustave Guitton) (4 vols.)
Jules Lermina. *Mysteryville; Panic in Paris; To-Ho and the Gold Destroyers; The Secret of Zippelius*
Jean-Marc & Randy Lofficier. *Edgar Allan Poe on Mars; The Katrina Protocol; Pacifica; Robonocchio; Tales of the Shadowmen 1-9*
Xavier Mauméjean. *The League of Heroes*
Joseph Méry. *The Tower of Destiny*
Hippolyte Mettais. *The Year 5865*
Louise Michel. *The Human Microbes; The New World*
José Moselli. *Illa's End*
John-Antoine Nau. *Enemy Force*
Marie Nizet. *Captain Vampire*
C. Nodier, A. Beraud & Toussaint-Merle. *Frankenstein*
Henri de Parville. *An Inhabitant of the Planet Mars*
Gaston de Pawlowski. *Journey to the Land of the 4th Dimension*
Georges Pellerin. *The World in 2000 Years*
Ernest Pérochon. *The Frenetic People*
Pierre Pelot. *The Child Who Walked on the Sky*
J. Polidori, C. Nodier, E. Scribe. *Lord Ruthven the Vampire*
P.-A. Ponson du Terrail. *The Vampire and the Devil's Son*
Henri de Régnier. *A Surfeit of Mirrors*
Maurice Renard. *The Blue Peril; Doctor Lerne; The Doctored Man; A Man Among the Microbes; The Master of Light*
Jean Richepin. *The Wing; The Crazy Corner*
Albert Robida. *The Adventures of Saturnin Farandoul; The Clock of the Centuries; Chalet in the Sky*

J.-H. Rosny Aîné. *Helgvor of the Blue River; The Givreuse Enigma; The Mysterious Force; The Navigators of Space; Vamireh; The World of the Variants; The Young Vampire*
Marcel Rouff. *Journey to the Inverted World*
Han Ryner. *The Superhumans*
Brian Stableford. *The New Faust at the Tragicomique;The Empire of the Necromancers (The Shadow of Frankenstein; Frankenstein and the Vampire Countess; Frankenstein in London); Sherlock Holmes & The Vampires of Eternity; The Stones of Camelot; The Wayward Muse.* (anthologist) *The Germans on Venus; News from the Moon; The Supreme Progress; The World Above the World; Nemoville; Investigations of the Future*
Jacques Spitz. *The Eye of Purgatory*
Kurt Steiner. *Ortog*
Eugène Thébault. *Radio-Terror*
C.-F. Tiphaigne de La Roche. *Amilec*
Théo Varlet. *The Golden Rock. The Xenobiotic Invasion; Timeslip Troopers* (w/André Blandin); *The Martian Epic* (w/Octave Joncquel)
Paul Vibert. *The Mysterious Fluid*
Villiers de l'Isle-Adam. *The Scaffold; The Vampire Soul*
Philippe Ward. *Artahe*
Philippe Ward & Sylvie Miller. *The Song of Montségur*

MYSTERIES & THRILLERS

M. Allain & P. Souvestre. *The Daughter of Fantômas*
A. Anicet-Bourgeois, Lucien Dabril. *Rocambole*
A. Bernède. *Belphegor; Judex* (w/Louis Feuillade)
A. Bisson & G. Livet. *Nick Carter vs. Fantômas*
V. Darlay & H. de Gorsse. *Lupin vs. Holmes: The Stage Play*
Séamas Duffy. *Sherlock Holmes in Paris*
Paul Féval. *Gentlemen of the Night; John Devil; The Black Coats ('Salem Street; The Invisible Weapon; The Parisian Jungle; The Companions of the Treasure; Heart of Steel; The Cadet Gang; The Sword-Swallower)*
Emile Gaboriau. *Monsieur Lecoq*
Goron & Emile Gautier. *Spawn of the Penitentiary*
Steve Leadley. *Sherlock Holmes: The Circle of Blood*

Maurice Leblanc. *Arsène Lupin vs. Countess Cagliostro; Lupin vs. Holmes (The Blonde Phantom; The Hollow Needle); The Many Faces of Arsène Lupin*
Gaston Leroux. *Chéri-Bibi; The Phantom of the Opera; Rouletabille & the Mystery of the Yellow Room Rouletabille at Krupp's*
Richard Marsh. *The Complete Adventures of Judith Lee*
William Patrick Maynard. *The Terror of Fu Manchu; The Destiny of Fu Manchu*
Frank J. Morlock. *Sherlock Holmes: The Grand Horizontals; Sherlock Holmes vs Jack the Ripper*
Antonin Reschal. *The Adventures of Miss Boston*
P. de Wattyne & Y. Walter. *Sherlock Holmes vs. Fantômas*
David White. *Fantômas in America*

SCREENPLAYS

Mike Baron. *The Iron Triangle*
Emma Bull & Will Shetterly. *Nightspeeder; War for the Oaks*
Gerry Conway & Roy Thomas. *Doc Dynamo*
Steve Englehart. *Majorca*
James Hudnall. *The Devastator*
Jean-Marc & Randy Lofficier. *Royal Flush*
J.-M. & R. Lofficier & Marc Agapit. *Despair*
J.-M. & R. Lofficier & Joël Houssin. *City*
Andrew Paquette. *Peripheral Vision*
Robert L. Robinson, Jr. *Judex*
R. Thomas, J. Hendler & L. Sprague de Camp. *Rivers of Time*

NON-FICTION

Stephen R. Bissette. *Blur 1-5. Green Mountain Cinema 1; Teen Angels*
Win Scott Eckert. *Crossovers* (2 vols.)
Jean-Marc & Randy Lofficier. *Shadowmen* (2 vols.)
Randy Lofficier. *Over Here*